P9-AEV-326

INVINCIBLE

ULTIMATE COLLECTION

VOLUME 6

Created by

Robert Kirkman & Cory Walker

Robert Kirkman
Writer

Ryan Ottley
Penciler (chapters 60-65, 68-70, Invincible Returns 1 main story)

Cory Walker
Penciler, Inker (chapters 66-67, Invincible Returns 1 backup story)

Cliff Rathburn
Inker (chapters 60-65, 68-70, Invincible Returns 1 main story)

FCO Plascencia
Colorist (chapters 60-65, 68-70, Invincible Returns 1 main story)

Dave McCaig
Colorist (chapters 66-67)

Rus Wooton
Letterer

Ryan Ottley & FCO Plascencia
Cover

Sina Grace
Editor

Aubrey Sitterson
Original Series Editor

WWW.SKYBOUND.COM WWW.IMAGECOMICS.COM

For international rights inquiries, please contact: foreign@skybound.com

INVINCIBLE, ULTIMATE COLLECTION, VOL 6. Second Printing. Published by Image Comics, Inc., Office of publication: 2134 Allston Way, 2nd Floor, Berkeley, California 94704.

PRINTED IN CANADA
ISBN: 978-1-60706-360-5

60
+fco

Months ago.
Oh, God.
Oh, God.
Oh, God.
Oh, God.
Oh, God.
Oh, God.

HKK.

HNNN--

FUUHIXSSS...
...MUHEEEE.

MONTHS LATER.

Now.
Day one.

ATTACK!
GO! SPREAD OUT! MOVE ACROSS THE GLOBE--DESTROY EVERYTHING IN YOUR PATH! MAKE THEM SEE INVINCIBLE. MAKE THEM FEAR INVINCIBLE.
MAKE THEM HATE INVINCIBLE!
DO THIS--FULFILL YOUR SIDE OF THE BARGAIN, AND EVERYTHING YOU WISH FOR WILL BE YOURS!

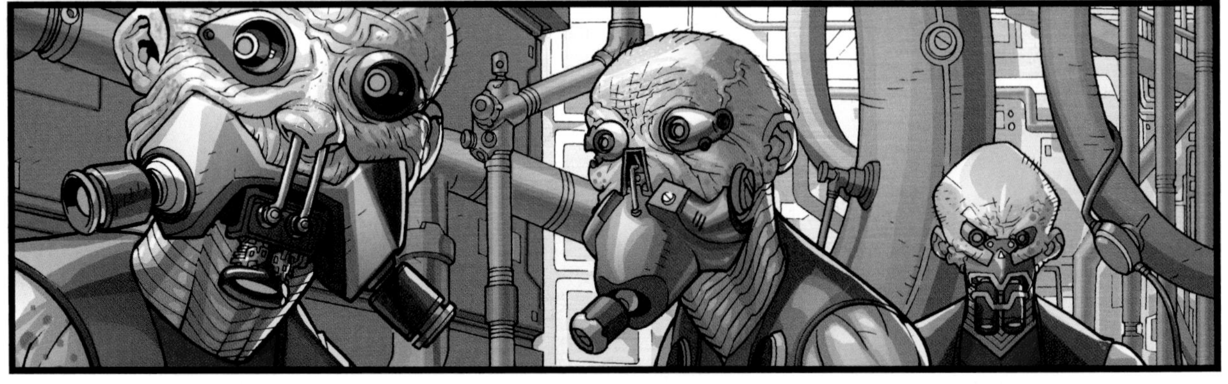

THE HOME OF SAMANTHA EVE WILKINS, OTHERWISE KNOWN AS ATOM EVE.

SO... WHAT'S THE DEAL, ANYWAY? WHY CAN'T I MEET THEM?
WHO?
YOUR PARENTS. YOU THINK I WOULDN'T NOTICE? YOU ONLY HAVE ME OVER WHEN THEY'VE GONE SOMEWHERE.

I'M SORRY, I'LL LET YOU MEET THEM IF YOU REALLY WANT TO. IT'S JUST... MY PARENTS ARE HORRIBLE.
YOU WOULDN'T UNDERSTAND.

UH... HELLO. THIS IS ME YOU'RE TALKING TO.
I WOULDN'T UNDERSTAND?

OH, CRAP-- UH.
I DIDN'T MEAN TO--
BEEPBEEPBEEPBEEP

WHOA--MY FIRST CALL. SWEET!
MUST BE SOMETHING GOING ON OVER AT STRONGHOLD PENITENTIARY.

YOU WANT ME TO COME WITH?

NAH. I'LL GIVE THEM A CALL ON THE WAY--SEE WHAT IT IS.
I'M SURE IT'S NOTHING SERIOUS.

KRAKOOM!!
IS THIS WHAT PASSES FOR A PRISON ON THIS WORLD?!

PATHETIC!
I WOULDN'T EVEN KEEP YOU AS A SLAVE IN MY EMPIRE!

AFTER NEARLY A YEAR IN A VILTRUMITE PRISON--I COULD USE THIS WARM-UP!
RUN! FLEE! THIS IS NOTHING COMPARED TO WHAT I'M GOING TO DO TO MY FATHER WHEN I FIND HIM!

I'VE KILLED YOU BEFORE AND I'LL DO IT AGAIN!

THE DUNCAN ROSENBLATT OF MY DIMENSION WOULD BE ASHAMED OF YOU! HE'S THE KING OF ALL MONSTERS-- ONE OF THE MOST FEROCIOUS VILLAINS I'VE FACED!
WHAT *HAPPENED* TO YOU?!
LOOP
202

CRAP!
WHO *IS* THIS GUY?!

STOP THIS! WE'RE TOO EVENLY MATCHED-- JUST STOP! THIS COULD GO ON FOREVER!
STOP FIGHTING AND TELL ME HOW YOU GOT HERE-- WHO BROUGHT YOU HERE?! HOW DID YOU GET TO THIS DIMENSION?!
KROOM!

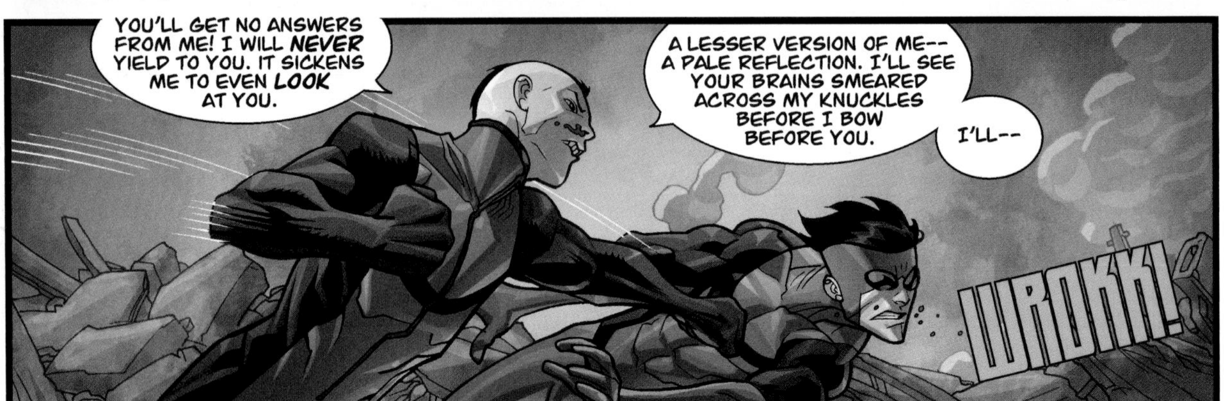
YOU'LL GET NO ANSWERS FROM ME! I WILL NEVER YIELD TO YOU. IT SICKENS ME TO EVEN LOOK AT YOU.
A LESSER VERSION OF ME-- A PALE REFLECTION. I'LL SEE YOUR BRAINS SMEARED ACROSS MY KNUCKLES BEFORE I BOW BEFORE YOU.
I'LL--
WROKK!

SHUT UP!
KROOM!

WHAT THE HELL IS--
HEY!

THERE'S ANOTHER ONE--GET HIM! WE'VE GOT TO STOP THESE BASTARDS BEFORE IT'S TOO LATE!
WHAT?!
GUYS-- IT'S ME!
IT'S--!

BOLT! KID THOR! IT'S ME--WHAT'S WRONG WITH YOU?!
KRAK!
YOU FOOL! YOU SHOULD BE RUNNING WITH US--WHY ARE YOU DOING THIS? YOU'RE NO BETTER THAN US--WIFE-KILLER!
YOU'RE IN HERE FOR A REASON, THRILL-KILL. IF KEEPING YOU INSIDE MEANS I STAY TOO--SO BE IT!
WHAT'S THE DEAL--YOU LIKE IT IN HERE?!

YOU!
GET BACK HERE!

NOT YOU OR ANYONE ELSE IS GOING TO KEEP ME IN HERE.

SOON, INVINCIBLE...
BUT NOT TODAY.

REPORTS ARE COMING IN FROM ACROSS THE GLOBE.

MULTIPLE SUPER-HUMANS, ALL RESEMBLING INVINCIBLE IN SOME WAY, HAVE BEEN WREAKING HAVOC IN CITIES ALL OVER THE WORLD.

AT FIRST THEY WERE BELIEVED TO ACTUALLY **BE** INVINCIBLE, UNTIL THE SIGHTINGS REVEALED MULTIPLE ATTACKERS--NOW TOTALING NEARLY TWENTY.

BREAKING NE

IT IS UNCLEAR WHAT THEIR MOTIVE FOR THESE ATTACKS IS--OR HOW LONG THEY WILL CONTINUE. THEY'VE MET WITH OPPOSITION IN MANY INSTANCES BUT THE OVERALL ATTACK SHOWS NO SIGNS OF ENDING.

WE'LL CONTINUE BROADCASTING AS LONG AS WE CAN, ALTHOUGH WE DON'T KNOW HOW LONG OUR LOCATION WILL REMAIN SECURE. WE NOW GO LIVE TO--

THIS TIME I'M KILLING YOU SLOWLY--I'M GOING TO **ENJOY** MYSELF!
ACK!
WRAMM!

YOU SUCK, I DON'T CARE HOW STRONG YOU ARE--I'M TAKING YOU OUT!
KEEP TELLING YOURSELF THAT, BOY--YOU'LL EVENTUALLY BELIEVE IT. YOU'RE GOING TO HAVE TO **EARN** THAT SYMBOL ON YOUR CHEST!

CALL IN WHOEVER YOU CAN--THIS IS HUGE, TOO BIG FOR ANY ONE OF US TO HANDLE.
I'M GOING TO TRY AND TAKE AS MANY OF THEM OUT AS I CAN--BUT IF I CAN'T DO IT--BE READY TO BACK ME UP.
WE'RE ON IT!

DEEP BELOW THE PENTAGON, THE HEADQUARTERS OF THE GLOBAL DEFENSE AGENCY, LED BY CECIL STEDMAN.
PENTAGON
Parking in Rear

CHRIST, I HOPE WE NEVER HAVE TO DO *THAT* AGAIN.
HAVE YOU BEEN WATCHING THE NEWS?

OKAY, BRIT--GRAB A SQUADRON AND SECURE THE PENTAGON--WE'VE GOT TO HAVE A PLACE TO STAGE A COUNTER ATTACK, THIS IS AS GOOD AS ANY--MAYBE ALL WE'VE GOT LEFT.
DONALD, I NEED YOU TO START MAKING CALLS. WE'RE GOING TO NEED EVERY OUNCE OF HELP WE CAN GET ON THIS ONE.

RIGHT AWAY, SIR. WHO DO YOU WANT ME TO CALL IN?

EVERYONE!

DAY TWO.
SPREAD OUT AND ENTER THE TRANSPORT WINDOWS, DOUBLE TIME! BE READY FOR WHATEVER FACES YOU WHEN YOU EMERGE, DROP POINTS ARE BEING CHOSEN AT RANDOM-- WE'VE GOT NO TIME FOR SPECIFIC MATCH-UPS.
WE'VE GOT MULTIPLE THREATS, MULTIPLE LOCATIONS-- THIS SITUATION IS DIRE, I WANT CONTINUAL UPDATES ON THE COMLINKS, IF YOU'RE DOWN WE NEED TO KNOW IMMEDIATELY SO REPLACEMENTS CAN BE DISPATCHED.
LET'S SAVE THE WORLD, PEOPLE!

EVERYONE LISTEN UP, THIS IS AGENT CECIL STEDMAN. MOST OF YOU HAVE NO CLUE WHO I AM SO JUST ASSUME I'M YOUR BOSS' BOSS BECAUSE IN MOST CASES THAT'S TRUE. I'LL BE COORDINATING THINGS FROM HERE.
IF YOU'RE INJURED, REPORT IN IMMEDIATELY. I'LL HAVE MISS POPPER ON STAND-BY TO RETRIEVE ANYONE NOT FIT FOR COMBAT.

THEY'RE JUST UP AHEAD, WON'T BE LONG NOW.
SORRY I'M PULLING YOU SO FAST.

IT'S OKAY, WE'VE GOTTA BE AS FAST AS POSSIBLE. ARE YOU OKAY?

RIGHT?

POPPER, YOU UP FOR THIS?
I'VE BEEN DRINKING ORANGE JUICE ALL MORNING.

THEY'RE ALL ***ME***. I'M NOT DOING THIS--BUT I CAN'T HELP BUT--I LOOKED IN HIS EYES AND I SAW MYSELF. I FEEL RESPONSIBLE FOR ALL OF THIS.
BEYOND THAT--IT'S OTHER VERSIONS OF ME. FROM OTHER DIMENSIONS...

NO. I'M NOT.

I ONLY KNOW OF ONE MAN WHO HAS THE POWER TO ACCESS OTHER DIMENSIONS AND HATES ME ENOUGH TO DO THIS.
BUT THAT'S IMPOSSIBLE...

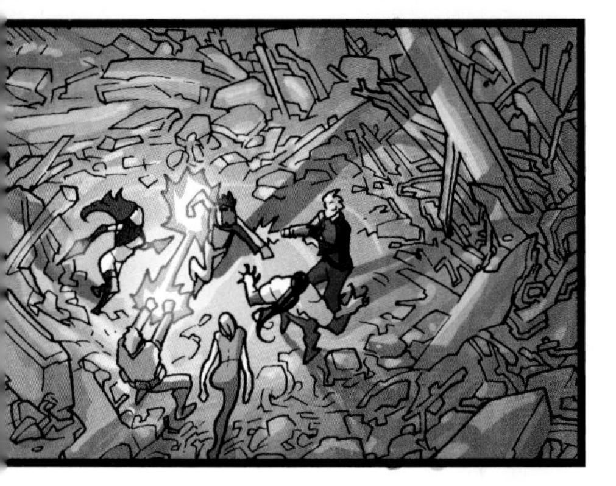

THIS WON'T BE ENOUGH! NOT NEARLY ENOUGH! CYBLADE, RIPCLAW, HEATWAVE, VELOCITY, BALLISTIC--IT'S AMUSING TO SEE YOU ALL WORKING TOGETHER AGAIN--CYBERFORCE, WAS IT?
IT DOESN'T MATTER, I KNOW EVERYTHING ABOUT YOU AND YOU CAN'T HOPE TO WIN THIS FIGHT!
THIS IS YOUR FINAL BATTLE--ENJOY IT WHILE IT LASTS!
OKAY, GUYS--CAN WE PLEASE SHUT HIM UP?

WRAKK

YOU'RE NOT INVINCIBLE-- I KNOW INVINCIBLE! WHO ARE YOU?!
JUST SHUT UP AND BEAT HIM, DAD!
KROOM!

YOU'RE MINE NOW!

YOU THINK THIS WILL WORK? YOU THINK YOU CAN STOP ME?!
I MURDERED MY FATHER! AN ADULT VILTRUMITE-- DO YOU REALLY THINK YOU CAN HOPE TO SURVIVE THIS?!

LOOK OUT!
SORRY!
ACK!
WHUMP!

REMATCH!
CHEERS!

SWOSH!

JERK!

OH, GOD-- JUST HANG ON, EVE!
WE'LL BE AT THE HOSPITAL IN NO TIME-- JUST HANG ON!!

KROOM!
PATHETIC! THEY CALL YOU CLOWNS THE GUARDIANS OF THE GLOBE HERE?!
YOU'RE AN EMBARRASSMENT!
I CAN'T BELIEVE I KILLED YOU ALL SO EASILY!

WE'RE NOT DEAD YET!
DARKWING?!

HELP!
I NEED HELP!

YOU GOING TO MAKE IT?
YEAH--UGH--I CAN PULL MYSELF TOGETHER. WHERE'S DARKWING? DID HE GET HIM?

DIE!
WROKK

SHE'S NOT HERE--WAS LOOKING FORWARD TO KILLING HER MYSELF, THIS TIME.

YOU'RE OBVIOUSLY SOME KIND OF LESSER VILTRUMITE--JUST LOOK AT YOU! HOW COULD YOU HOPE TO DEFEAT ME?!
KROOM!

SHE'S BREATHING! SHE'S STILL BREATHING!
I THINK I CAN FIX THAT...

LEAVE THEM ALONE!
WRAMM!

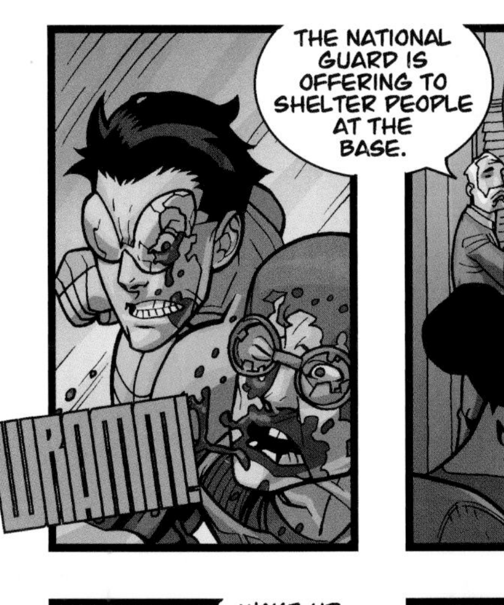
THE NATIONAL GUARD IS OFFERING TO SHELTER PEOPLE AT THE BASE.
WRAMM!

NO--WE'LL BE FINE HERE. I DON'T WANT TO BE LOCKED AWAY AS LONG AS THEY'RE STILL BROADCASTING UPDATES.

WAKE UP, AMANDA-- PLEASE BE OKAY--
MONSTER GIRL!

CHOOM!

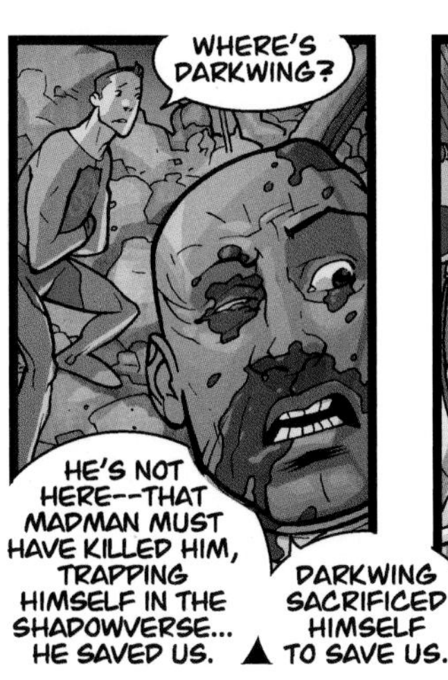
WHERE'S DARKWING?
HE'S NOT HERE--THAT MADMAN MUST HAVE KILLED HIM, TRAPPING HIMSELF IN THE SHADOWVERSE... HE SAVED US.

JUST FIX HER! PLEASE!
FIX HER!
DARKWING SACRIFICED HIMSELF TO SAVE US.

NO! GET THEM OUT OF HERE BEFORE HE KILLS ALL OF US. LEAVE HIM TO ME.

NO! GO BACK!
IT'S THE ONLY WAY-- GO!
WE CAN'T LEAVE HIM!!

THAT WAS A FUTILE GESTURE, REX. I'M GOING TO POP YOUR HEAD OFF AND THEN FLY OFF TO MURDER ALL THREE OF THEM.
WHAT DO YOU HOPE TO ACCOMPLISH AGAINST ME? YOU'RE OUT OF BATONS AND GOLF BALLS AND WHATEVER YOU KEPT IN YOUR POCKETS--YOUR WRIST LAUNCHER IS SPENT--YOU'VE GOT NOTHING. NO WAY OF ATTACKING ME.
SO TELL ME--HOW ARE YOU GOING TO KILL ME? WHAT ARE YOU GOING TO CHARGE AND EXPLODE?
MY SKELETON.

BRAKKA-CHOOM!!!

REX!
NO!

YOU CAN'T BE HERE.

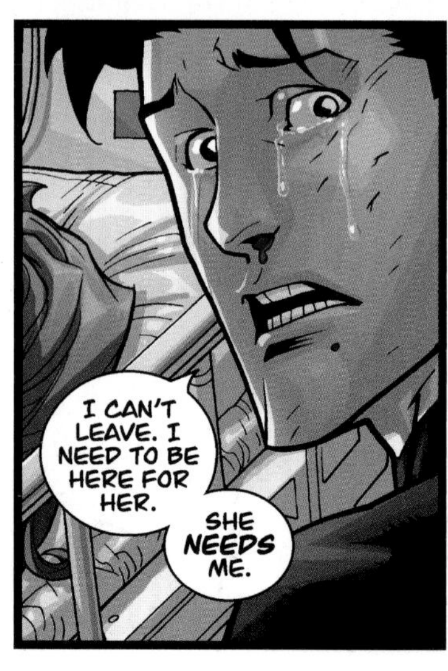
I CAN'T LEAVE. I NEED TO BE HERE FOR HER.
SHE **NEEDS** ME.

WE'RE LOSING THIS, KID.
THE **WORLD** NEEDS YOU.

I DON'T CARE.
YOU'VE GOT EVERY GODDAMN SUPERHERO ON THE PLANET WORKING ON THIS. YOU CAN DO THIS WITHOUT ME.

JESUS, KID.
LET'S HOPE YOU'RE RIGHT.

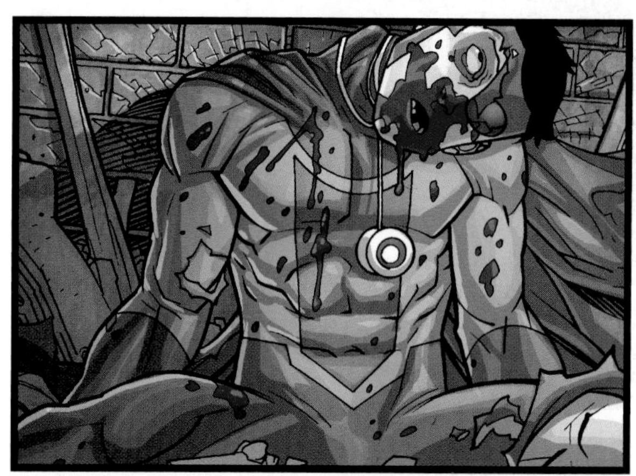

JESUS.

DAY THREE.

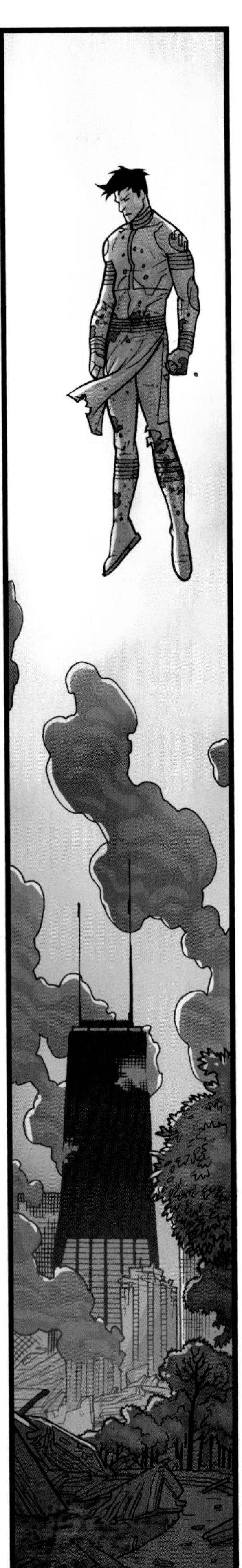

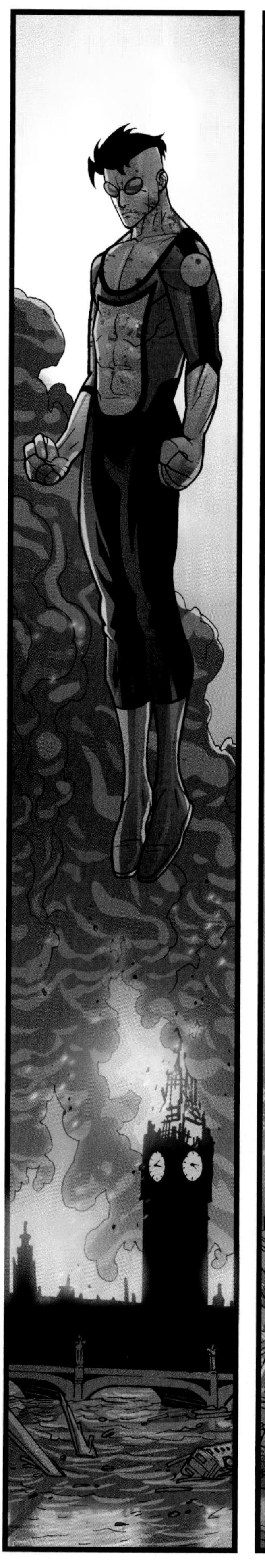

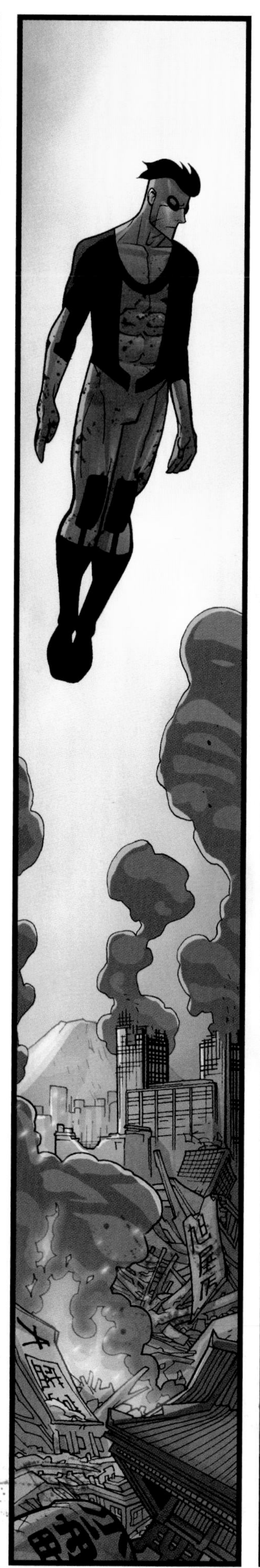

PHASE ONE IS COMPLETE.
GATHER AND PREPARE FOR MY ARRIVAL.

WHY ARE WE MEETING ABOVE MY HOUSE? I HATE COMING BACK TO THIS PLACE.
NOT ALL OF US KILLED OUR MOTHER HERE. MY FATHER DESTROYED THIS PLACE BEFORE I COULD KILL HIM. I'M HAPPY TO SEE IT.
WHAT IS TAKING HIM SO LONG?

SORRY. I PREFER TO MAKE AN ENTRANCE.
THIS WORLD IS IN RUINS, THIS INVINCIBLE'S REPUTATION IS DESTROYED. THE PEOPLE HERE WILL ALWAYS HATE AND FEAR HIM BECAUSE OF WHAT YOU'VE DONE. NOW ALL THAT IS LEFT IS TO DISFIGURE HIM. I WANT HIM TO KNOW WHAT PAIN HE'S CAUSED ME.
FIND HIM, AND BRING HIM TO ME.

HOW ABOUT WE ***DON'T?*** YOUR STUPID PLAN WEEDED US DOWN TO EIGHT. YOU SAID IF WE DID THIS FOR YOU, IN RETURN YOU'D HELP US EXPAND OUR EMPIRES INTO COUNTLESS DIMENSIONS.
THIS PLACE IS IN SHAMBLES. I SAY WE MOVE ON--***NOW,*** OR WE KILL YOU.

WRAMM!

HOW DISAPPOINTING.

ANGSTROM! YOU CAN'T STRAND US HERE!!
WE WILL FIND A WAY OUT OF HERE! WE WILL FIND YOU--AND WE WILL KILL YOU!

YOU!
I KNEW IT WAS YOU!!
OH, GOOD, YOU CAME TO ME.

YOU WON'T BE SO HAPPY TO SEE US IN A MINUTE.
WE'RE GONNA KICK YOUR--!

HCKK!
THWAPP!
THWAPP!

ACK!!
WROKK!
WRAMM!

IT WAS YOU! YOU'VE BEEN SPYING ON ME FOR WEEKS!
YOU'RE GOING TO PAY FOR WHAT HAPPENED TO ATOM EVE!

WRAMM!
UNPH!

ARE YOU HIM?! THE ANGSTROM I THOUGHT WAS DEAD--THAT I THOUGHT I'D BEATEN TO DEATH?!
HOW ARE YOU HERE?! HOW DID YOU SURVIVE?!

BECAUSE I'M BRILLIANT.
FWOOM

I WAS PREPARED FOR YOU TO DEFEAT ME. MY STRENGTH AND DURABILITY HAD BEEN AUGMENTED--BUT I HAD NO WAY OF KNOWING IF IT WOULD BE ENOUGH.
I HAD SURGEONS IN A PARALLEL DIMENSION ON STAND-BY. THEY PATCHED ME UP.
NOW I KNOW THAT SENDING YOU THROUGH DIMENSIONS ONLY GIVES YOU ENOUGH TIME TO EVENTUALLY OUTWIT ME...SO THIS TIME I BROUGHT WEAPONS.
DO YOU LIKE THEM?

CHOOM! CHOOM!

KROOM!

WROKK!

KROK! KROK!

Thap.
NO.
NOT AT ALL.

SKROOM

YOU THOUGHT THAT WOULD BE ENOUGH?! YOU THOUGHT YOU COULD DEFEAT ME WITH **THAT?**
YOU BROUGHT EVIL VERSIONS OF ME TO THIS DIMENSION TO WHAT--DISCREDIT ME? DID YOU SEE WHAT THEY'VE DONE?! GOOD GOD, MAN--IS THIS WHAT YOU **WANTED?!**
YOU'VE CAUSED THE DEATHS OF **THOUSANDS!** I COULD--

KILL HIM!

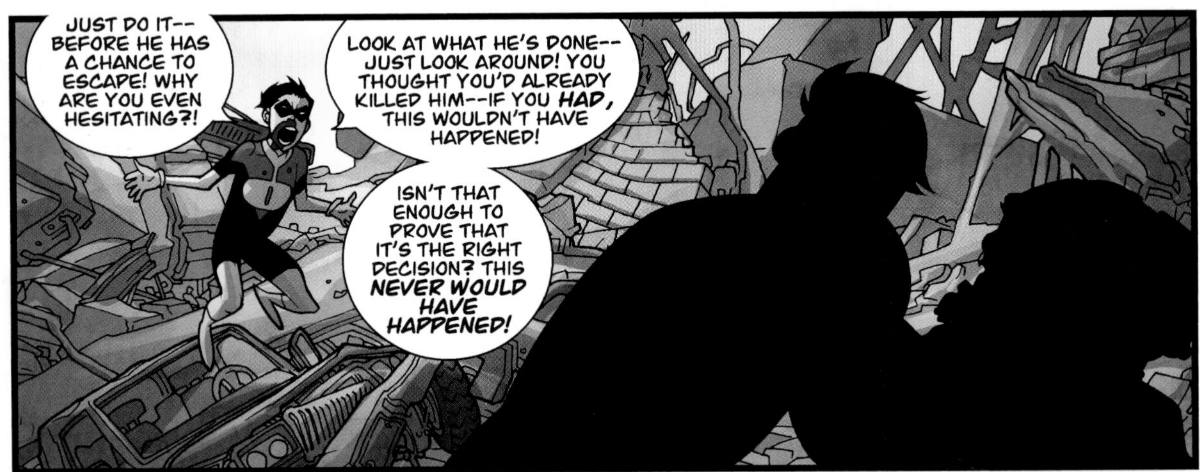
JUST DO IT-- BEFORE HE HAS A CHANCE TO ESCAPE! WHY ARE YOU EVEN HESITATING?!
LOOK AT WHAT HE'S DONE-- JUST LOOK AROUND! YOU THOUGHT YOU'D ALREADY KILLED HIM--IF YOU **HAD,** THIS WOULDN'T HAVE HAPPENED!
ISN'T THAT ENOUGH TO PROVE THAT IT'S THE RIGHT DECISION? THIS **NEVER WOULD HAVE HAPPENED!**

OKAY.
ANGSTROM, I'M SORRY-- BUT YOU'VE GIVEN ME NO CHOICE.

WRAKK! KROOM!
MARK!
TRUER WORDS...

NO!
NO WAY!

YOU'RE NOT GETTING AWAY WITH THIS!
I WON'T LET YOU!
DON'T BE SO SURE.

NO!
NO!

SHUKK!
NO!

...
GROSS.

I NEED YOU TO PATCH ME UP. I'M GETTING THE REMAINING EIGHT INVINCIBLES FROM THAT DIMENSION I STRANDED THEM IN--AND WE'RE GOING BACK--WE'LL HIT HIM ALL AT ONCE.
I WANT HIS BLOOD! HURRY, WE'VE GOT TO GET BACK.
NO.

PROMISES WERE MADE, ANGSTROM LEVY. YOU GAVE US ASSURANCES, WE HAD A DEAL AND YOU FAILED.
YOU DO NOT GET A SECOND CHANCE. YOU DO NOT GET TO GIVE US ORDERS.
YOU WORK FOR US NOW.

DAY FOUR.

REGINAL
VEL JOHNSO
HIGH SCHOOL

MY GOD...

61

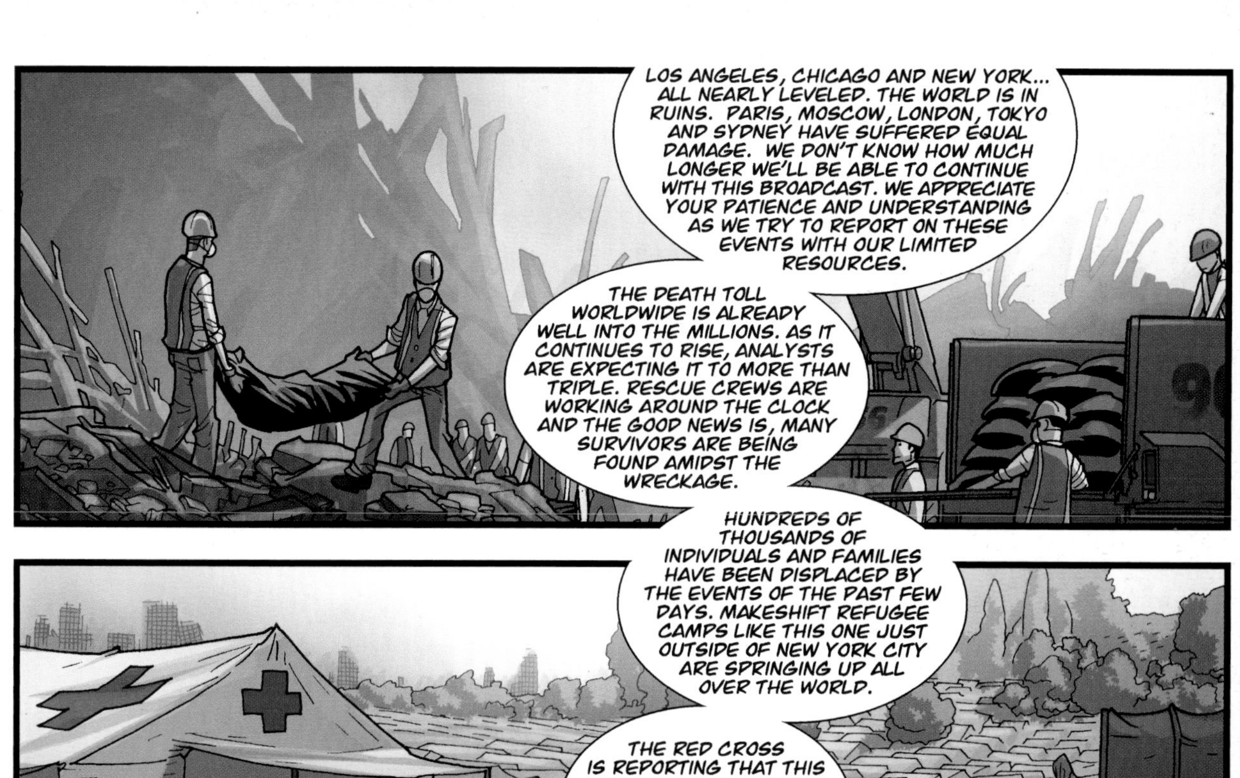
LOS ANGELES, CHICAGO AND NEW YORK... ALL NEARLY LEVELED. THE WORLD IS IN RUINS. PARIS, MOSCOW, LONDON, TOKYO AND SYDNEY HAVE SUFFERED EQUAL DAMAGE. WE DON'T KNOW HOW MUCH LONGER WE'LL BE ABLE TO CONTINUE WITH THIS BROADCAST. WE APPRECIATE YOUR PATIENCE AND UNDERSTANDING AS WE TRY TO REPORT ON THESE EVENTS WITH OUR LIMITED RESOURCES.
THE DEATH TOLL WORLDWIDE IS ALREADY WELL INTO THE MILLIONS. AS IT CONTINUES TO RISE, ANALYSTS ARE EXPECTING IT TO MORE THAN TRIPLE. RESCUE CREWS ARE WORKING AROUND THE CLOCK AND THE GOOD NEWS IS, MANY SURVIVORS ARE BEING FOUND AMIDST THE WRECKAGE.

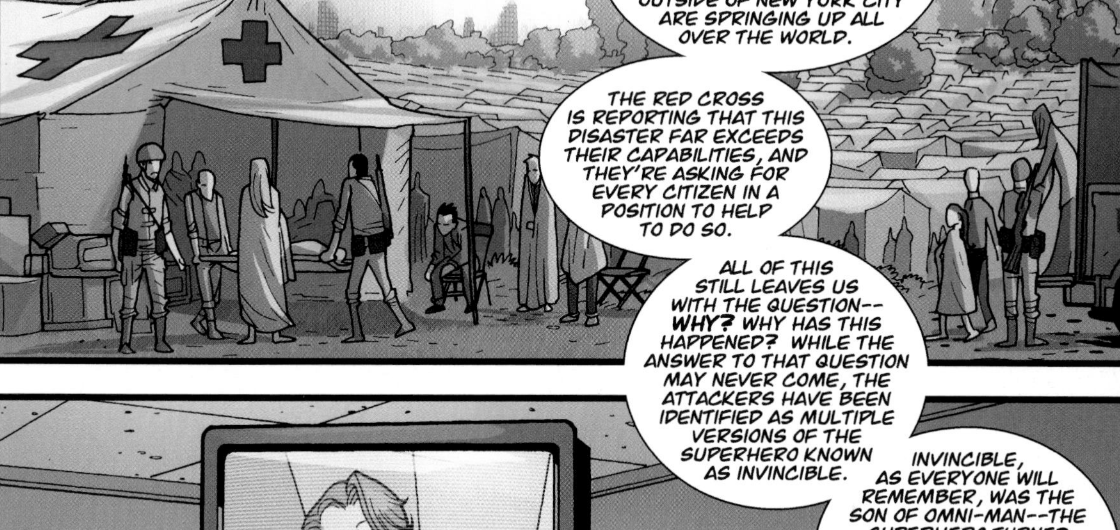
HUNDREDS OF THOUSANDS OF INDIVIDUALS AND FAMILIES HAVE BEEN DISPLACED BY THE EVENTS OF THE PAST FEW DAYS. MAKESHIFT REFUGEE CAMPS LIKE THIS ONE JUST OUTSIDE OF NEW YORK CITY ARE SPRINGING UP ALL OVER THE WORLD.
THE RED CROSS IS REPORTING THAT THIS DISASTER FAR EXCEEDS THEIR CAPABILITIES, AND THEY'RE ASKING FOR EVERY CITIZEN IN A POSITION TO HELP TO DO SO.
US-3

ALL OF THIS STILL LEAVES US WITH THE QUESTION-- **WHY?** WHY HAS THIS HAPPENED? WHILE THE ANSWER TO THAT QUESTION MAY NEVER COME, THE ATTACKERS HAVE BEEN IDENTIFIED AS MULTIPLE VERSIONS OF THE SUPERHERO KNOWN AS INVINCIBLE.
INVINCIBLE, AS EVERYONE WILL REMEMBER, WAS THE SON OF OMNI-MAN--THE SUPERHERO TURNED SUPER-VILLAIN WHO TRIED TO TAKE OVER THE WORLD UNTIL HE WAS THWARTED BY HIS SON AND THEN DISAPPEARED, NEVER TO BE SEEN AGAIN.
SUSPICIONS HAVE ALWAYS RUN WILD WITH SOME BELIEVING INVINCIBLE WAS ACTUALLY WORKING WITH OMNI-MAN--WITH PLANS TO CONQUER THE WORLD AT A LATTER TIME.
WORLD DISASTER
WE HAVE REPORTS OF INVINCIBLE WORKING ALONGSIDE THESE ATTACKERS, BUT NOTHING HAS BEEN CONFIRMED AND HE COULDN'T BE REACHED FOR COMMENT.

I SAW HIM WITH MY OWN EYES. HE WAS WORKING WITH THEM. INVINCIBLE HAS FINALLY SHOWN HIS TRUE COLORS. IT'S OBVIOUS NOW THAT HIM DEFENDING THE WORLD AGAINST HIS FATHER WAS ALL JUST AN ACT.

THIS IS ABSURD. THESE THINGS WERE DOPPELGANGERS--EVIL TWINS. I KNOW INVINCIBLE AND HE WASN'T WORKING WITH THEM.
THIS IS SLOPPY REPORTING. IF YOU REVIEWED FOOTAGE FOR TEN MINUTES I'M SURE YOU'D FIND INVINCIBLE, ON CAMERA, FIGHTING AGAINST THESE MONSTERS.

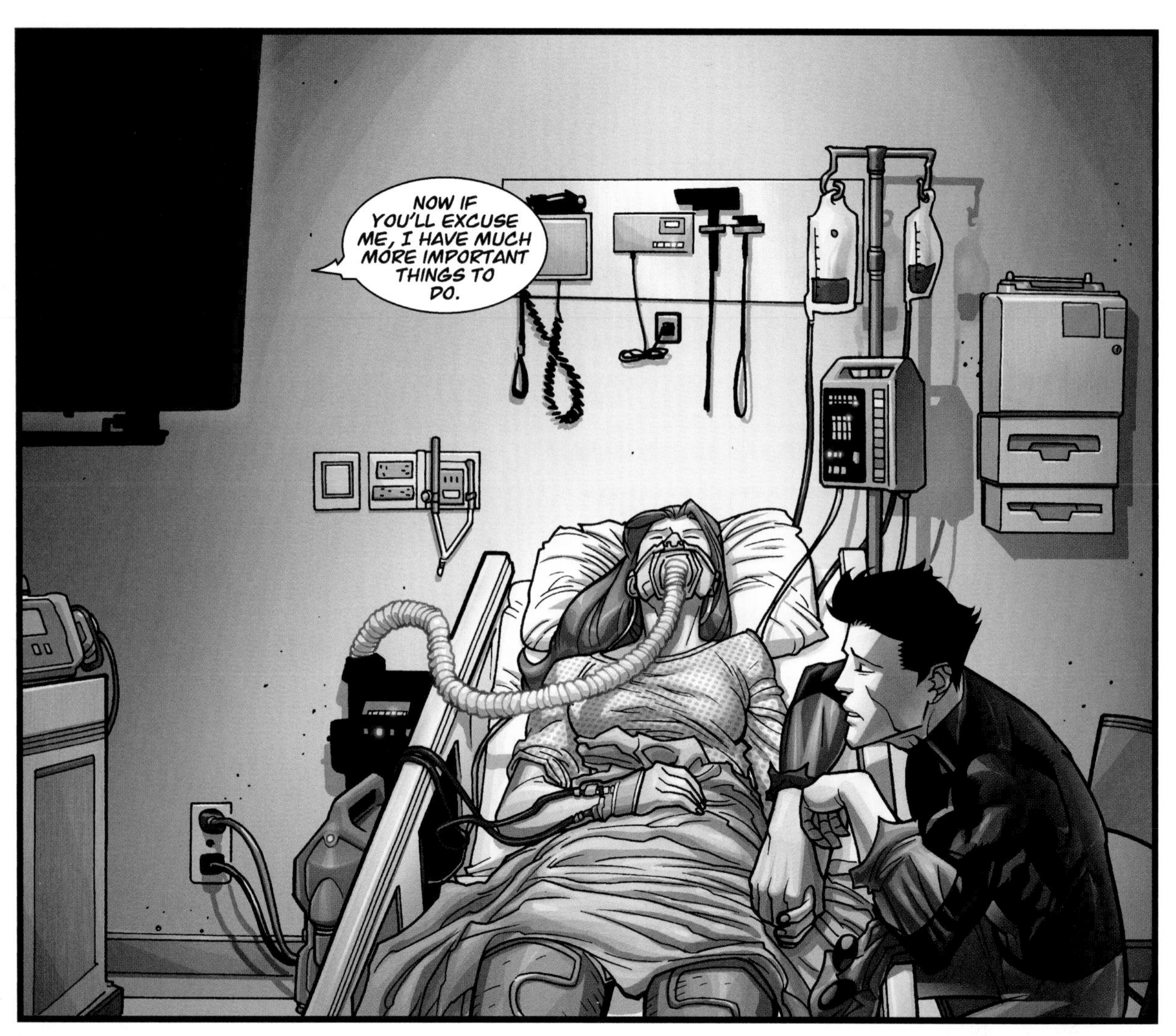
NOW IF YOU'LL EXCUSE ME, I HAVE MUCH MORE IMPORTANT THINGS TO DO.

PLEASE WAKE UP, EVE. PLEASE... IF YOU'RE IN THERE, IF YOU CAN HEAR ME... WAKE UP.
...
I'M SO SORRY, BUT... I DON'T THINK I CAN STAY HERE MUCH LONGER. I CAN'T, I'VE GOT TO HELP PEOPLE-- THERE'S TOO MUCH TO BE DONE.

I CAN'T BE HERE FOR YOU.
I'M SORRY.
YOU READY?

IS SHE GOING TO BE **SAFE** HERE?
IT'S NOT SAFE TO MOVE HER TO ONE OF MY SECURE FACILITIES YET, SO I'VE MOVED A MEDICAL TEAM HERE. THE STAFF OF THIS HOSPITAL WON'T EVEN COME INTO THIS AREA--AND HER IDENTITY HAS BEEN PROTECTED.
HER PARENTS ARE BEING BROUGHT IN. SHE WON'T BE ALONE.

HAVE YOU FOUND MY MOTHER?

OLIVER DID. SHE WAS AT HER BOYFRIEND'S HOUSE THE WHOLE TIME--MOST SUBURBAN AREAS WEREN'T HIT, THANKFULLY.
HE'S MEETING UP WITH US ON LOCATION. OLIVER, NOT YOUR MOM'S BOYFRIEND.

AFTER THIS IS OVER... WE'RE THROUGH.
THIS IS ONLY TEMPORARY.

UNDERSTOOD.

I'M GLAD WE COULD PUT OUR DIFFERENCES BEHIND US FOR NOW, THOUGH.
THIS SITUATION IS BIGGER THAN EITHER OF US.

BRAKOWW!

YOU! I CAN'T BELIEVE YOU'D SHOW YOUR FACE HERE AFTER ALL THE PAIN AND SUFFERING YOU'VE CAUSED!
HOW DARE YOU!
BZZACKT!

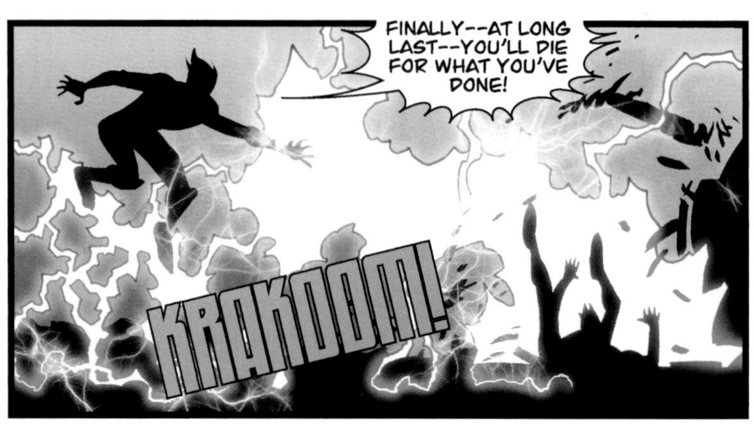
FINALLY--AT LONG LAST--YOU'LL DIE FOR WHAT YOU'VE DONE!
KRAKOOM!

WHAT THE--?!

WHERE DID HE COME FROM?!
HE WAS HELPING US. IS HE NOT A SUPERHERO? I DON'T RECOGNIZE ALL OF THEM.

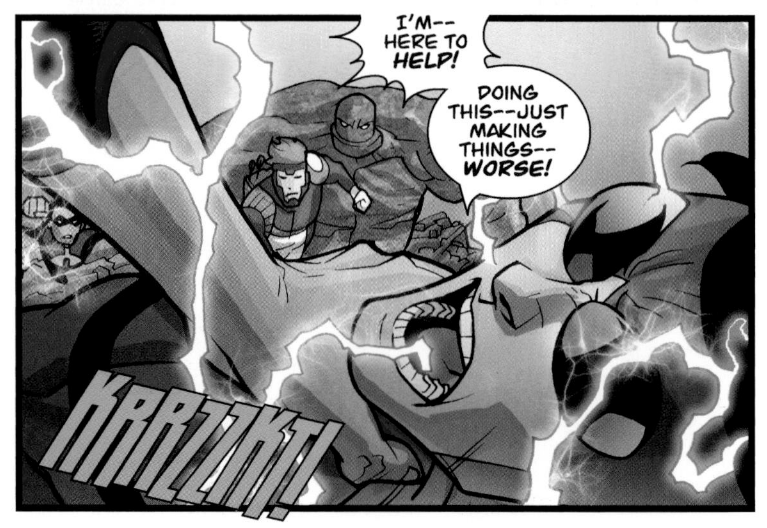
I'M-- HERE TO HELP!
DOING THIS--JUST MAKING THINGS-- WORSE!
KRRZZAKT!

WE DON'T HAVE TIME FOR THIS-- TAKE HIM DOWN HARD AND FAST, PEOPLE!
LET'S GO!

AAGGH!
KROOM!

THINK THEY'VE GOT THIS ONE COVERED, KID THOR.
C'MON, THERE'S WORK TO BE DONE, LIVES TO SAVE.

YOU'VE JUST GIVEN ME ALL THE ENERGY I NEED TO TAKE YOU DOWN!
IDIOT!
BZZZK!

POW!
HERE'S MORE, JERK!

QUICK-- SOMEONE PIN HIM DOWN!
DON'T LET HIM MOVE!

ON IT, DUDE!
KROOOM!!

NO! YOU CAN'T STOP ME!
POWERPLEX WILL HAVE HIS REVENGE!
BZZACKKT!

JUST HOLD HIM DOWN UNTIL HE USES UP ALL HIS STORED ENERGY. FIGHT THROUGH THE PAIN AS BEST YOU CAN!

I'M GOOD, BRO.
I'M MADE OF SOLID, AWESOME ROCK-- THIS STUFF BARELY TICKLES.

NO.
NO!
NO!

NO.
THIS ISN'T RIGHT...

BRING HIM HERE.
WHAT IS WRONG WITH ALL OF YOU?!

WHY WOULD YOU HELP *HIM?!* WHY NOW--AFTER EVERYTHING HE'S DONE--WOULD YOU STOP ME FROM TAKING HIM DOWN?!
LOOK AROUND YOU! LOOK AT THIS! THIS IS ALL HIS FAULT! HE CAUSED THIS!
EVERY DEAD BODY YOU FIND IS A PERSON HE'S KILLED! HE'S A MURDERER!
HE HAS TO BE STOPPED!!

THIS IS ALL HIS FAULT!
WHY CAN'T YOU SEE THAT?!

DON'T LISTEN TO HIM, MARK.

THE CLEAN-UP IS GOING WELL. WE'VE ALMOST GOT ALL OF MANHATTAN CLEARED AWAY AND READY FOR RECONSTRUCTION. I SEE WHAT THE SUPERHERO COMMUNITY IS CAPABLE OF WHEN WE ALL WORK TOGETHER AND... IT'S *INSPIRING.*
BUT...
I DON'T HAVE ANYONE ELSE I CAN TALK TO ABOUT THIS... I HOPE YOU WAKE UP SOON. I REALLY--OH, GOD, EVE... I MISS YOU SO MUCH.

I SEE THE DESTRUCTION, THE LIVES LOST... I CAN'T HELP BUT THINK... POWERPLEX IS ABSOLUTELY RIGHT. THIS IS ALL MY FAULT.
I DON'T KNOW WHAT TO DO... ANGSTROM LEVY, POWERPLEX... THESE GUYS ARE OUT THERE BECAUSE OF *ME.* THERE'S NO DISPUTING THAT. THEIR ACTIONS ARE A DIRECT RESULT OF THINGS I'VE DONE, WHETHER I WAS TRYING TO DO GOOD OR NOT IS IRRELEVANT.
I CAN'T IGNORE THIS GUILT ANYMORE. I CAN'T ESCAPE IT.

I DON'T KNOW WHAT I'M GOING TO DO...
UM... EXCUSE US-- WE DIDN'T KNOW YOU WERE--

NONSENSE, SHE'S *OUR* DAUGHTER. EXCUSE ME.
I WAS-- JUST LEAVING ANYWAY.

UM... MARK-- RIGHT? I REMEMBER YOU COMING TO SEE SAMANTHA AT THE HOUSE.
YEAH, SORRY. I DIDN'T MEAN TO JUST WALK AWAY IN THERE.

NO, IT'S OKAY. ADAM, SAMANTHA'S FATHER--HE'S NOT HANDLING THIS WELL.
HE--

YOU'RE HERE--SO YOU KNOW, SAMANTHA... YOU KNOW SHE'S ATOM EVE.
YEAH.

ADAM NEVER APPROVED--WE WERE ALWAYS WORRIED SOMETHING LIKE... THIS WOULD HAPPEN. THIS IS OUR WORST FEARS REALIZED.
YOU SEEM LIKE A NICE BOY, I'M SORRY HE WAS SO RUDE.

NO--IT'S OKAY. I'M REALLY SORRY ABOUT WHAT HAPPENED. IF THERE'S ANYTHING I CAN DO FOR YOU OR YOUR HUSBAND, LET ME KNOW.
THAT'S VERY KIND OF YOU. NO, WE'RE FINE. THE DOCTOR HAS SAID HE'S VERY OPTIMISTIC--HER INJURIES AREN'T AS SEVERE AS THEY COULD HAVE BEEN.
IT'S FUNNY... NO, THAT'S A HORRIBLE THING TO SAY...IT'S IRONIC--BUT THAT STILL DOESN'T SEEM RIGHT...

THERE WAS A GIRL, LIVED ACROSS THE STREET FROM US. LUCY WAS HER NAME. SAMANTHA AND HER PLAYED TOGETHER WHEN THEY WERE YOUNGER--BUT SHE WENT OFF TO COLLEGE IN CHICAGO. SHE WAS A COUPLE YEARS OLDER THAN SAM...
SHE DIED. SHE WAS JUST A NORMAL GIRL, SHE WASN'T OUT FIGHTING ANYONE--AND SHE'S DEAD... AND OUR LITTLE GIRL IS ALIVE.

I DON'T KNOW WHAT TO SAY...

I'M SORRY, DEAR. I DIDN'T MEAN TO BE SO MORBID. WE JUST--
I SHOULD PROBABLY GO, I DIDN'T MEAN TO KEEP YOU.

WHAT'S LEFT OF THE APARTMENT OF FORMER ASTRONAUT, RUS LIVINGSTON.

THIRD FLOOR'S CLEAR.
YEAH-- I THINK THAT'S IT.

DID YOU SEE THAT?!
YEAH! WHAT THE HELL WAS THAT THING?!

I NEED A NEW PLACE TO LIVE--A BIGGER PLACE.
YOU WILL HELP ME FIND IT.
GRAAAGH!
YEEAAGH!!

THE PENTAGON, CURRENTLY UNDER CONSTRUCTION.
UNITED STATES PENTAGON
Parking in Rear

OKAY, OKAY... HE'S REVIVING.
IMMORTAL? IMMORTAL CAN YOU HEAR ME?

I'M-- I'M HERE... I'M--
KATE, I-- I'M VERY HAPPY TO SEE YOU.
I HURRIED HERE AS FAST AS I COULD ONCE ALL MY COPIES WERE KILLED. I WANTED TO BE HERE FOR YOUR REVIVAL.
IT'S GOOD TO SEE YOU, IMMORTAL. I'M HERE TO ASSURE YOU THAT WE'LL GIVE YOU AS MUCH TIME TO RECOVER AS YOU NEED. THE GUARDIANS WILL BE OKAY WITHOUT YOU.

I HOPE THAT IS TRUE BECAUSE I AM NOT COMING BACK.
I AM THROUGH WITH THIS LIFE. MY WIFE WANTS TO START A FAMILY, I'M READY TO GIVE THAT TO HER.

OH, MY GOD!
OH, MY GOD--I LOVE YOU SO MUCH!

IMMORTAL AND DUPLI-KATE ARE RETIRING. DARKWING IS DEAD, SHAPESMITH IS INJURED--THE GUARDIANS OF THE GLOBE ARE OUT OF COMMISSION.
THE WORLD IS LARGELY UNDEFENDED.
WE NEED TO DO SOMETHING ABOUT THAT, FAST. THAT'S WHY I CALLED YOU ALL HERE, DESPITE THE PAST DIFFERENCES I'VE HAD WITH SOME OF YOU.

SHAPESMITH SHOULD BE BACK UP TO SPEED SOON, HE HAS SOMETHING HE CALLS A "CORE" AND AS LONG AS THAT'S NOT DAMAGED HE SAYS HE'LL BE FINE. SO HE WAS LUCKY.
MORE LIKE WE WERE LUCKY. IF WE'RE TALKING ABOUT FORMING A NEW TEAM, WE HAVE VERY FEW OPTIONS RIGHT NOW.
THAT'S THE MAIN ISSUE-- WE NEED A NEW TEAM RIGHT NOW. I DON'T THINK THE ENEMIES OF THE WORLD WILL BE KIND ENOUGH TO TAKE A BREAK WHILE WE REBUILD.

I UNDERSTAND THIS SITUATION IS BIGGER THAN MY COMPLAINTS WITH YOU, CECIL... SO YOU CAN COUNT ON ME.
I'M TOLD BULLETPROOF'S NEW HAND IS COMPLETE--HE WASN'T INJURED OTHERWISE. I THINK I COULD CONVINCE HIM TO JOIN AT LEAST TEMPORARILY.
I'M CURRENTLY IN THE HOSPITAL WITH MONSTER GIRL AND THE DOCTORS TELL ME THEY'RE OPTIMISTIC THAT SHE'LL MAKE A FULL RECOVERY SOON. WE COULD COUNT HER IN AS WELL.

WHAT ABOUT REX SPLODE?

REX IS DEAD.

THERE'S NO TIME FOR THAT NOW.

WE NEED TO GET THIS TEAM UP AND RUNNING BEFORE ANYONE REALIZES HOW VULNERABLE WE ARE.

I DON'T FEEL COMFORTABLE WORKING FOR YOU UNDER ANY CIRCUMSTANCES.
WHY AM I HERE?

I WAS GOING TO ASK YOU TO LEAD THE TEAM.

WHAT? **ME?** I'M NOT READY FOR SOMETHING LIKE THAT.
WHAT MAKES YOU THINK I'D BE QUALIFIED FOR THAT?

YOU STOOD UP TO ME, KID. THAT MEANS SOMETHING.
I NEED SOMEONE WITH A STRONG WILL WHO'S ABLE TO MAKE TOUGH DECISIONS WHEN HE HAS TO. I **KNOW** YOU'RE READY FOR THIS.

I CAN'T-- NOT WITH EVE HURT LIKE SHE IS.
MY HEAD'S NOT IN IT RIGHT NOW.

BRIT? THINK YOU COULD HANDLE LEADING THE TEAM?

I'M HERE FOR YOU, CECIL-- BUT IT'S NICE TO KNOW YOU WENT TO THE ROOKIE FIRST.
NO OFFENSE, KID.

YOU WERE ALWAYS GOING TO BE IN CHARGE--WE JUST DIDN'T THINK YOU'D WANT TO BE THE FIELD LEADER.

I WISH YOU GUYS THE BEST OF LUCK. AND YOU CAN COUNT ON ME IF SOMETHING BIG COMES ALONG-- BUT FOR NOW, I THINK I'D BE OF BEST USE IN THE CLEAN-UP EFFORT.

CAN SOMEONE SHOW ME HOW TO GET OUT OF HERE WITHOUT JUST FLYING **UP?**
I'LL SHOW YOU OUT.

IF IT'S A GUARDIANS OF THE GLOBE TEAM... YOU KNOW YOU CAN COUNT ON ME.
I APPRECIATE THAT, SAMSON. IT WOULDN'T FEEL RIGHT WITHOUT YOU INVOLVED.
THAT INVINCIBLE-- MOODY LITTLE CUSS, AIN'T HE?

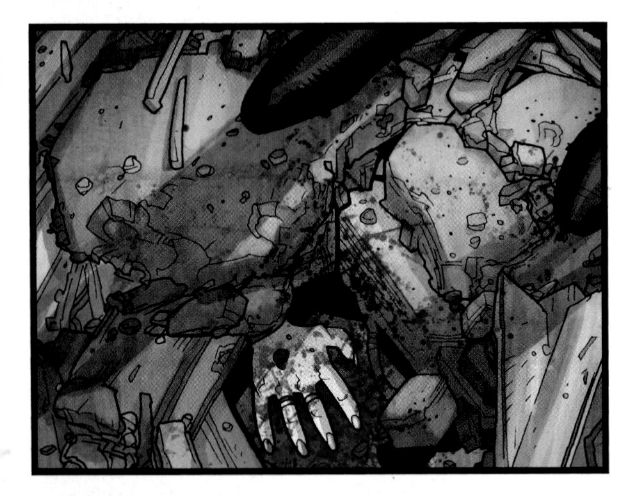

GOT ANOTHER BODY OVER HERE!

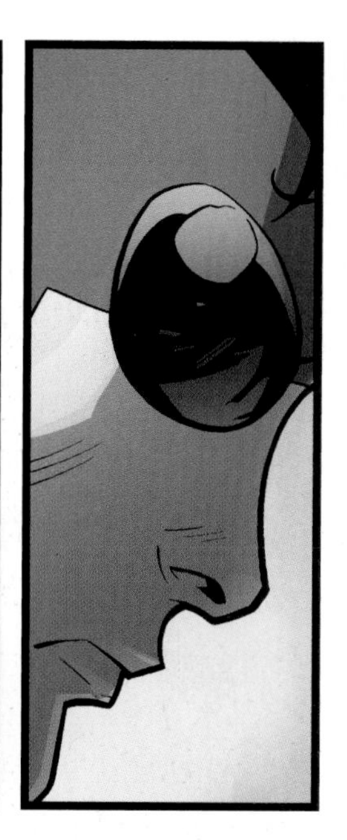

STAND READY FOR MY ARRIVAL, WORM!

YOU HAVE BEEN APPOINTED THE VILTRUMITE AGENT OF THIS PLANET, CHARGED WITH PREPARING IT FOR EVENTUAL TAKEOVER BY OUR EMPIRE.
I AM HERE TO CONFIRM YOUR PROGRESS MADE TOWARD THAT TASK... IF THERE IS NONE, I WILL ASSUME YOUR DUTIES AND TAKE OVER.
IF YOU OPPOSE ME. *I WILL KILL YOU.*

THIS ISN'T A GOOD TIME.

MAYBE YOU DO NOT UNDERSTAND THE SITUATION. THE VILTRUM EMPIRE ANTICIPATED YOUR RESISTANCE-- THAT IS WHY THEY SENT ME, SPECIFICALLY.
I AM CONQUEST. I HAVE NEVER FAILED TO ASSIMILATE A CHOSEN PLANET, NO MATTER ITS STRENGTH.
IF YOU CHOOSE TO OPPOSE ME, YOU WILL NOT SURVIVE.

MAYBE YOU DO NOT UNDERSTAND. I HAVE CAUSED ALL THE DESTRUCTION YOU SEE AROUND YOU. THE LIVES LOST ARE A DIRECT RESULT OF MY ACTIONS.
I CAN'T DESCRIBE THE GUILT, SHAME... AND MOST IMPORTANTLY ANGER THAT I FEEL RIGHT NOW.
ALL I HAVE THOUGHT ABOUT-- THE ONLY THING I'VE WANTED SINCE ALL OF THIS HAPPENED...

...WAS SOMETHING TO HIT AS HARD AS I CAN.

VERY WELL.

62
RYAN
+fco

KRA-KOOM!!

RUMMM

RIGHT NOW, ANISSA WOULD BE TELLING YOU ABOUT HOW THE VILTRUM EMPIRE WOULD TURN THIS PLANET INTO A UTOPIA. SHE'D TELL YOU YOU'RE A FOOL TO TRY AND PREVENT THIS--THAT WE WOULD BE HELPING THE PEOPLE YOU BELIEVE YOU ARE PROTECTING FROM US.
I WILL NOT TELL YOU ANY SUCH THING.
THE TRUTH IS, I WANT YOU TO RESIST. I'M NOT HERE BECAUSE I WANT TO SPREAD THE VILTRUM EMPIRE. I'M NOT HERE BECAUSE I BELIEVE IN ONE CAUSE OR THE OTHER, OR THAT I'M FULFILLING SOME KIND OF HONORABLE DUTY.
I'M HERE BECAUSE I ENJOY THIS.

I LONG TO FEEL MY FISTS DRENCHED IN BL--

WRAMM!

HA HA!
YOU'RE GETTING THERE.

VOOSH!

KROOM!!

RRRRMMMMMBBLE!

KKRRRGGGG!

KKGGGG!

BOOM!!

Krik.
Krakkle.

KRRGG!

MORE!
I WANT MORE!

THOOM!
ARRGH!

VERY GOOD.

THAT WAS A WARM UP.

KRAK!

KROOM!

WROKK!

WRAMM

KRAK!

KRAK!

YOU TRIED THIS ALREADY!
WRAMM!

ENOUGH GAMES.

DOOM!!!

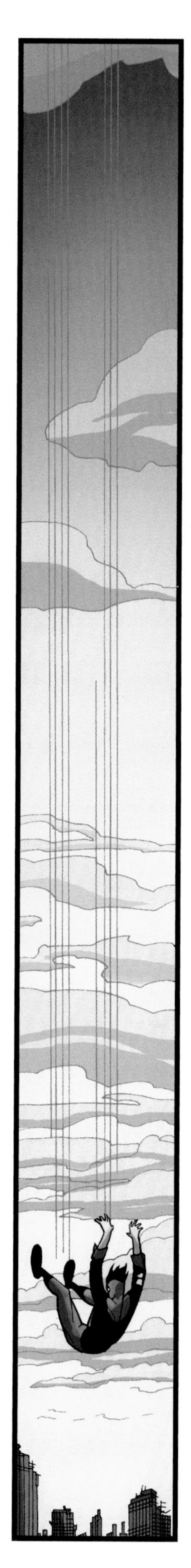

THERE--THEY'VE FOUND HIM AGAIN--THAT'S NOT TOO FAR AWAY!
I CAN HELP HIM!
OLIVER, DON'T--
LIVE!

--GO.
VOOSH!

YOUR BOYS ARE STRONG, DEB. THEY'LL BE OKAY.
YOU'LL SEE.

AGH.
JESUS.
OUCH.

KROOM!

WRAMM!

THERE!

TOO FAST--
CAN'T--

KRA-KOOM!

BOOM!!

WROKK!
WRUNK!
SKRRRGGG

STOP!

LISTEN TO ME--
JUST LISTEN.

ARE YOU CRAZY?

YOU THINK I'M GOING TO GIVE YOU A CHANCE TO SURRENDER SO THAT I HAVE TO STOP?
HAVE I GIVEN YOU ANY INDICATION THAT I WANT TO QUIT? I'M HAVING THE TIME OF MY LIFE!
COME ON-- KEEP GOING! WHEN I'M DONE WITH YOU I'M GOING TO KILL EVERYONE ELSE--DON'T FORGET THAT! YOU'RE ALL THAT STANDS BETWEEN ME AND THESE FEEBLE BEINGS YOU'VE GROWN TO LOVE.
GOOOM!

BIG-ASS BEAT DOWN COMING UP!
CHOOOM!!

WHO THE HELL ARE YOU?
I LIKE TO KNOW WHO I'M DISMEMBERING.
SCREW YOU. YOUR BREATH SMELLS LIKE FEET.

CHOOM!
OLIVER-- GET OUT OF HERE!

LET GO OF ME!
I'M HERE TO HELP! TOGETHER WE CAN BEAT THIS GUY!

NO!
HE'LL KILL YOU!

YOU IDIOT! YOU NEED ALL THE HELP YOU CAN GET!
WRAMM!
THE TIME I SPENT KILLING HIM MIGHT HAVE GIVEN YOU A MOMENT TO GATHER YOUR THOUGHTS-- MAYBE EVEN OUTWIT ME. YOU ARE AN EMBARRASSMENT.

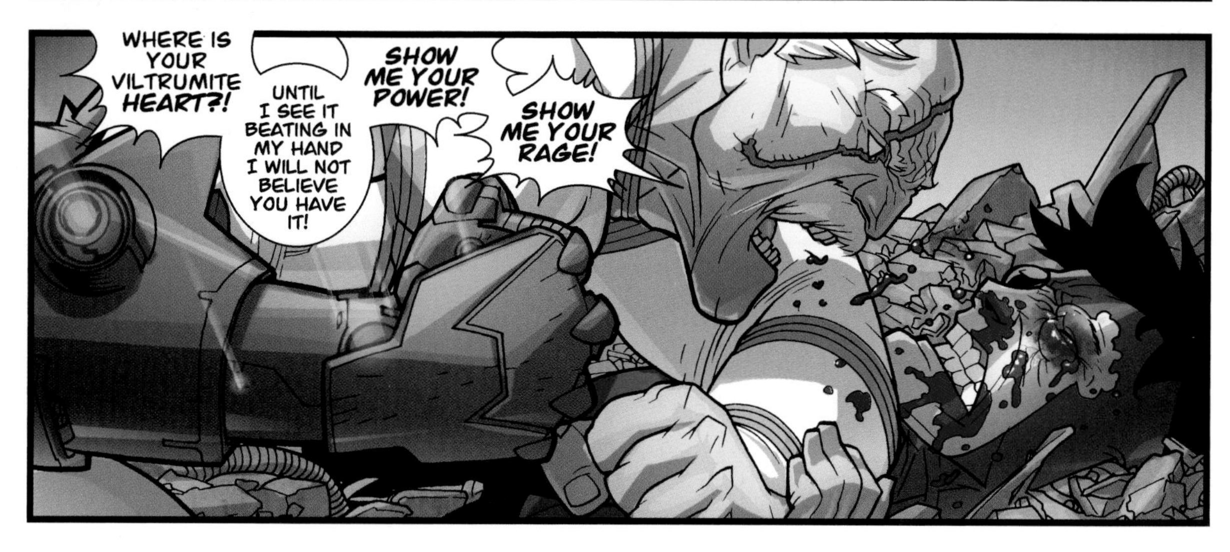
WHERE IS YOUR VILTRUMITE HEART?!
UNTIL I SEE IT BEATING IN MY HAND I WILL NOT BELIEVE YOU HAVE IT!
SHOW ME YOUR POWER!
SHOW ME YOUR RAGE!

WROKK!

ALMOST THERE.

GROKK!

KRAKK!

BRAKK!

CHILD...
...IF THAT IS ALL THE STRENGTH YOU POSSESS, THIS IS NOT GOING TO END WELL FOR YOU.
THAPP!

DEEP BELOW THE PENTAGON, THE HEADQUARTERS OF THE GLOBAL DEFENSE AGENCY.
UNITED STATES PENTAGON
Parking in Rear

NOW?!
THIS HAS TO HAPPEN NOW OF ALL TIMES?!

OUT OF MY WAY!

HEADS UP!

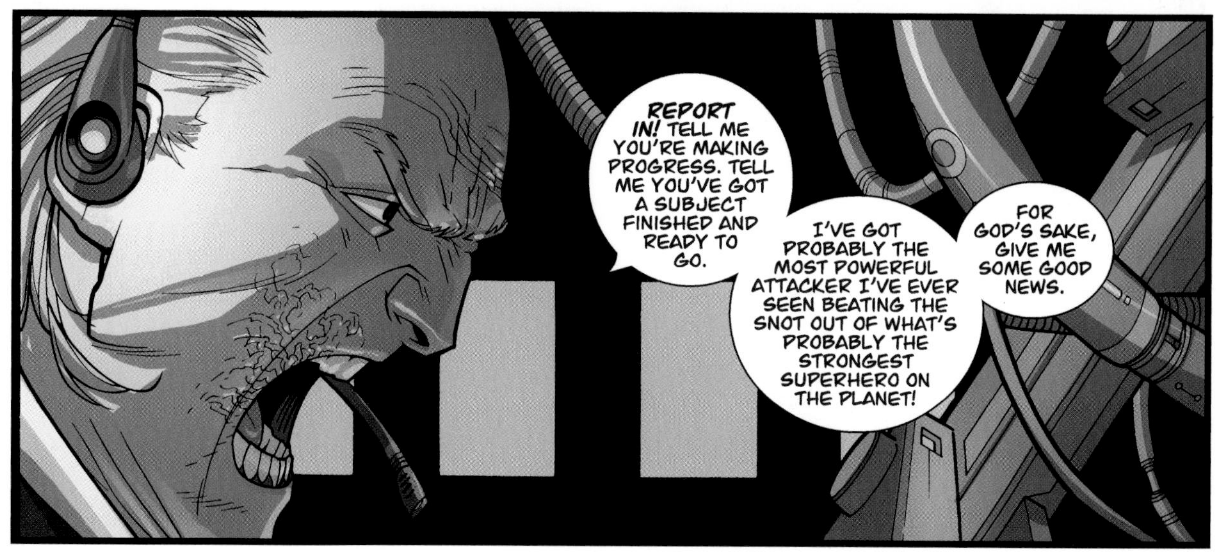
REPORT IN! TELL ME YOU'RE MAKING PROGRESS. TELL ME YOU'VE GOT A SUBJECT FINISHED AND READY TO GO.
I'VE GOT PROBABLY THE MOST POWERFUL ATTACKER I'VE EVER SEEN BEATING THE SNOT OUT OF WHAT'S PROBABLY THE STRONGEST SUPERHERO ON THE PLANET!
FOR GOD'S SAKE, GIVE ME SOME GOOD NEWS.

I'M AFRAID I CAN'T HELP YOU THERE. IT WOULD TAKE MY TEAM AND I TWO WEEKS OF NON-STOP WORK JUST TO GET SO MUCH AS **ONE** OF THESE ALTERNATE DIMENSION INVINCIBLES UP AND RUNNING.
YOU HAVE NO IDEA HOW DENSE THEIR MUSCLE TISSUE IS--IT'S LIKE CUTTING THROUGH ROCK.
THERE'S SIMPLY NOTHING I CAN DO TO SPEED THINGS ALONG.

THEN GOD HELP US ALL...

63

WHILE THE CLEAN-UP EFFORT CONTINUES ALL ACROSS THE GLOBE, AIDED IN LARGE PART BY THE SUPERHERO COMMUNITY OF THE WORLD, IT APPEARS THE CRISIS THAT CAUSED THIS DESTRUCTION HAS YET TO REACH A CONCLUSION.
WE'VE BEEN BRINGING YOU WHAT FOOTAGE WE CAN OF THE FIGHT BETWEEN WHO WE ORIGINALLY BELIEVED TO BE THE NEW HERO **INVINCIBOY**, BUT IS NOW KNOWN TO ACTUALLY BE INVINCIBLE AND AN UNKNOWN ATTACKER.
THE FIGHT HAS MOVED ACROSS THE GLOBE AT ENORMOUS SPEEDS. BECAUSE OF THIS, WE'VE ONLY BEEN ABLE TO PROVIDE YOU WITH SNIPPETS FROM VARIOUS SOURCES ACROSS THE WORLD.

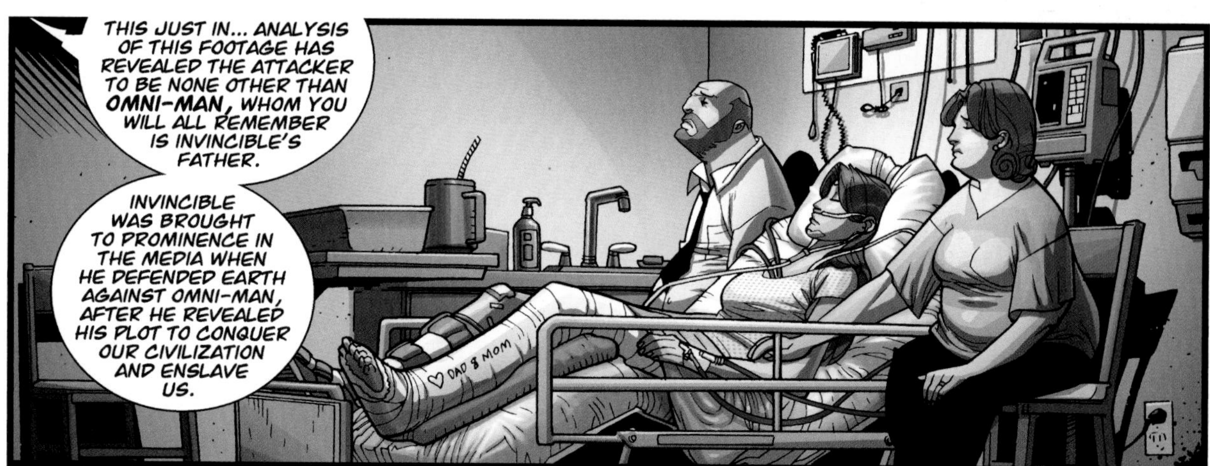
THIS JUST IN... ANALYSIS OF THIS FOOTAGE HAS REVEALED THE ATTACKER TO BE NONE OTHER THAN **OMNI-MAN**, WHOM YOU WILL ALL REMEMBER IS INVINCIBLE'S FATHER.
INVINCIBLE WAS BROUGHT TO PROMINENCE IN THE MEDIA WHEN HE DEFENDED EARTH AGAINST OMNI-MAN, AFTER HE REVEALED HIS PLOT TO CONQUER OUR CIVILIZATION AND ENSLAVE US.
♡ DAD & MOM

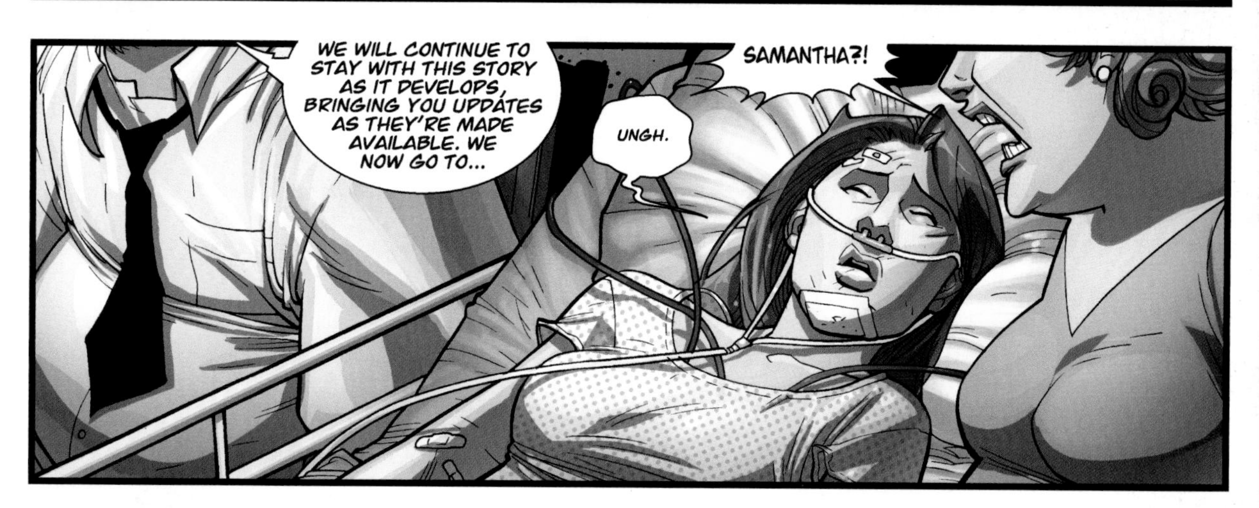
WE WILL CONTINUE TO STAY WITH THIS STORY AS IT DEVELOPS, BRINGING YOU UPDATES AS THEY'RE MADE AVAILABLE. WE NOW GO TO...
UNGH.
SAMANTHA?!

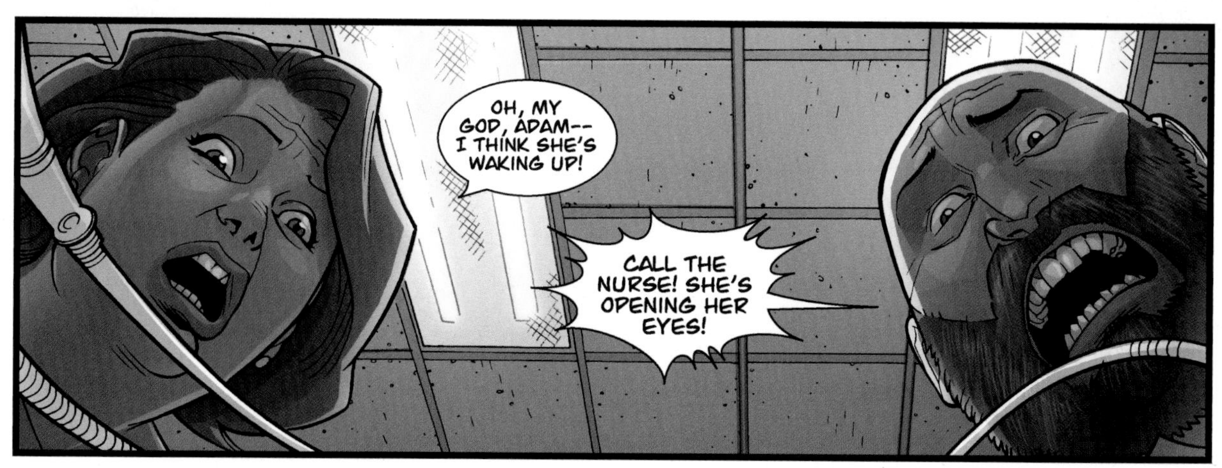
OH, MY GOD, ADAM-- I THINK SHE'S WAKING UP!
CALL THE NURSE! SHE'S OPENING HER EYES!

UNGH...
KOFF!
OH, MY GOD! WHERE'S MARK?!
WHAT HAPPENED?!

WAIT...

MOM?
DAD?
HOW LONG HAVE I BEEN OUT?
TWO DAYS.
SAMANTHA, HONEY-- EVERYTHING'S OKAY. THIS IS A SPECIAL PLACE-- THEY'RE KEEPING YOUR IDENTITY SECRET... THEY TOLD US NOT TO WORRY.

OH, MY GOD--WHAT IS *THAT?*

OH, THAT POOR INVINCIBLE BOY IS FIGHTING HIS DAD AGAIN.
YOU KNOW HIM, RIGHT?

OH, MY GOD-- MARK!
HE'S GOING TO KILL HIM THIS TIME! I HAVE TO HELP HIM!
MARK? YOU MEAN--?
YOUR BOYFRIEND?
CRAP.
YOU CAN'T BE DOING THIS-- YOUR INJURIES, YOU COULD MAKE THEM WORSE. THERE ARE TESTS--YOU CAN'T EVEN WALK!
DO I LOOK LIKE I NEED TO WALK?! LISTEN--IF YOU GUYS ARE PROTECTING MY IDENTITY, I NEED TO SPEAK TO THE MAN WHO SET THIS UP. GRAY HAIR-- WEIRD SCAR ON HIS MOUTH.
YOU KNOW WHO I'M TALKING ABOUT. GET HIM ON THE PHONE-- NOW!
I'LL--
I'LL SEE WHAT I CAN DO.

I'M COMING, MARK.

UP UNTIL NOW, I'VE BEEN PLAYING WITH YOU-- GETTING TO KNOW THE NEW TOY.
I TIRE OF THAT GAME.

WRAMM!

NOT THAT I'M NOT HAVING FUN--BUT I'M STARTING TO QUESTION WHY THEY SENT ME HERE. THIS TASK IS BENEATH ME.
BEATING YOU-- CONQUERING YOUR PATHETIC PLANET--IT'S TOO EASY.

FUN-- BUT EASY!

WRAMM!

KRAKKA-DOOM!

I'VE MET YOUR FATHER, YOU KNOW. NEVER SPENT MUCH TIME WITH HIM--BUT I KNEW HIM WHEN HE WAS YOUNGER. HE SHOWED SO *MUCH* PROMISE.
NOW HE'S DEAD. HEARD HIS EXECUTION WAS FINALLY ORDERED JUST BEFORE I WAS SENT HERE.
SAD REALLY--I'D LOVE TO SEE THE LOOK ON HIS FACE AFTER I TOLD HIM I'VE KILLED ***YOU.***
MY... FATHER...?

EAT ONE, YOU OLD SACK OF TURDS!
WROKK!
C'MON-- HURRY!
WHY DID YOU COME BACK? HE'LL KILL YOU, OLIVER. PLEASE, JUST RUN!
YOU CAN'T FIGHT HIM ALONE--HE'S OLD AS DIRT-- WE CAN TAKE HIM DOWN TOGETHER.
TRUST ME, YOU **CAN'T**. I'M OLD-- NOT **WEAK**.
I DO THANK YOU FOR COMING BACK. I WELCOME THE SECOND CHANCE.
I'M GOING TO SPLIT YOU IN HALF AND EAT YOUR HEART. HOW'S THAT SOUND?

I THINK THAT SOUNDS LIKE A BUNCH OF BULL--
TAKE A BREAK WHILE I FOCUS ON THE BOY.
WRAM!
GOOM!
AAGH!!
KRAKK!
NGGG.
DO YOU FEEL YOUR BODY STARTING TO RIP APART? IT STARTS WITH YOUR VERTEBRAE SEPARATING--THEN YOU'LL FEEL YOUR MUSCLES STARTING TO STRETCH--IF YOU'RE ABLE TO FOCUS THROUGH THE PAIN YOU'LL FEEL YOUR SKIN PULLED TO ITS BREAKING POINT...
THIS IS GOING TO BE AMAZING.

NO!
NO!
NO!
NO!

CHOOM

WELL...
FASTER THAN I ANTICIPATED...

NO MATTER.
KROOM!

I'LL EAT *YOUR* HEART INSTEAD!
WRAMM!

I'VE GOT HIM, SEND A MED-UNIT RIGHT AWAY. TELL HIS MOTHER HE'S STILL BREATHING.
SIR, I'VE GOT AN URGENT CALL COMING IN. IT'S THE REDHEAD. SHE WANTS A TELEPORT INTO THE HOT ZONE. WHAT SHOULD I SAY?

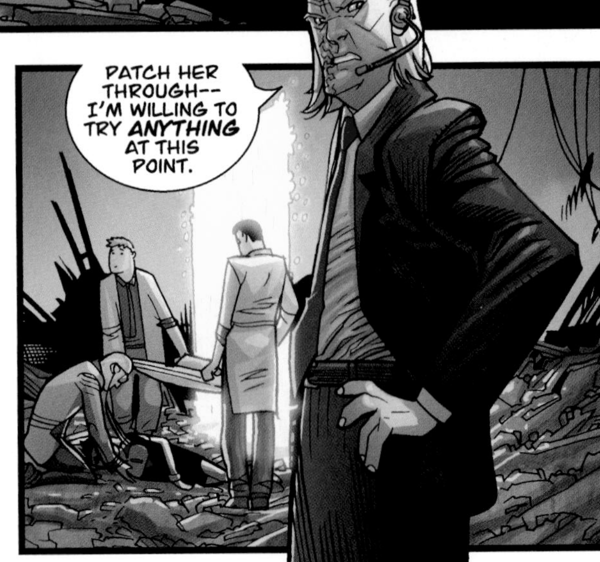
PATCH HER THROUGH-- I'M WILLING TO TRY *ANYTHING* AT THIS POINT.

THAT WAS THEM, THEY SAID HE'S HURT BUT BREATHING--THEY SAY HE'S GOING TO BE OKAY.
THERE, THERE...

DESTRUCTINATOR

HALF OF THE SUPERHERO COMMUNITY IS EITHER IN THE HOSPITAL OR COMPLETELY SHELL-SHOCKED BY THE EVENTS THAT LEVELED THE WORLD.
OTHERWISE, I'D HAVE SUPERHEROES POPPING OUT OF PORTALS A MILE APART TRYING TO ANTICIPATE WHERE THIS FIGHT IS GOING--NEVER MIND THE FACT THAT WE'VE GOT MAYBE **SIX** PEOPLE ON THE PLANET WHO COULD HOLD THEIR OWN WITH THIS GUY FOR MORE THAN A MINUTE.
WHAT I'M SAYING IS--I CAN SEND YOU, BUT BY THE TIME YOU STEP OUT OF THAT PORTAL THEY COULD BE GONE. THEY'RE MOVING AT INCREDIBLE SPEEDS--WE'VE BEEN BEHIND AS MUCH AS FIVE MINUTES TRYING TO FOLLOW THEIR FIGHT ON SATELLITE FEEDS.
I DON'T CARE--I HAVE TO TRY. IF I GET THERE IN TIME--I CAN HOLD THE MAN DOWN WITH MY FORCE FIELDS.
DO IT.

LOOK BEHIND YOU!
SPUTT!
SPUTT!
SPUTT!

BWAKA-DOOM!

FSSSHH!

WRRRKK!

SHHHGG!

KRRMMM

GOOOM!!!
WHAMM!
PLEASE, NO--
YOU'RE NOT OMNI-MAN!
YEAH, BAD NEWS FOR YOU.

MARK!
GET OUT OF HERE! GO!
NOW!
WRAMM!
SO CONCERNED FOR OTHERS' SAFETY...
YOU REALLY ARE PATHETIC.
WRUKK!
AAAGGH!
NO!
YOU'VE GOT PROBLEMS OF YOUR OWN, KITTEN.
CHOOM!

GOO

SPLUGCK!

HEH.
SO PRETTY...

...SUCH A WASTE.
NO.
EVE, PLEASE-- I CAN'T DO THIS WITHOUT YOU.
I CAN'T LIVE WITHOUT YOU...

PLEASE.
PLEASE.
PLEASE.

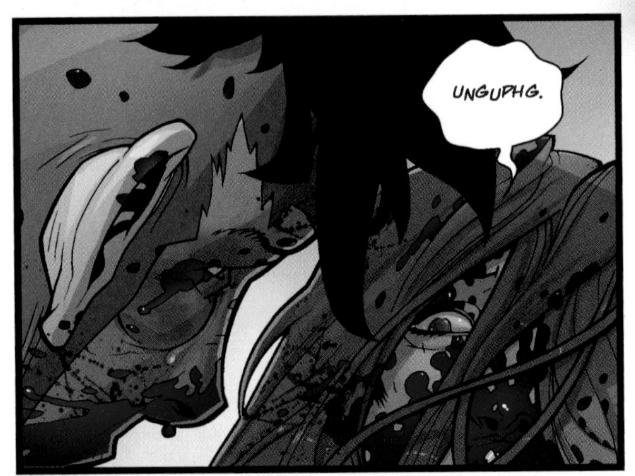
UNGUPHG.

DON'T TRY TO TALK-- SAVE YOUR STRENGTH.
IF CECIL'S WATCHING HE'LL SEND HELP!

PLEASE, JUST KEEP BREATHING.
KEEP--

--BREATHING.

SHE MUST HAVE REALLY CARED FOR YOU--TO DO WHAT SHE DID HERE. SURELY SHE WASN'T STUPID ENOUGH TO THINK SHE COULD ACTUALLY HURT ME.
SHE MUST HAVE DONE ALL THIS FOR YOU.
SUCH A STRONG BOND, WE VILTRUMITES HAVE NOTHING LIKE THIS. IT BREEDS WEAKNESS. STILL, IT'S ADMIRABLE. I AM BEGINNING TO UNDERSTAND YOUR AFFINITY FOR THESE CREATURES.

DELICIOUS.

EVE!
EVE--DON'T!

NOT LONG NOW, EH?
IF YOU'VE GOT ANYTHING IMPORTANT TO TELL HER--BETTER GET IT OFF YOUR CHEST NOW.

I SHOULD DO THIS NOW--DON'T KNOW WHEN I'LL GET THE CHANCE AGAIN.
I WANT TO **THANK** YOU, MARK GRAYSON... INVINCIBLE.
REALLY.
FROM THE BOTTOM OF MY HEART.
IT'S NOT VERY OFTEN THAT I GET TO CUT LOOSE LIKE THIS. I MEAN **REALLY** CUT LOOSE LIKE I HAVE HERE. USUALLY, THERE ARE SO MANY MISSION PARAMETERS.
"DON'T DESTROY THIS."
"KEEP THIS PERSON ALIVE."
BUT NOT HERE--NOT WITH **THIS** PLANET. FOR WHATEVER REASON, I DON'T REALLY CARE WHY, TO BE HONEST, I WAS TOLD--TAKE CONTROL, NO MATTER WHAT IT TAKES... TAKE CONTROL OF THE PLANET.
SO WHATEVER YOU DID TO PISS US OFF--**THANK YOU.** THIS HAS BEEN **FUN.**

DEAD?
GOOD. I TAKE IT I HAVE YOUR FULL ATTENTION, NOW?

I DON'T CARE HOW STRONG YOU ARE.
I DON'T CARE HOW FAST YOU ARE.
I CAN SEE THE FUTURE... YOU DON'T LIVE TO SEE TOMORROW.

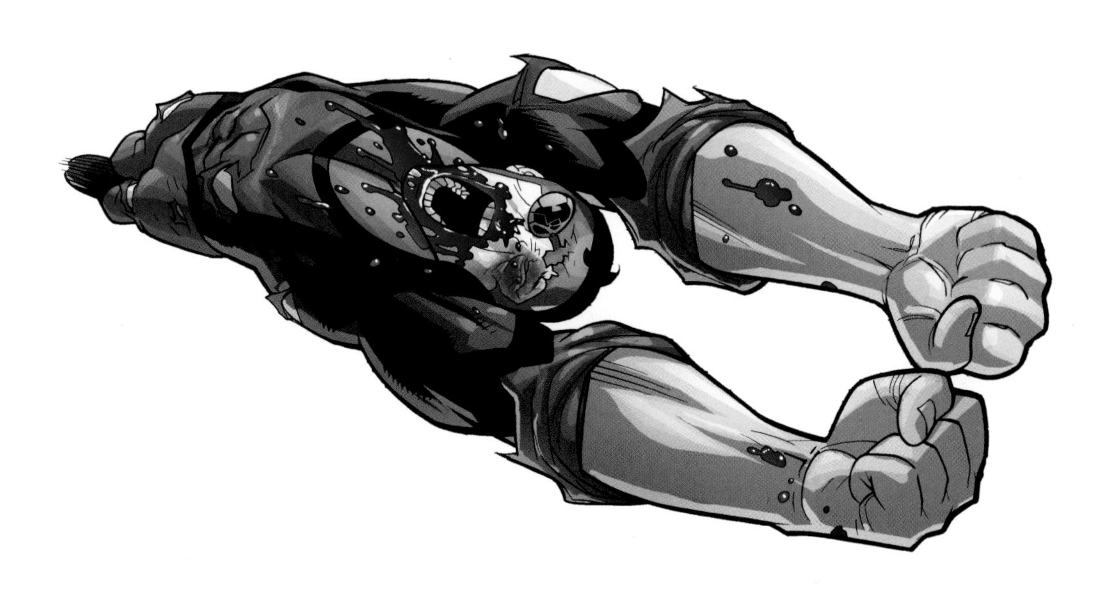

64
Ryan 09
+fco

HA HA HA HA HA!
AFTER ALL I'VE DONE-- AFTER EVERYTHING YOU'VE ENDURED AT MY HAND--STILL, YOU THREATEN ME.
I DARE SAY, CHILD-- YOU ARE BEGINNING TO IMPRESS ME.
OKAY, THEN.
DO YOUR WORST.

THOOM!

NOW WE'RE GETTING SOMEWHE--

KROK!

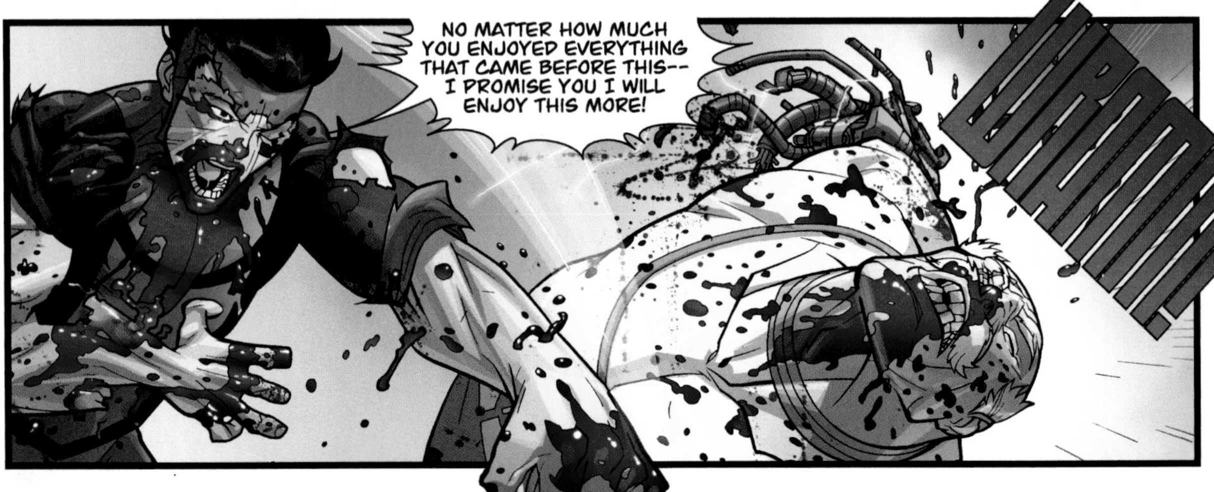
NO MATTER HOW MUCH YOU ENJOYED EVERYTHING THAT CAME BEFORE THIS-- I PROMISE YOU I WILL ENJOY THIS MORE!
WHAM!

CHILD, PLEASE.
BEING ENRAGED AT ME DOESN'T MAKE YOU STRONGER. THAT'S NOT HOW IT WORKS.

YOU DON'T STAND A--

YEEEAAAAAAGH!!

GRAAGH!

SHHK

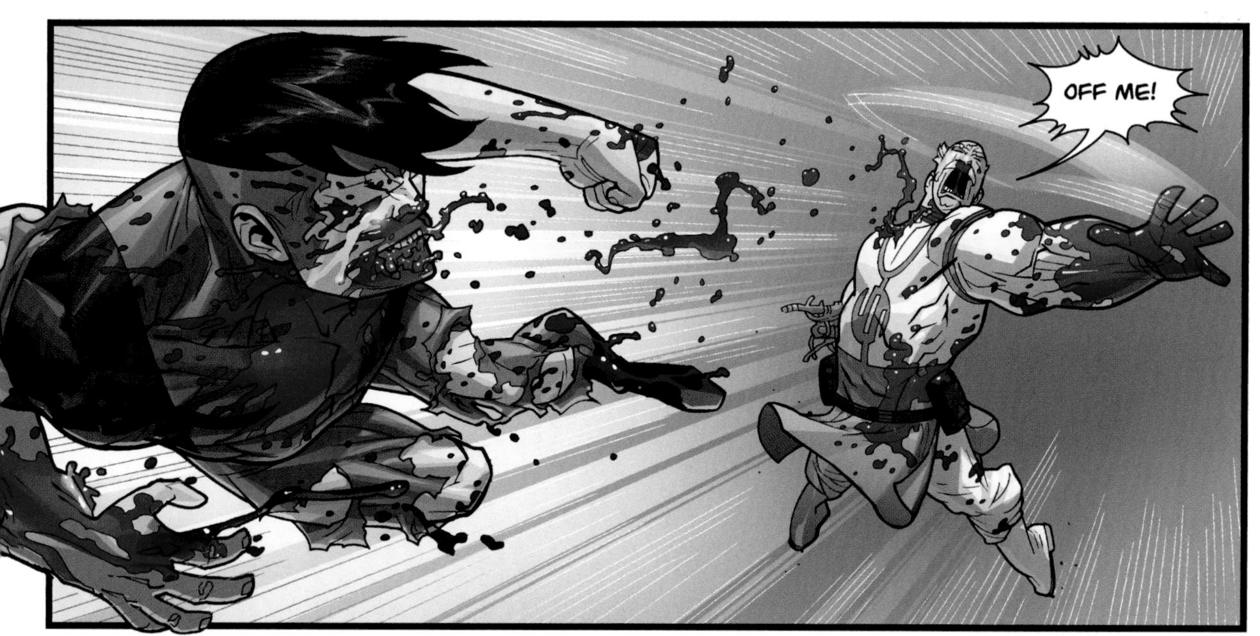
OFF ME!

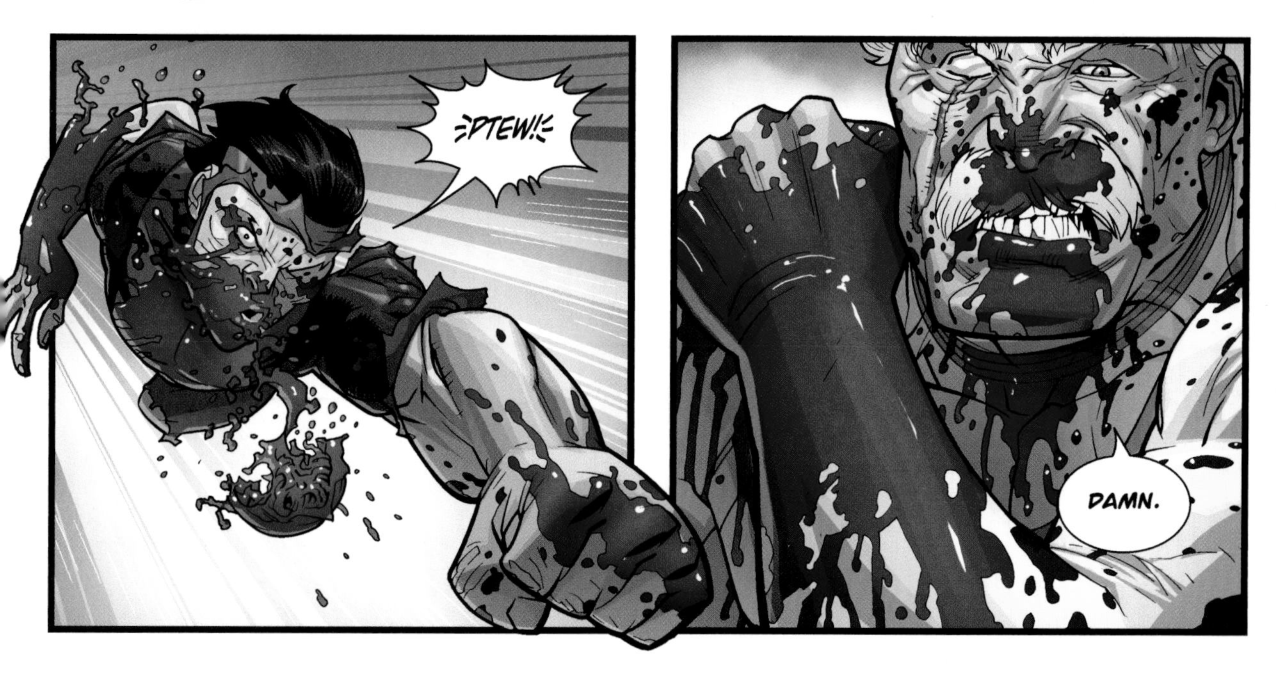
PTEW!
DAMN.

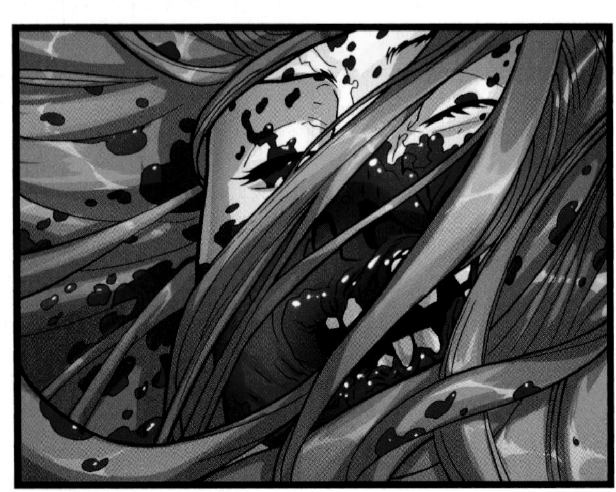

DIE!
DIE!
WRAM!
WRAMM!

DIE!

EVE?

PAY ATTENTION!!
KROOOM!

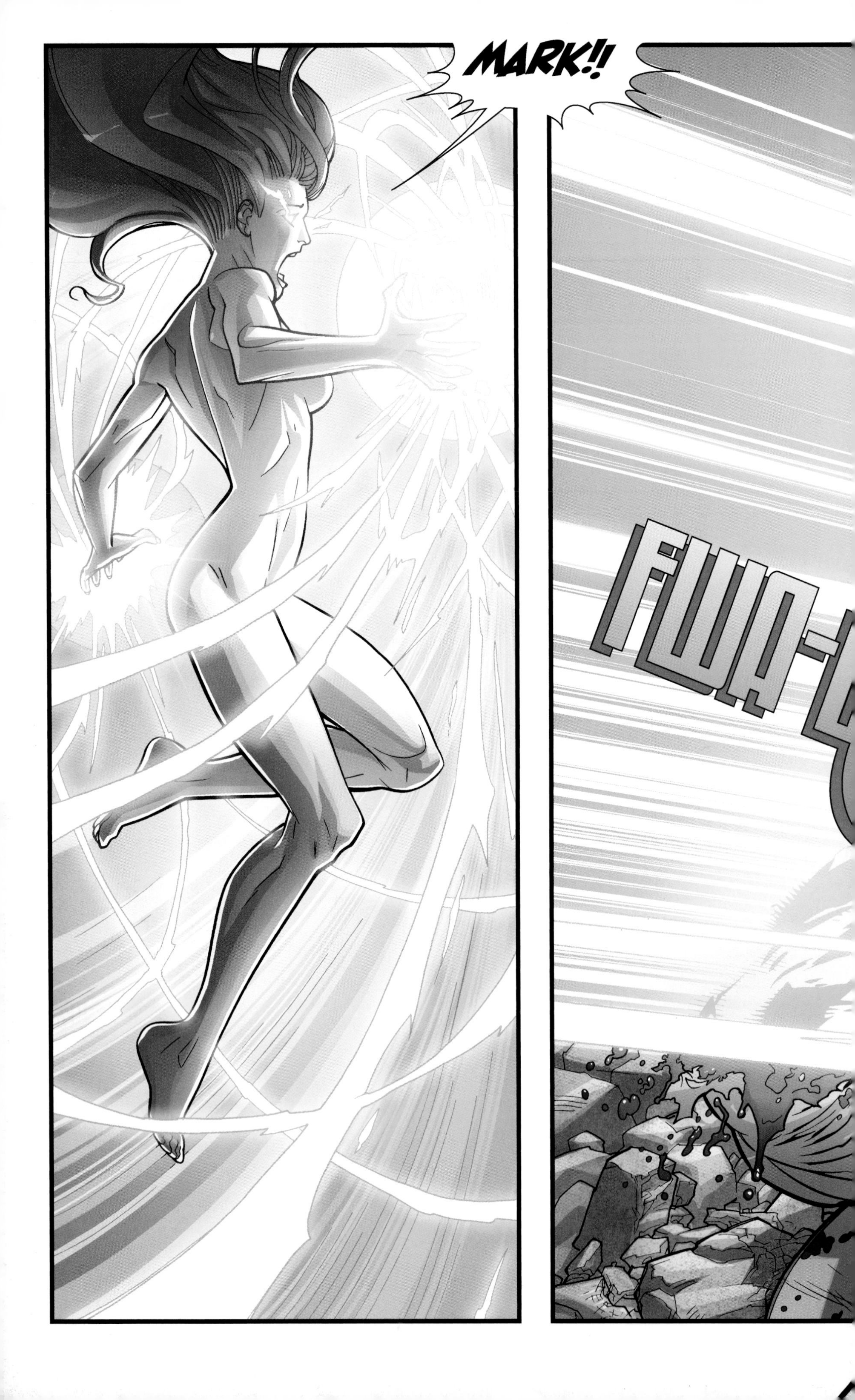
MARK!!
FWA-

HURRGGGH!!
OOSH!!

JERK.

WHAT WAS--?

THIS TIME I'LL MAKE **SURE** YOU'RE DEAD...

YOU WILL NOT TOUCH HER!
HNGH?

WRAMM!

UNGH.
WHUMP!

KRAK! KRAK!

KRAK! KRAK!

THAP!
GOT MORE THAN ENOUGH FIGHT LEFT IN ME FOR YOU, BOY.

RUNKK!

YEAAAGGHH!!

HUFF!
HUFF!
SEE?
MORE THAN ENOUGH.

NOT ENOUGH.
NOT NEARLY.

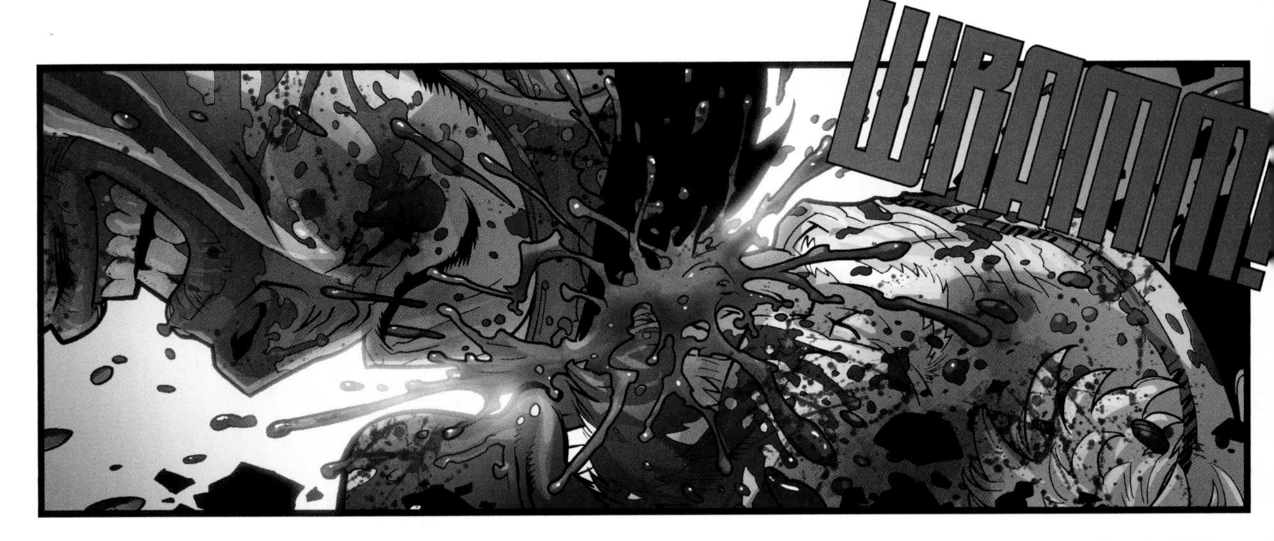
WRAMM!

IS THIS STILL FUN?!
ARE YOU ENJOYING YOURSELF?!
HAVING FUN?!

WELL?!
ANSWER ME!

HEH.
I TAKE THE GOOD WITH THE BAD...

CHOOM!
CHOOM!
CHOOM!

CHOOM!
CHOOM!
CHOOM!
CHOOM!
CHOOM!

HUFF!
HUFF!
HUFF!
HUFF!

EVE?

HOLD ON...
I'M COMING...

PLEASE...

...

EVE?
HOW?

I SAW--
HOW ARE YOU--?
UGHN?
MARK?

YOU'RE ALIVE.

I AM.
YOU TOO.

YEAH...
LOVE YOU...
LOVE YOU, TOO...

I THOUGHT...
...
I THOUGHT YOU WERE...

MARK? MARK, ARE YOU...?
HEY.
AM I...?

...NAKED?
...

HUH.

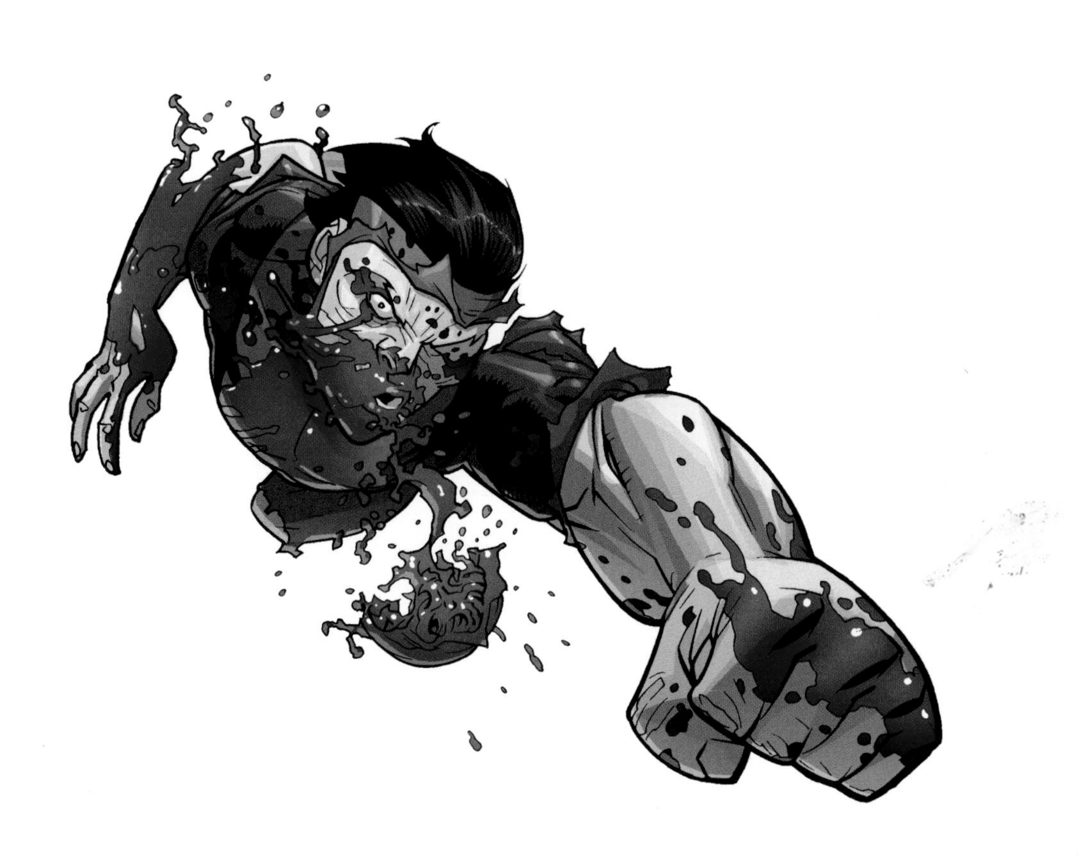

65

UNITED STATES
PENTAGON
Parking in Rear

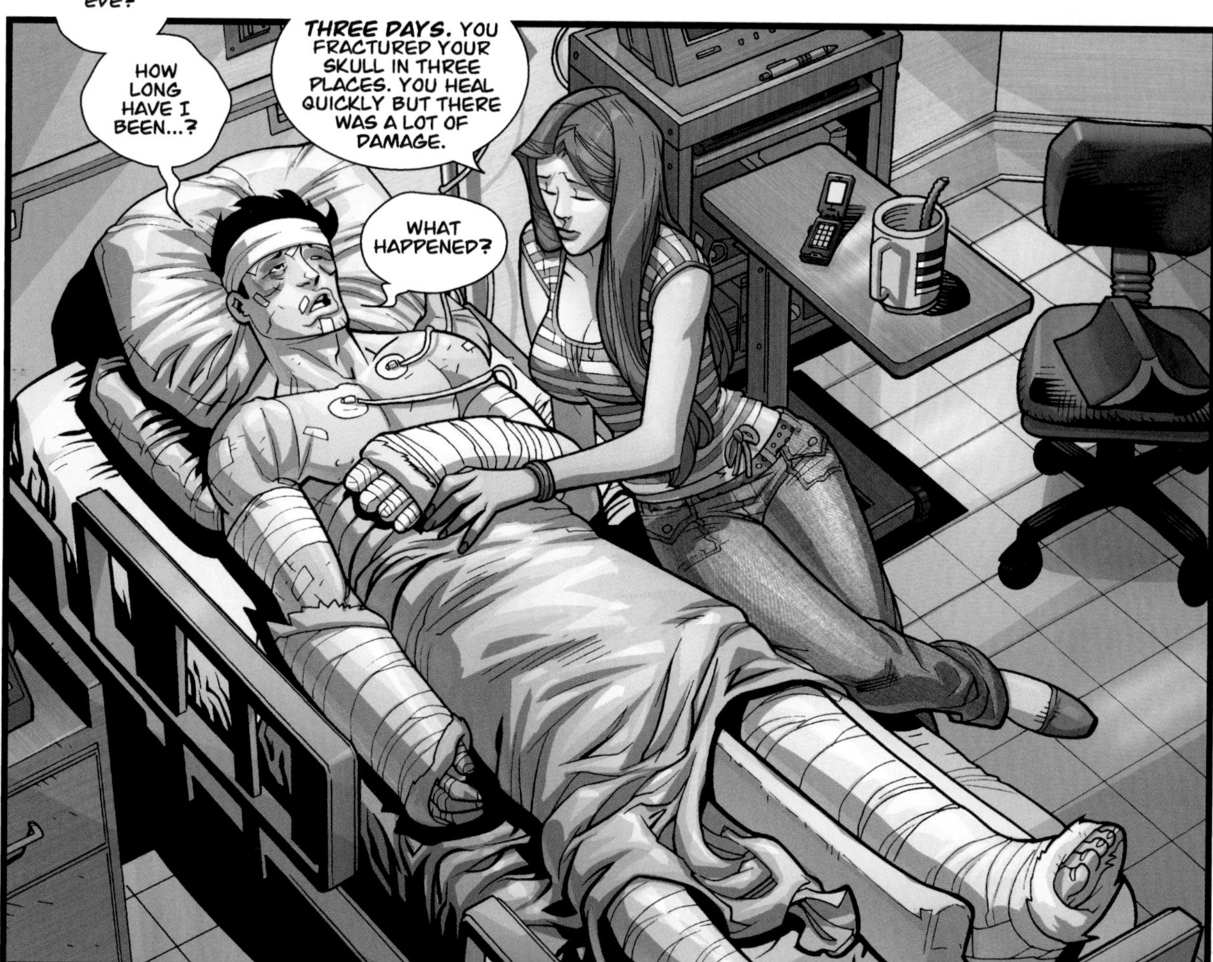
UNGH... EVE?
HOW LONG HAVE I BEEN...?
THREE DAYS. YOU FRACTURED YOUR SKULL IN THREE PLACES. YOU HEAL QUICKLY BUT THERE WAS A LOT OF DAMAGE.
WHAT HAPPENED?

YOU MEAN... YOU DON'T REMEMBER?
DO YOU REMEMBER ANYTHING?

NO... I REMEMBER EVERYTHING.

I REMEMBER YOU... I REMEMBER THAT YOU DIED.
ARE YOU REALLY HERE? ARE YOU ALIVE?
YES. I'M ALIVE AND WELL. I NEVER ACTUALLY DIED... I JUST GOT REALLY CLOSE.
H-- HOW?

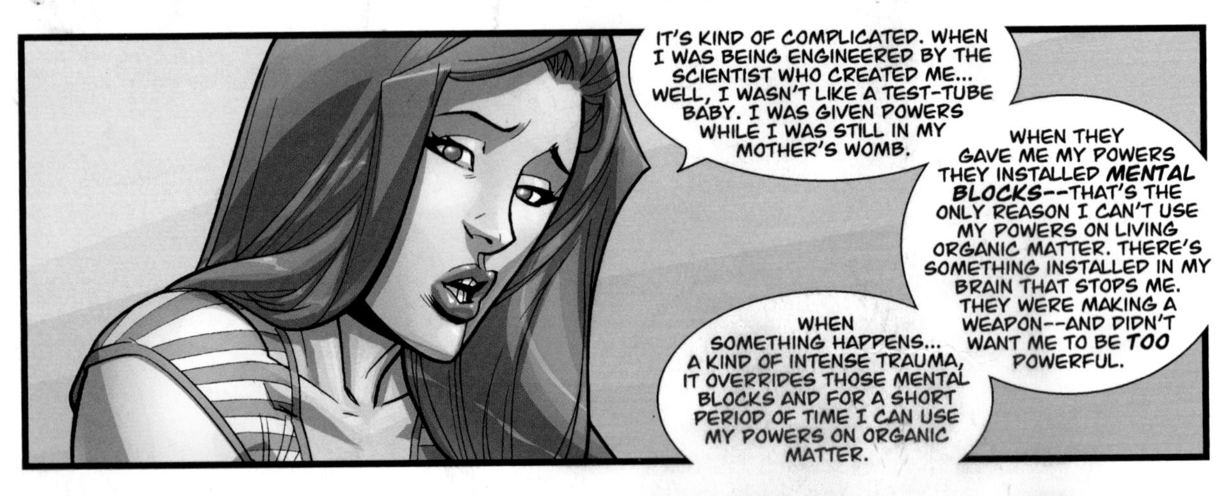
IT'S KIND OF COMPLICATED. WHEN I WAS BEING ENGINEERED BY THE SCIENTIST WHO CREATED ME... WELL, I WASN'T LIKE A TEST-TUBE BABY. I WAS GIVEN POWERS WHILE I WAS STILL IN MY MOTHER'S WOMB.
WHEN THEY GAVE ME MY POWERS THEY INSTALLED MENTAL BLOCKS--THAT'S THE ONLY REASON I CAN'T USE MY POWERS ON LIVING ORGANIC MATTER. THERE'S SOMETHING INSTALLED IN MY BRAIN THAT STOPS ME. THEY WERE MAKING A WEAPON--AND DIDN'T WANT ME TO BE TOO POWERFUL.
WHEN SOMETHING HAPPENS... A KIND OF INTENSE TRAUMA, IT OVERRIDES THOSE MENTAL BLOCKS AND FOR A SHORT PERIOD OF TIME I CAN USE MY POWERS ON ORGANIC MATTER.

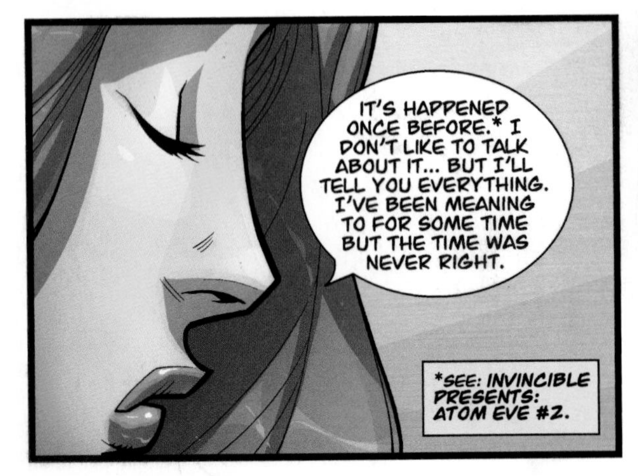
IT'S HAPPENED ONCE BEFORE.* I DON'T LIKE TO TALK ABOUT IT... BUT I'LL TELL YOU EVERYTHING. I'VE BEEN MEANING TO FOR SOME TIME BUT THE TIME WAS NEVER RIGHT.
*SEE: INVINCIBLE PRESENTS: ATOM EVE #2.

SO BASICALLY... BEING NEAR DEATH WAS STRESSFUL ENOUGH TO ALLOW ME TO REBUILD MY BODY.

AND, UH... ARE YOUR BOOBS?
A LITTLE. I WASN'T THINKING CLEARLY. I GUESS IN THE SPUR OF THE MOMENT I MADE SOME... IMPROVEMENTS.

HEH.
UGH--IT HURTS TO LAUGH.

I DON'T THINK I COULD HAVE SURVIVED WITHOUT--

SHHH.

OW.

I'LL BE GENTLE.

I DON'T THINK YOU UNDERSTAND. I WOULD LOVE TO HAVE SO MUCH AS ONE OF THESE GUYS COMPLETED AND OPERATIONAL... BUT IT'S JUST NOT FEASIBLE.
I'M DOING MY BEST--REALLY. THERE'S JUST--SO MUCH WORK INVOLVED IN REBUILDING THESE BODIES. I'M ESSENTIALLY INVENTING NEW TOOLS TO MAKE THIS JOB POSSIBLE.
IT SIMPLY CAN'T BE RUSHED.

NO, I THINK YOU DON'T UNDERSTAND.
HAVE YOU BEEN WATCHING THE FOOTAGE? DID YOU SEE WHAT THIS MONSTER DID TO INVINCIBLE? DO YOU HAVE ANY IDEA WHAT JUST ONE OF THESE THINGS IS CAPABLE OF?
THIS IS ONE OF AN ENTIRE ALIEN RACE. COUNTLESS SOLDIERS--JUST LIKE HIM, WHO ARE, NOW THAT THIS ONE HAS FAILED, SOONER RATHER THAN LATER...
COMING HERE.

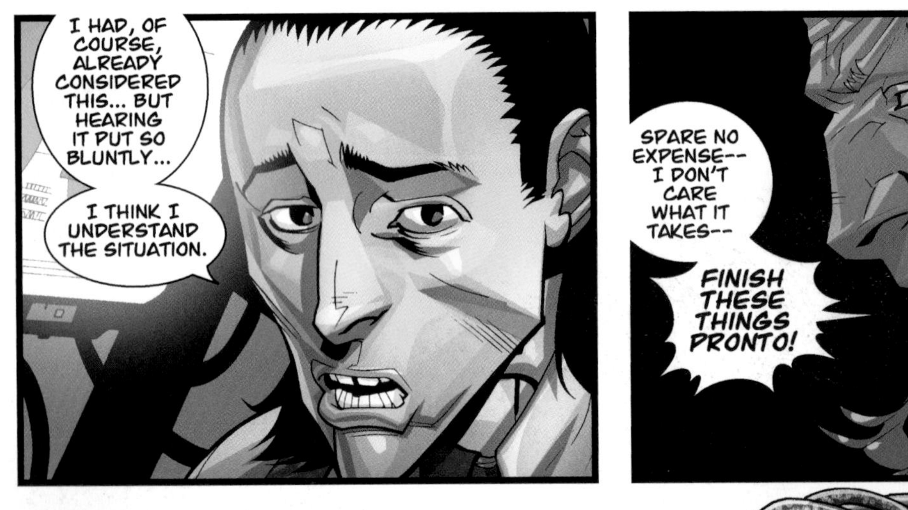
I HAD, OF COURSE, ALREADY CONSIDERED THIS... BUT HEARING IT PUT SO BLUNTLY...
I THINK I UNDERSTAND THE SITUATION.

SPARE NO EXPENSE-- I DON'T CARE WHAT IT TAKES--
FINISH THESE THINGS PRONTO!

INSTEAD OF DINNER AND A MOVIE... I THINK WE'LL BE WORKING TONIGHT.
I GATHERED...

UH...

IT **SOUNDED** LIKE YOU WERE AWAKE FROM THE HALL.
WE HEARD **RUSTLING.**

SORRY, MS. GRAYSON. I WAS GOING TO COME GET YOU IN A MINUTE.
HE **JUST** WOKE UP.

IT'S OKAY-- AND, PLEASE, CALL ME DEBBIE.

OH, MARK... I'M SO GLAD YOU'RE OKAY.
I WAS SO WORRIED...I THOUGHT...
...
IT'S **OKAY,** MOM.

NO, IT'S NOT.
I'M SO SORRY, MARK.

I DON'T UNDERSTAND, MOM.
WHY?

WHEN I MARRIED YOUR FATHER... I KNEW ABOUT HIS POWERS--WHAT HE DID. I DIDN'T KNOW EVERYTHING...
...BUT I KNEW ENOUGH.
I BROUGHT YOU INTO THIS LIFE. I RAISED YOU, KNOWING THAT THIS WOULD BE YOUR LIFE. WE PRACTICALLY ENCOURAGED YOU. EVERY TIME I SEE YOU OUT THERE... GETTING HURT, FIGHTING FOR YOUR LIFE...
I FEEL LIKE IT'S MY FAULT.

MOM, IT'S NOT YOUR--
I COULD HAVE TAKEN YOU AWAY FROM ALL THIS... WE COULD HAVE HIDDEN YOUR FATHER'S POWERS LONGER.

I SHOULDN'T HAVE LET HIM CONVINCE ME THIS WOULD BE OKAY. YOU COULD BE DOING SOMETHING ELSE WITH THESE POWERS--ANYTHING...
...ANYTHING BUT THIS.

BUT WHAT I'M DOING IS GOOD.
PEOPLE NEED ME--

PEOPLE NEED HEROES AND THERE ARE PLENTY!
THEY DON'T NEED YOU!
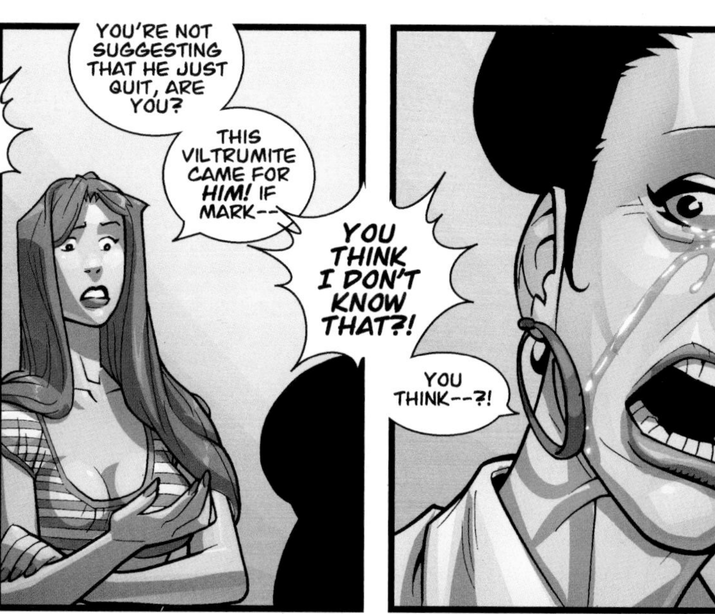
YOU'RE NOT SUGGESTING THAT HE JUST QUIT, ARE YOU?
THIS VILTRUMITE CAME FOR HIM! IF MARK--
YOU THINK I DON'T KNOW THAT?!
YOU THINK--?!

I'M SORRY. I DON'T KNOW WHAT I'M DOING. I'M JUST UPSET.
LET'S GO, PAUL.
UM, GET WELL SOON.
DEBBIE, WAIT--
JUST LET HER GO. SHE'S NOT MAD AT YOU.

OH, EXCUSE ME.

I KNOW WE'RE NOT ON THE BEST OF TERMS, BUT I WANTED TO TALK TO YOU ABOUT WHAT HAPPENED.
THERE'S A LOT AT STAKE HERE.

ANSWER THIS RIGHT NOW.
WHERE IS THE BODY?

HERE.
HE'S DEAD.
HE'S **REALLY** DEAD.

...
YEAH.

DID YOU REALLY HAVE TO SEE IT?
I HAD TO BE SURE... HAD TO SEE HIM WITH MY OWN EYES... TO KNOW HE'S DEAD.

AFTER ANGSTROM--

I UNDERSTAND. I JUST--I DON'T KNOW IF I COULD STAND SEEING THAT MAN AGAIN.
ALIVE OR DEAD.

I DIDN'T WANT TO, I JUST HAD TO BE SURE.
I'M GOING TO CHECK ON OLIVER. HE'S JUST DOWN THE HALL. WANNA COME?

I CAN'T.
I NEED TO LEAVE, MARK.

WHY? WHERE ARE YOU GOING?

REX'S FUNERAL IS TODAY.

OH, UH... CAN I COME? WOULD YOU MIND?
I FEEL LIKE I SHOULD BE THERE.

I'D LIKE THAT.

...WE DIDN'T GET ALONG AT FIRST. HE WAS ALWAYS PUSHING MY BUTTONS.
HUH.
BUTTONS... ROBOT... HE WOULD HAVE THOUGHT THAT WAS FUNNY. I'D BE LYING IF I SAID I DIDN'T LIKE HIM AT FIRST, THE TRUTH IS, I IDOLIZED HIM. HE WAS ALWAYS SO CONFIDENT, SO SURE OF HIMSELF AT ALL TIMES.
HE WAS EVERYTHING I WANTED TO BE...
AND NOW HE'S GONE. I WILL MISS HIM MORE THAN I CAN EVER SAY.

I'VE LIVED MOST OF MY LIFE THROUGH DRONES LIKE THE ONE YOU SEE BEFORE YOU NOW. I HAVE ALWAYS SIMPLY BEEN "ROBOT." I HAVE NEVER BEEN COMFORTABLE USING MY GIVEN NAME--IT REMINDS ME OF THE DISFIGURED BODY I INHABITED MOST OF MY LIFE... BEFORE I TRANSFERRED MYSELF INTO A CLONED BODY OF MY OLDEST FRIEND.
IN HONOR OF THIS FALLEN HERO, I'VE DECIDED THAT I WILL TAKE HIS NAME. I AM CHANGING MY NAME TO "REX." THAT MUCH OF HIM, AT LEAST, WILL LIVE ON.
I ONLY HOPE THAT I CAN LIVE UP TO HIS SACRIFICE. HE DIED AS HE LIVED--SAVING LIVES.
HE WILL BE MISSED.

NOW I BELIEVE ATOM EVE WANTED TO SAY A FEW WORDS.

WHY ARE YOU DOING IT LIKE THIS?
I'M STILL NOT--COMFORTABLE OUT IN THE--
CRYING--I CAN TRANSMIT MY THOUGHTS--BUT NOT TALK--

OH, HONEY, I DIDN'T--YOU'RE ADORABLE.
I LOVE YOU... "REX."

REX SPLODE WAS...
HE WAS MY FIRST... EVERYTHING...

HE WAS...

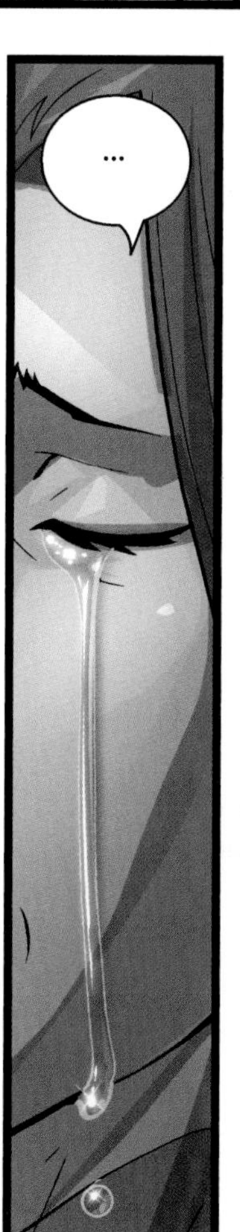
...

I'M SORRY.

EVE? ARE YOU OKAY?
MARK?

NO, I'M--I JUST CAN'T BELIEVE HE'S **DEAD**. REX IS **REALLY** GONE. HE'S JUST... GONE. I NEVER EVEN GOT TO SAY **GOODBYE**.
I DON'T EVEN REMEMBER THE LAST CONVERSATION WE HAD.
I'M SURE I WAS RUDE TO HIM. I TREATED HIM LIKE HE WAS THAT BRASH YOUNG JERK HE WAS WHEN WE FIRST MET.

THAT'S THE PROBLEM WHEN YOU KNOW SOMEONE FOR THAT LONG... WHEN YOU MEET THEM THAT YOUNG.
THEY'RE ALWAYS THE SAME... ***TO YOU.*** YOU DON'T LET THEM CHANGE OR MATURE. YOU KNOW THEM ONE WAY AND THAT NEVER CHANGES.
REX WAS GROWING UP. HE'D STOPPED BEING SUCH A JERK. HE WAS KIND, CONSIDERATE... RESPONSIBLE.

HE WAS AN **ADULT**... AND I NEVER GAVE HIM A CHANCE.
I NEVER ALLOWED MYSELF TO SEE HOW MUCH HE'D CHANGED. HE MEANT SO MUCH TO ME AND HE--

WHAT? WHAT IS IT?
I'M SORRY. I DON'T MEAN TO TALK ABOUT HIM LIKE THIS IN FRONT OF YOU.
I FEEL GUILTY BEING **SAD** IN FRONT OF YOU...

WHY?

CAN I SAY I LOVED HIM?
IS THAT TOO WEIRD FOR YOU? HE MEANT SO MUCH TO ME BEFORE HE CHEATED ON ME. IF I'M HONEST, I WAS ALREADY STARTING TO HAVE FEELINGS FOR YOU BEFORE HE DID THAT.
THAT JUST MAKES ME FEEL MORE GUILTY...

I'M A WRECK, I JUST--IT'S BEEN SO HARD, I CAME OUT OF MY COMA, YOU WERE FIGHTING CONQUEST--I REBUILT MYSELF.
I ONLY RECENTLY LEARNED HE'D BEEN KILLED.
IT'S ALL HAPPENED SO FAST, I JUST CAN'T--
ARE YOU... SMILING?
I'M SORRY, I JUST... I THOUGHT I'D LOST YOU. I CAN'T STOP THINKING ABOUT HOW YOU'RE HERE AND OKAY AND...
I CAN'T HELP IT.

Later...

UH...
THIS IS GOING TO BE AWKWARD.

UH?

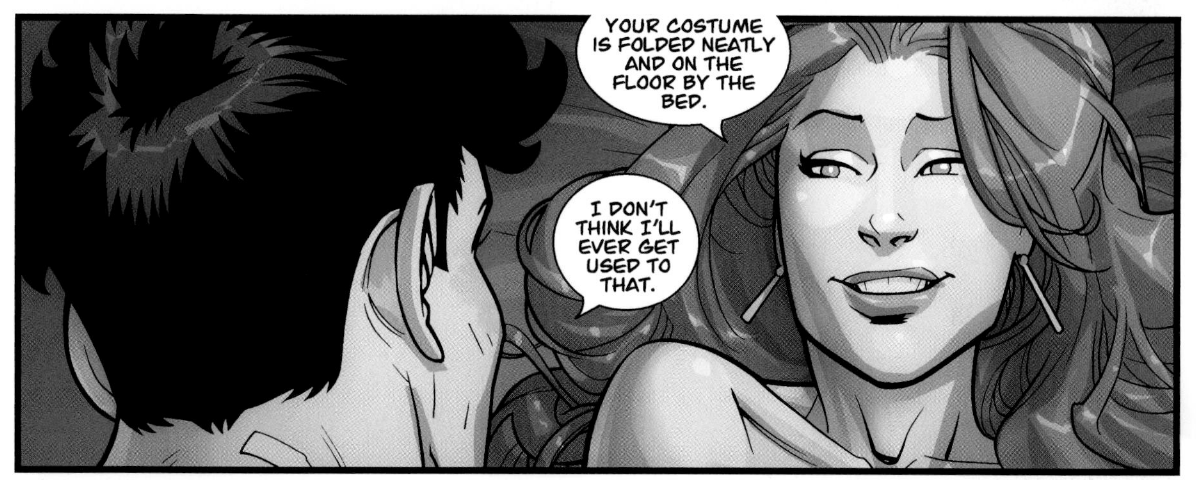
YOUR COSTUME IS FOLDED NEATLY AND ON THE FLOOR BY THE BED.
I DON'T THINK I'LL EVER GET USED TO THAT.

WELL?

REMARKABLE.
IT BARELY FEELS LIKE IT'S NOT MY OWN HAND--I HAVE COMPLETE CONTROL AND FEELING. VERY IMPRESSIVE.

NOW.
WHAT IS IT YOU WANT FROM ME?

ANGSTROM LEVY, YOU HAVE WITNESSED FIRST HAND WHAT OUR... AMBITIONS HAVE DONE TO THIS WORLD.
YOU HAVE BORNE WITNESS TO WHAT WE HAVE HAD TO DO TO OURSELVES IN ORDER TO SURVIVE HERE.
WHAT MAKES YOU THINK WE WOULD WANT TO STAY HERE?

AND THAT IS ONLY THE BEGINNING OF WHAT WE REQUIRE FROM YOU.

NOT LONG NOW...

THE BLOCK. REMOTE GLOBAL DEFENSE AGENCY OUTPOST IN THE MOJAVE DESERT.

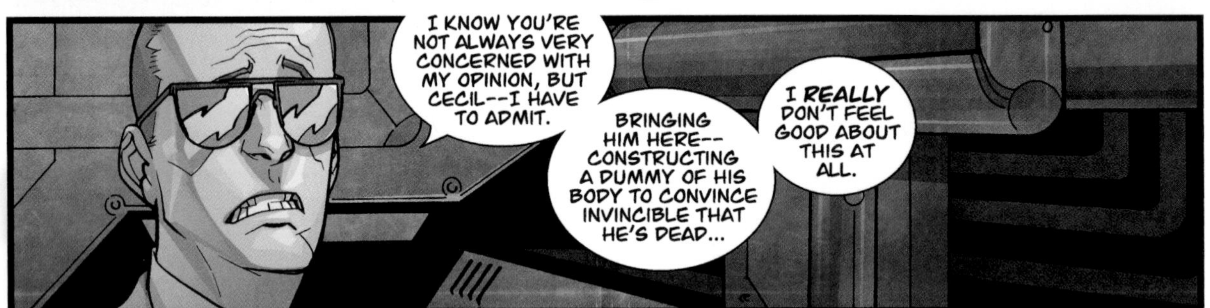
I KNOW YOU'RE NOT ALWAYS VERY CONCERNED WITH MY OPINION, BUT CECIL--I HAVE TO ADMIT.
BRINGING HIM HERE--CONSTRUCTING A DUMMY OF HIS BODY TO CONVINCE INVINCIBLE THAT HE'S DEAD...
I **REALLY** DON'T FEEL GOOD ABOUT THIS AT ALL.

WHAT'S THERE TO WORRY ABOUT? HIS BODY IS CAST IN A **FOUR-HUNDRED TON** BLOCK OF SOLID TEMPERED STEEL. HE'S IN AN UN-MANNED STATION SIX MILES BELOW THE EARTH'S SURFACE. HE SO MUCH AS TWITCHES AND THIS PLACE IMPLODES.
HE'S NOT GOING ANYWHERE.
AND AS SOON AS HIS HEAD HEALS ENOUGH FOR HIM TO REGAIN CONSCIOUSNESS...
...HE'S GOING TO TELL ME EVERYTHING THERE IS TO KNOW ABOUT THE VILTRUM EMPIRE AND THE THREAT IT POSES TOWARD THIS PLANET.

UNITED STATES
PENTAGON
Parking in Rear

THEY'RE LETTING ME GO TOMORROW. I SHOULD BE READY TO HELP YOU IN THE CLEAN-UP EFFORT IN A FEW DAYS. THANKS FOR ASKING.
I'M SORRY, I CAME HERE TO CHECK UP ON YOU--I DON'T MEAN TO BE SO--DISTANT. IT'S JUST--SOMETHING'S GOING ON. EVE'S POWERS... THEY MIGHT NOT BE WORKING RIGHT.

HOW SO?

SHE TRIES TO MAKE SOMETHING--AND IT DOESN'T WORK. I DON'T REALLY KNOW HOW TO EXPLAIN IT.

IS SHE OKAY?

SHE SEEMS FINE. IT'S JUST HER POWERS--AT LEAST, THAT'S HOW IT SEEMS NOW.
FROM WHAT I HEAR, SHE HAD TO REBUILD HERSELF. I WOULDN'T TRUST MYSELF TO DO THAT WITHOUT MESSING SOMETHING UP.

DAMN IT! I THOUGHT EVERYTHING WAS OKAY. I THOUGHT IT WAS ALL OVER.
HE MAY NOT HAVE TAKEN HER LIFE--BUT THAT MONSTER GOT SOMETHING IN THE END!

I'M SORRY, MARK.
I'M SORRY ABOUT EVERYTHING THAT HAPPENED.

NO, I'M THE ONE WHO SHOULD BE APOLOGIZING TO *YOU*, OLIVER.
THE PAST FEW WEEKS, I'VE BEEN TRAINING YOU... I THINK I'VE LEARNED MORE THAN *YOU* HAVE.

I SCOLDED YOU... I YELLED AT YOU--THOUGHT I KNEW BETTER. I THOUGHT YOU WERE MISGUIDED, NAIVE--
I WAS **WRONG.**
YOU WERE RIGHT THE WHOLE TIME--BUT I'VE LEARNED MY LESSON.
SOMEONE TRIES TO HURT MY FAMILY--SOMEONE I LOVE--IF THERE'S ANOTHER VILLAIN OUT THERE PUTTING LIVES IN DANGER--WHO'S JUST GOING TO KEEP COMING AT ME UNTIL THEY FINALLY SUCCEED...

I WON'T HESITATE TO *KILL* THEM.

66

THERE ARE LESS THAN FIFTY FULL-BLOODED VILTRUMITES LEFT IN THE UNIVERSE... BUT IT WAS NOT ALWAYS THIS WAY.
ALLEN, MY FRIEND... IT IS TIME SOMEONE KNEW THE TRUTH ABOUT THE VILTRUM EMPIRE.

YOU KNOW A GREAT DEAL ABOUT THE PLANET VILTRUM, OUR HISTORY AND OUR EMPIRE...
...AND MUCH OF IT IS TRUE.

WE WERE A VIOLENT RACE WHO VALUED STRENGTH ABOVE ALL ELSE.
TO RID OURSELVES OF ANY WEAKNESS WE SLAUGHTERED EACH OTHER UNTIL WE WERE BRED INTO THE VILTRUMITES YOU KNOW TODAY.

EVENTUALLY, OUR PEOPLE UNITED, AND WE TURNED OUR ATTENTION OUTWARD, ESTABLISHING THE VILTRUM EMPIRE.

AN EMPIRE THAT CONTINUED TO EXPAND AT AN ASTOUNDING RATE FOR NEARLY *ONE-THOUSAND YEARS*.

UNTIL OUR ENEMIES MADE A WEAPON CAPABLE OF HURTING US.
THEY MADE A *VIRUS*.

UNIQUE TO OUR GENETIC CODE, THE VIRUS WAS DEVASTATING. IT SWEPT THROUGH MY PEOPLE AT AN ALARMING RATE.
IT APPEARED THERE WAS NO WAY OF STOPPING IT. OUR ENTIRE EMPIRE WAS IN JEOPARDY.

ATTEMPTS WERE MADE TO QUARANTINE THOSE WHO BECAME INFECTED... BUT IT WAS TOO LATE.
ALMOST THE ENTIRE POPULATION WAS INFECTED WITH WHAT WOULD BECOME KNOWN AS THE SCOURGE VIRUS.

THOSE WHO SURVIVED THE VIRUS DISCOVERED ITS DEADLY AFTER EFFECTS.
THERE WAS A SHORT PERIOD OF TIME AFTER THE VIRUS HAD LEFT THEIR SYSTEM, WHERE THEIR STRENGTH AND INVULNERABILITY HAD BEEN GREATLY DIMINISHED.

THEY WERE THE LUCKY ONES.

FOR DECADES THIS VIRUS RAVAGED MY PEOPLE. EACH YEAR, IT WOULD TAKE COUNTLESS LIVES, EITHER BY SUCCUMBING TO THE VIRUS ITSELF OR BEING MURDERED DURING THE WEAKENING AFTER EFFECT.
IN THE END, WE LOST NINETY-NINE POINT NINE PERCENT OF OUR POPULATION. WE WERE LEFT ON THE BRINK OF EXTINCTION.

MIRACULOUSLY, THE VILTRUM EMPIRE ENDURED.

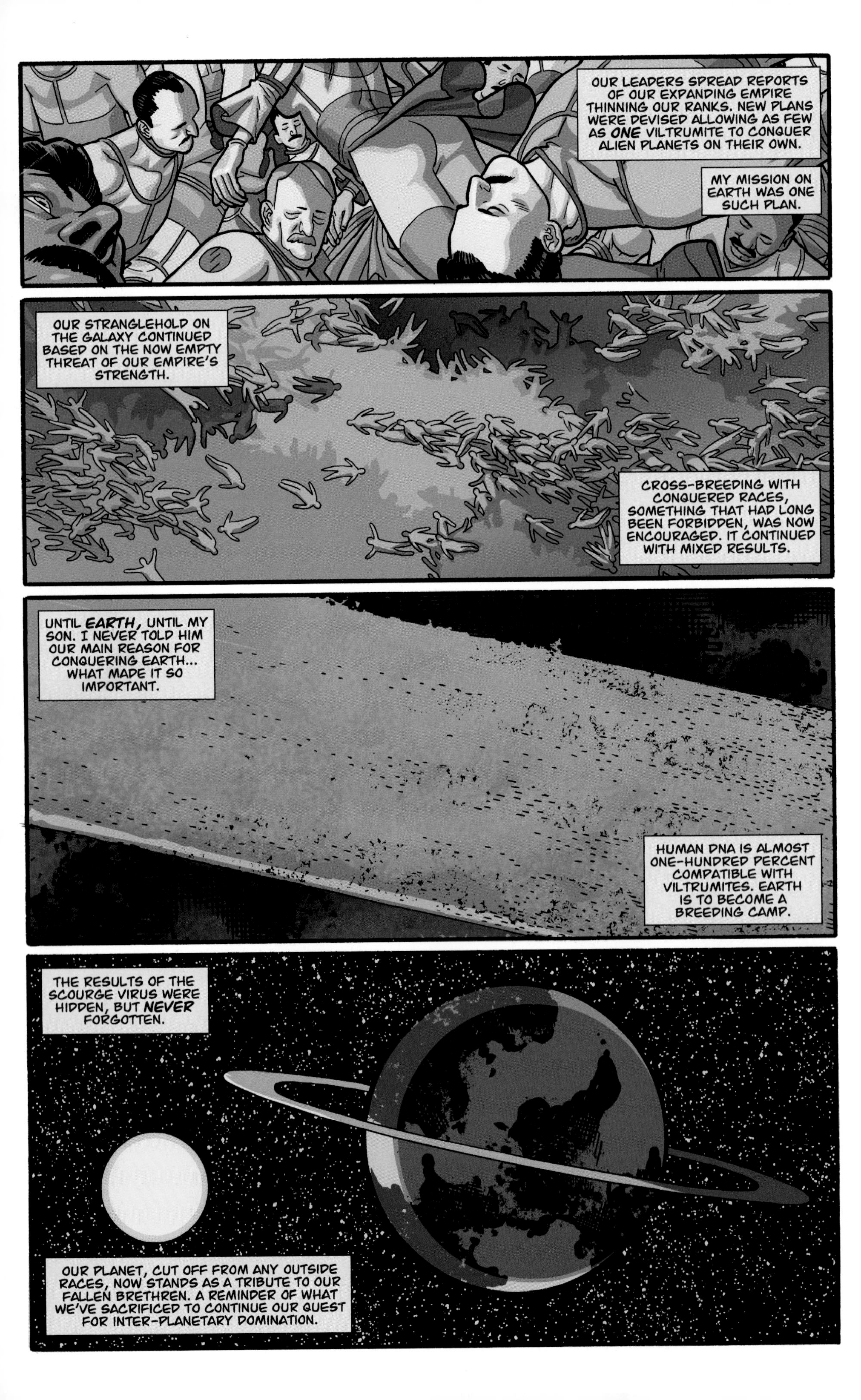
OUR LEADERS SPREAD REPORTS OF OUR EXPANDING EMPIRE THINNING OUR RANKS. NEW PLANS WERE DEVISED ALLOWING AS FEW AS ONE VILTRUMITE TO CONQUER ALIEN PLANETS ON THEIR OWN.
MY MISSION ON EARTH WAS ONE SUCH PLAN.
OUR STRANGLEHOLD ON THE GALAXY CONTINUED BASED ON THE NOW EMPTY THREAT OF OUR EMPIRE'S STRENGTH.
CROSS-BREEDING WITH CONQUERED RACES, SOMETHING THAT HAD LONG BEEN FORBIDDEN, WAS NOW ENCOURAGED. IT CONTINUED WITH MIXED RESULTS.
UNTIL EARTH, UNTIL MY SON. I NEVER TOLD HIM OUR MAIN REASON FOR CONQUERING EARTH... WHAT MADE IT SO IMPORTANT.
HUMAN DNA IS ALMOST ONE-HUNDRED PERCENT COMPATIBLE WITH VILTRUMITES. EARTH IS TO BECOME A BREEDING CAMP.
THE RESULTS OF THE SCOURGE VIRUS WERE HIDDEN, BUT NEVER FORGOTTEN.
OUR PLANET, CUT OFF FROM ANY OUTSIDE RACES, NOW STANDS AS A TRIBUTE TO OUR FALLEN BRETHREN. A REMINDER OF WHAT WE'VE SACRIFICED TO CONTINUE OUR QUEST FOR INTER-PLANETARY DOMINATION.

A QUEST I NOW SEE AS THE POINTLESS ENDEAVOR THAT IT IS...
WHAT THEY PLAN TO DO WITH EARTH... I WAS BORN IN A BREEDING CAMP. I WOULDN'T WISH THAT ON ANYONE. WE HAVE TO WARN MARK.

NO.
YOU HAVE TO TAKE ME TO YOUR PEOPLE. I NEED TO MEET WITH THE COALITION OF PLANETS. IMMEDIATELY.

I TRUST YOU, BUT I DON'T KNOW IF MY BOSS WILL. THIS WON'T BE EASY.

IT DOESN'T MATTER. IF WE'RE GOING TO BE ABLE TO SAVE EARTH AND STOP THE VILTRUM EMPIRE ONCE AND FOR ALL, THE COALITION NEEDS TO KNOW EVERYTHING I KNOW.

WE'LL ALSO NEED THE INFORMATION CONTAINED IN MY BOOKS THAT YOU SCANNED. I WROTE EVERYTHING DOWN SO I WOULDN'T NEED TO REMEMBER IT ALL--AND THERE IS VALUABLE INFORMATION ENCODED IN THE WORDS.
INFORMATION THAT WILL GAIN YOUR BOSS'S TRUST.
OKAY, LET ME GET MY GEAR AND THEN WE'LL GO.

SOME TIME LATER, THE PLANET TELESCRIA, THE SECRET HOME BASE OF THE COALITION OF PLANETS.

WHERE HAVE YOU BEEN?!

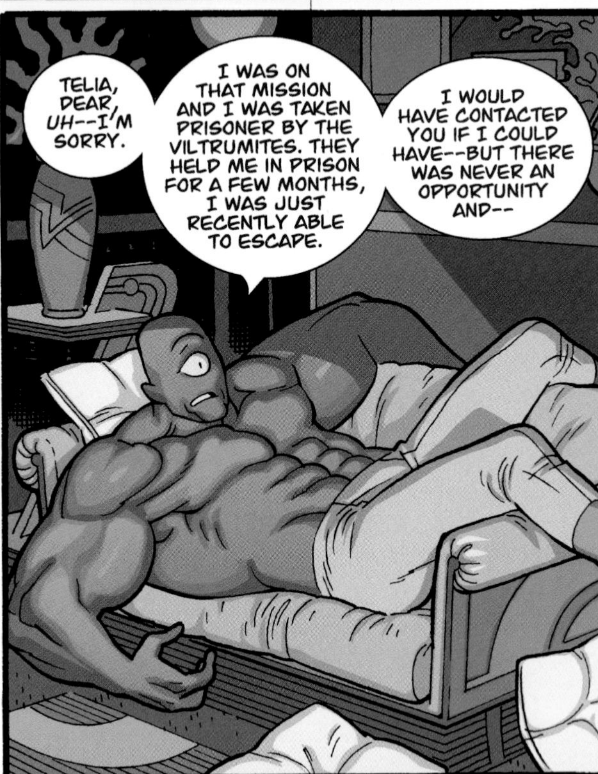
TELIA, DEAR, UH--I'M SORRY.
I WAS ON THAT MISSION AND I WAS TAKEN PRISONER BY THE VILTRUMITES. THEY HELD ME IN PRISON FOR A FEW MONTHS, I WAS JUST RECENTLY ABLE TO ESCAPE.
I WOULD HAVE CONTACTED YOU IF I COULD HAVE--BUT THERE WAS NEVER AN OPPORTUNITY AND--

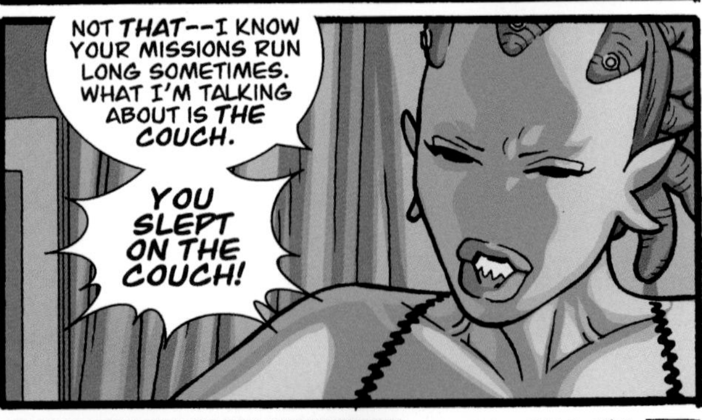
NOT THAT--I KNOW YOUR MISSIONS RUN LONG SOMETIMES. WHAT I'M TALKING ABOUT IS THE COUCH.
YOU SLEPT ON THE COUCH!

OH, UH... THAT. I'M SORRY. THE THING IS, WE GOT IN REALLY LATE AND--

I DON'T CARE **HOW** LATE YOU GET BACK FROM A MISSION. YOU KNOW THE **RULES.** YOU WAKE ME UP!
I'VE BEEN LIVING WITHOUT FOR **MONTHS** AND I AM HUNGRY! NOW GIVE IT TO ME YOU UNOPAN GOD.
GIVE IT TO ME **NOW!**

TELIA, PLEASE. I CAN'T RIGHT NOW.
STOP--!

CAN WE PLEASE, JUST ONCE... NOT DO THIS? I'M SICK OF ALL THE PRETENSE.
DO I **REALLY** HAVE TO HEAR ABOUT THE UNOPAN POPULATION AND HOW YOUR STRICT PROCREATION LAWS FORBID OUR UNION BEFORE EVERY SINGLE TIME WE HAVE SEX?
DON'T SAY YOU CAN'T. YOU **CAN**--YOU ALWAYS **DO.** CUT THE CRAP AND LET'S GET TO IT!

NO, THAT'S NOT IT--

WAIT A MINUTE... DID YOU SAY **"WE"** GOT IN REALLY LATE?

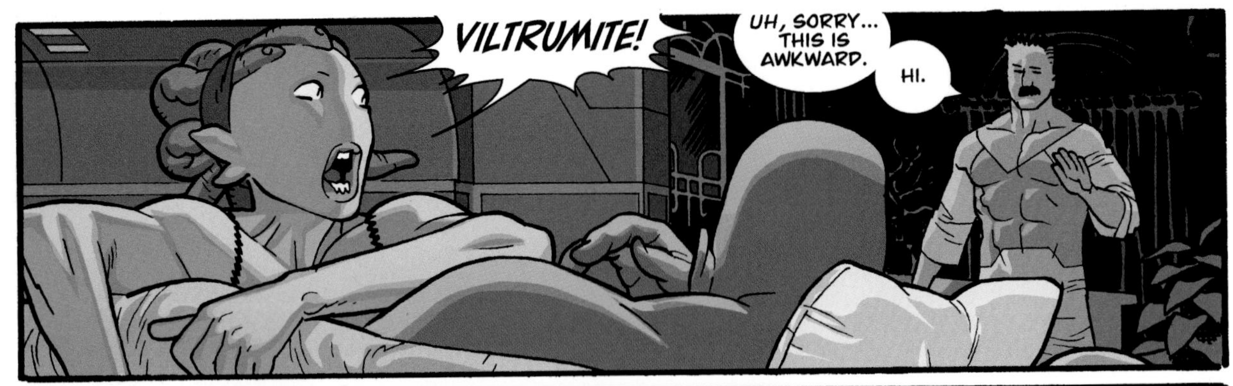
VILTRUMITE!
UH, SORRY... THIS IS AWKWARD.
HI.

DIE, WORLD-CONQUERING SCUM!
VOPP! VOPP!

SORRY TO STARTLE YOU-- I'M REALLY NOT HERE TO HURT YOU. I PROMISE.

I CAN VOUCH FOR HIM. HE'S A GOOD GUY. I MET HIM IN PRISON. HE'S HERE TO HELP THE COALITION.
AND, HONEY...

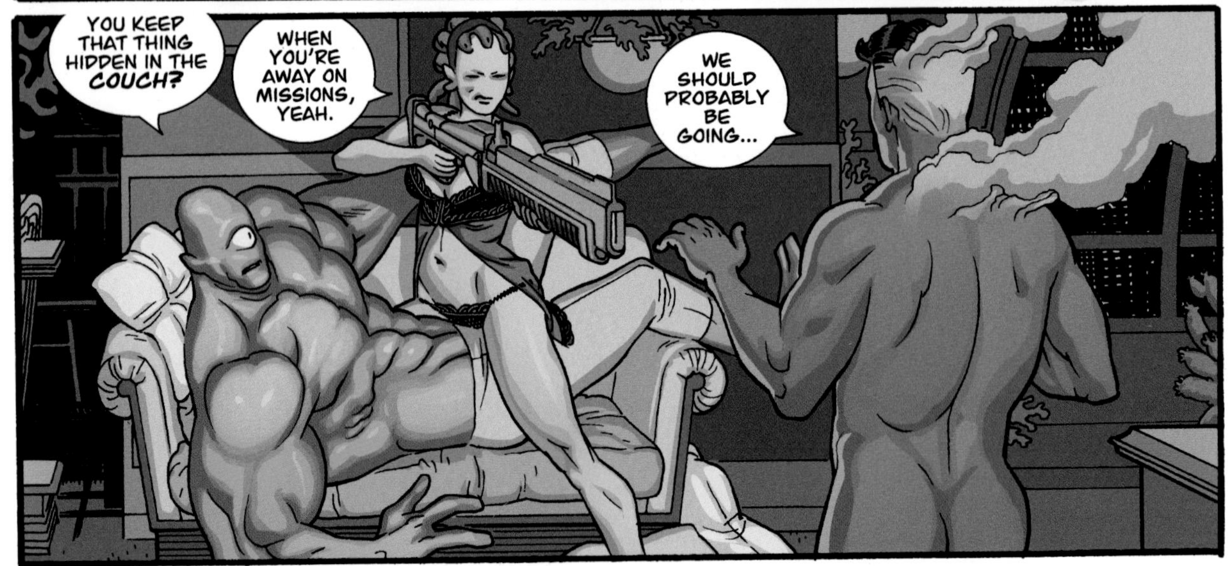
YOU KEEP THAT THING HIDDEN IN THE COUCH?
WHEN YOU'RE AWAY ON MISSIONS, YEAH.
WE SHOULD PROBABLY BE GOING...

HIDDEN AMONG THE TOWERING SKY SCRAPERS OF TELESCRIA IS CENTRAL BASE OF THE COALITION OF PLANETS.

FASCINATING--SIMPLY FASCINATING. ARE YOU CROSS REFERENCING THE VISUAL MARKERS HIDDEN IN THE STORIES WITH STAR MAPS?
NO, WHY? OOOOH. THEY LINE UP EXACTLY. AMAZING.
THIS COULD BE THE FINAL PIECE THE COALITION NEEDS TO END THE VILTRUMITE THREAT ONCE AND FOR ALL.
DOWNLOAD COMPLETE IN THREE, TWO...

MAYBE WE SHOULD CANCEL THE CHOOMBAK MATCH TONIGHT. I'M GOING TO BE PROCESSING DATA IN THE BACK OF MY MIND ALL NIGHT.
I WON'T BE ABLE TO ENJOY MYSELF.

YOU'RE PROBABLY RIGHT. WAS LOOKING FORWARD TO IT-- BUT, DUTY CALLS!
HOW MUCH LONGER DO YOU THINK THEY'LL BE IN WITH THAEDUS? WE NEED TO DISCUSS THIS WITH HIM.

WHO KNOWS, HE'S BEEN MEETING WITH ALLEN AND THE ROGUE VILTRUMITE FOR HOURS.
EVER SINCE HIS TRANSFORMATION, I FIND ALLEN UNSETTLING. HE TERRIFIES ME.

INTIMIDATING, SURE... BUT AGENT ALLEN IS ON OUR SIDE.
WHY WOULD YOU BE SCARED OF HIM?

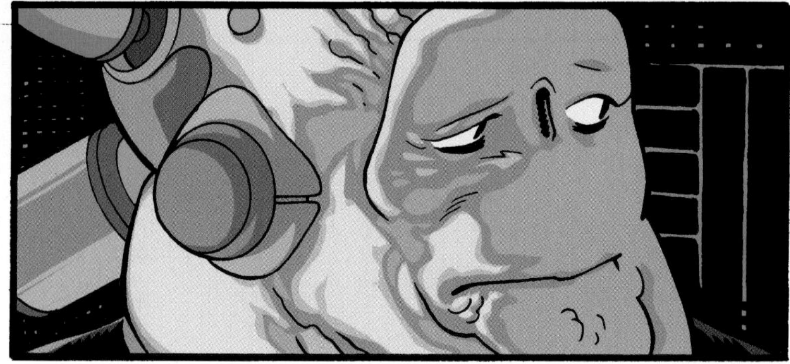

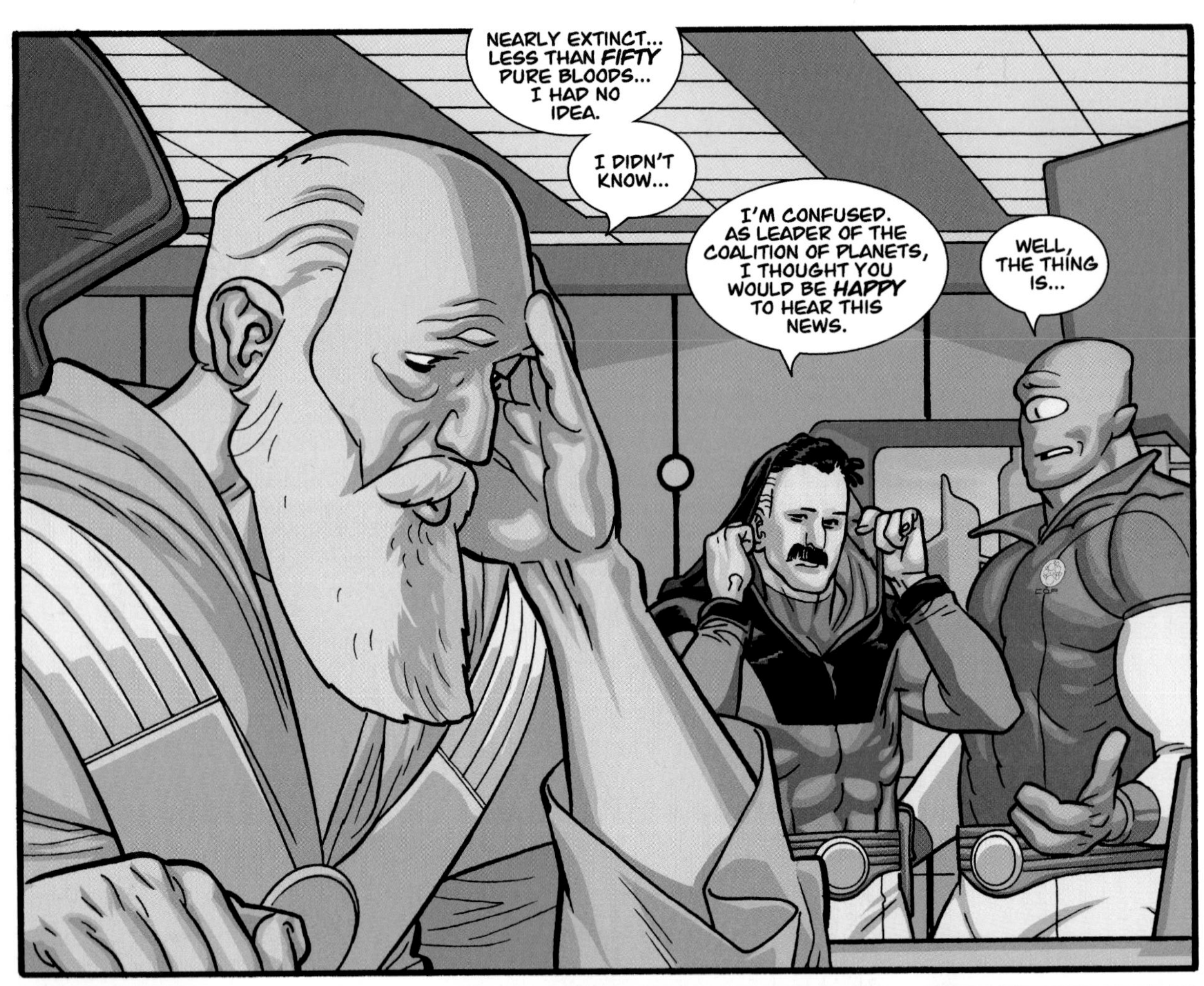
NEARLY EXTINCT... LESS THAN FIFTY PURE BLOODS... I HAD NO IDEA.
I DIDN'T KNOW...
I'M CONFUSED. AS LEADER OF THE COALITION OF PLANETS, I THOUGHT YOU WOULD BE HAPPY TO HEAR THIS NEWS.
WELL, THE THING IS...

I AM CONFLICTED.
I AM LEADER OF THE COLALITION OF PLANETS, SWORN TO BRING DOWN THE VILTRUM EMPIRE ONCE AND FOR ALL.
AND I AM ALSO A VILTRUMITE.

I DO NOT BELIEVE IT.
I DEMAND THAT YOU PERFORM THE TOOLOCK PULL TO PROVE YOURSELF AS AN UNDERCOVER VILTRUM AGENT.

I WILL GLADLY DO SO IF YOU INSIST.
BUT I HAVE ALREADY DONE THIS FOR ALLEN IN THE PAST AND I DID NOT CARE FOR IT.

IT'S TRUE, DUDE-- PULLED HIS BEARD RIGHT OUT.
IT WAS CRAZY.

BUT I THOUGHT--I ALWAYS FEARED THAT THERE WAS SOMETHING WRONG WITH ME, FOR TURNING MY BACK AGAINST THE EMPIRE--VILTRUMITES HAVE ALWAYS BEEN LOYAL...
...I THOUGHT I WAS THE FIRST.
MY BETRAYAL WAS HIDDEN, REMOVED FROM HISTORY'S RECORD.
BUT THERE IS NO TIME FOR THIS. WE HAVE ALREADY BEEN CONVERSING TOO LONG. PEOPLE WILL BECOME SUSPICIOUS THAT THIS ISN'T JUST A STANDARD BRIEFING.
I CAN'T HAVE THAT.

THERE IS AT LEAST ONE VILTRUMITE AGENT AMONG US, REPORTING BACK TO THE EMPIRE.
THE WORK YOU WILL DO WITH ALLEN MUST REMAIN SECRET.
THE DATA FROM MY INFO POD... IT'S GOING INTO THE MAIN DATABASE?

NO.
MY TRUSTED INNER-CIRCLE HAS A SEPARATE DATABASE FOR MORE SENSITIVE DATA. AND EVEN THEY WILL BE UNAWARE OF YOUR MISSION USING THIS DATA.

WE NOW HAVE A LIST OF WEAPONS AND BEINGS THAT CAN HURT A VILTRUMITE--THINGS THAT WILL BECOME VERY VALUABLE TO THE COALITION OF PLANETS.
I CHARGE YOU TWO WITH THE TASK OF GATHERING AS MUCH OF THESE THINGS THAT STILL REMAIN.
ALLEN, I'M GIVING YOU ACCESS TO OUR ARMORY FOR THE NEXT HOUR--THAT'S AS MUCH TIME AS I CAN KEEP SECRET FROM THE COUNCIL.
GO.

SWEET!
IT LOOKS COOL, BUT WITH YOUR STRENGTH AREN'T ALL THOSE GADGETS A LITTLE... UNNECESSARY? SEEMS LIKE THEY'LL JUST... SLOW YOU DOWN.
YEAH, AND YOUR SUIT'S ALL ABOUT PRACTICALITY. NICE CAPE, DUDE.
COP
COP

ARE YOU SURE YOU WANT TO TRY THIS ONE *FIRST?*
THIS ONE IS RELATIVELY CLOSE AND SHOULD BE EASY. I CONSIDER THIS ONE A... WARM UP.
CLOSE? **GOOD.** MY GIRLFRIEND ISN'T TOO HAPPY ABOUT ME LEAVING FOR ANOTHER MISSION SO SOON.
CAN'T BE TOO MAD, THOUGH. SHE PACKED ME SOME FRESH KANZLOK FOR THE TRIP. ***YUM.***
HM? WHAT IS IT?

ONLY THE MOST DELICIOUS THING IN THE ***UNIVERSE.***
WANT SOME?

PASS.

THERE IT IS, THE NEBULOID BELT. IT'S BEEN... ALMOST A HUNDRED YEARS SINCE I WAS HERE.
LOOKS EXACTLY THE SAME.
IT'S... A BUNCH OF ROCKS.

HAND ME YOUR INFO POD.

JUST SAYING...

THERE'S A CODE HIDDEN IN THE TEXT. THE NUMBER OF WORDS IN THESE PARAGRAPHS I WROTE ABOUT THE ASTEROIDS WILL SPELL OUT THE COORDINATES OF THE SPECIFIC ASTEROID WE'RE LOOKING FOR.
FOLLOW ME.

SO, IF IT'S BEEN ONE-HUNDRED YEARS, GIVE OR TAKE, AND THE ASTEROIDS ARE DRIFTING AT THIS SPEED, THEIR RELATIVE DISTANCE TO EACH OTHER WOULD BE SHIFTING...
AND...
YOU GOING TO BE ABLE TO FIND THIS... WHATEVER IT IS WE'RE AFTER?

ABSOLUTELY. JUST GIVE ME A MINUTE.

...
ANYTHING I CAN DO TO HELP?

NO, NO... ALMOST GOT IT.
THERE.

THIS IS IT.
HOW CAN YOU BE SURE? IT'S A ROCK-- THEY ALL LOOK THE SAME.

I'M NOT SURE... BUT THIS LOOKS FAMILIAR.

AH!

THERE IT IS.
WAIT, WHAT?

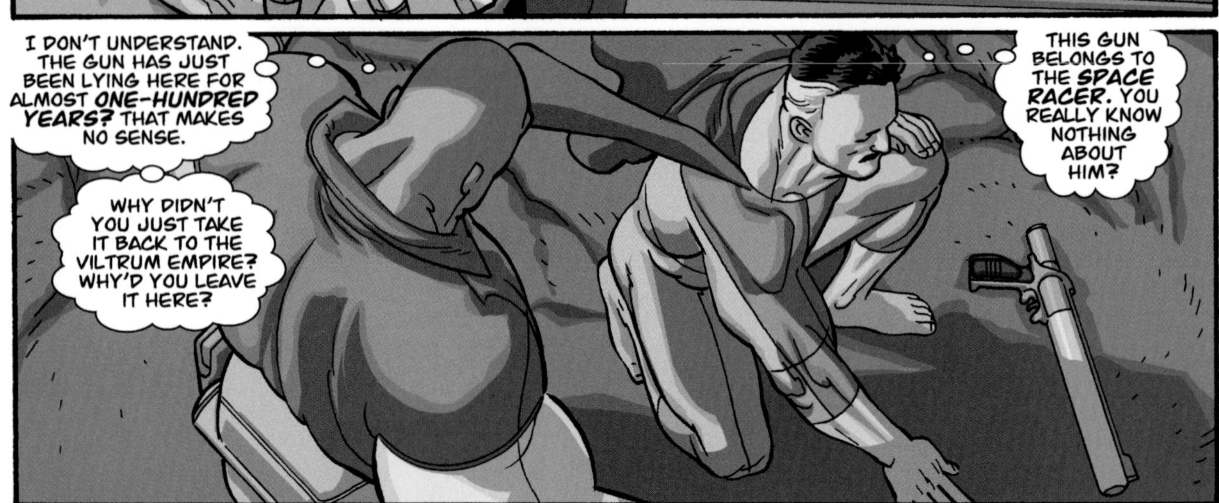
I DON'T UNDERSTAND. THE GUN HAS JUST BEEN LYING HERE FOR ALMOST ONE-HUNDRED YEARS? THAT MAKES NO SENSE.
WHY DIDN'T YOU JUST TAKE IT BACK TO THE VILTRUM EMPIRE? WHY'D YOU LEAVE IT HERE?
THIS GUN BELONGS TO THE SPACE RACER. YOU REALLY KNOW NOTHING ABOUT HIM?

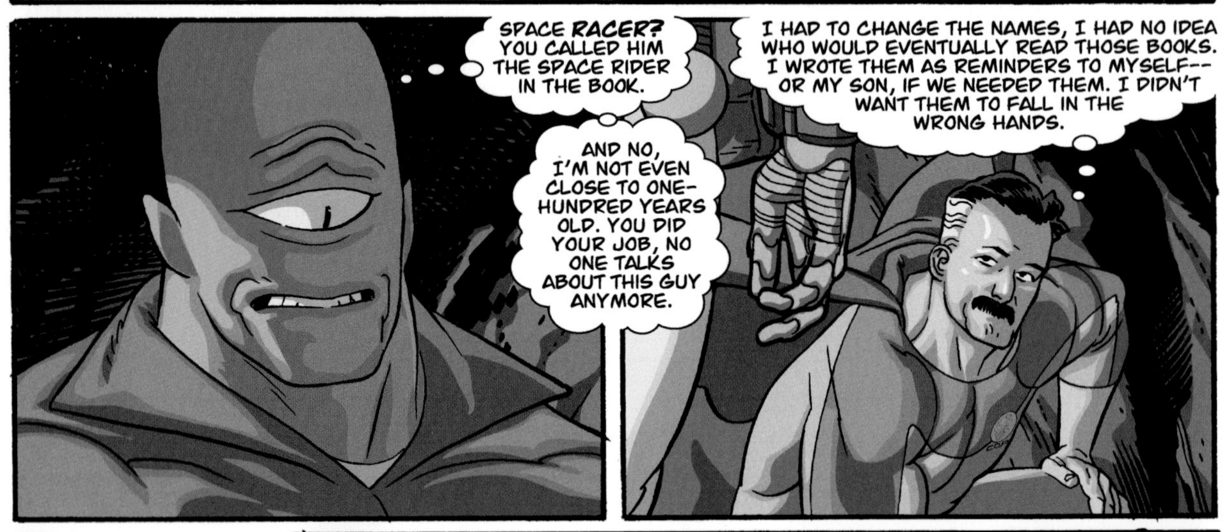
SPACE RACER? YOU CALLED HIM THE SPACE RIDER IN THE BOOK.
I HAD TO CHANGE THE NAMES, I HAD NO IDEA WHO WOULD EVENTUALLY READ THOSE BOOKS. I WROTE THEM AS REMINDERS TO MYSELF-- OR MY SON, IF WE NEEDED THEM. I DIDN'T WANT THEM TO FALL IN THE WRONG HANDS.
AND NO, I'M NOT EVEN CLOSE TO ONE-HUNDRED YEARS OLD. YOU DID YOUR JOB, NO ONE TALKS ABOUT THIS GUY ANYMORE.

THE SPACE RACER'S GUN--THE ONE THAT FIRES INDESTRUCTIBLE BLASTS THAT WILL SHOOT THROUGH ANYTHING--CAN ONLY BE FIRED BY HIM.
HE'S GOT SOME KIND OF BOND WITH THE GUN--IF ANYONE TRIES TO TAKE IT OR USE IT... IF I HAD TOUCHED IT WHILE HE WAS STILL ALIVE IT WOULD HAVE FLOWN INTO THE CENTER OF THE PILE OF RUBBLE I BURIED HIM UNDER AND GIVEN HIM THE MEANS TO ESCAPE.
MY ONLY OPTION WAS TO LEAVE IT EXACTLY WHERE HE DROPPED IT.

THANKFULLY, BY NOW HE'S SURELY...

...DEAD.

CRAP!

WHAT WAS THAT ALL ABOUT?
THIS IS GOING TO BE A PAIN--IT SEEMS THE GUN STILL GOES TO HIS CORPSE WHEN YOU TOUCH IT.

HELP ME DIG.

UH, ALLEN... DON'T...
...MOVE.

NOLAN OF VILTRUM-- GIVE ME ONE REASON NOT TO KILL YOU WHERE YOU STAND.

UH...
BOY, THIS GUY SURE CAN GO A LONG TIME WITHOUT EATING.

67

HOLD THE THREATS, SPACE RACER! YOU COULDN'T KILL ME LAST TIME AND THIS TIME I BROUGHT HELP!
UH... YEAH!
DON'T--!
WAIT! YOU CAN'T HEAR IT-- BUT I CAN FEEL IT! THIS ASTEROID IS BREAKING APART-- AND THE PIECES ARE COLLIDING WITH THE REST OF THE ASTEROIDS IN THE BELT!
IT'S CAUSING A CHAIN REACTION! THIS ISN'T GOING TO BE PRETTY!

MOVE! MOVE! MOVE!

THAT SHOULD BE FAR ENOUGH...
TO ME.
WHAT'S HE--?

WHAT THE--?!

AGH-- CRAP! DON'T SHOOT.
HEAR ME OUT.

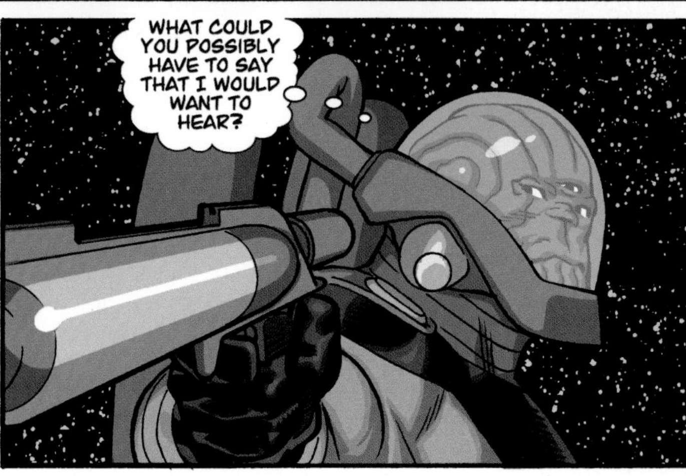
WHAT COULD YOU POSSIBLY HAVE TO SAY THAT I WOULD WANT TO HEAR?

WHY DO YOU THINK I'M HERE? WE CAME HERE TO FREE YOU--NOT TO FIGHT YOU.
WHY WOULD WE HAVE COME OTHERWISE?

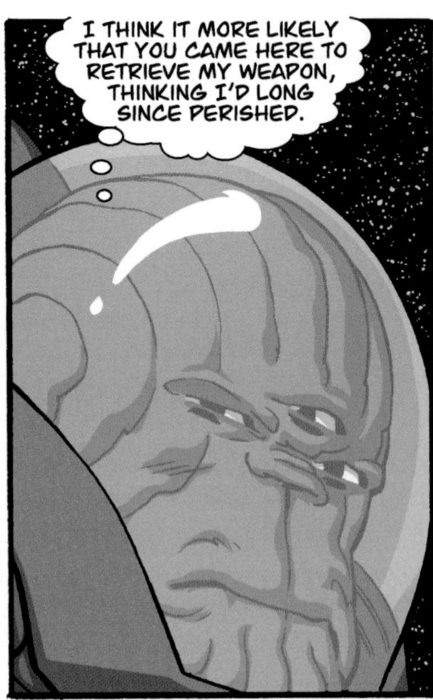
I THINK IT MORE LIKELY THAT YOU CAME HERE TO RETRIEVE MY WEAPON, THINKING I'D LONG SINCE PERISHED.

HE'S GOT YOU THERE.
MIND IF I STEP IN?

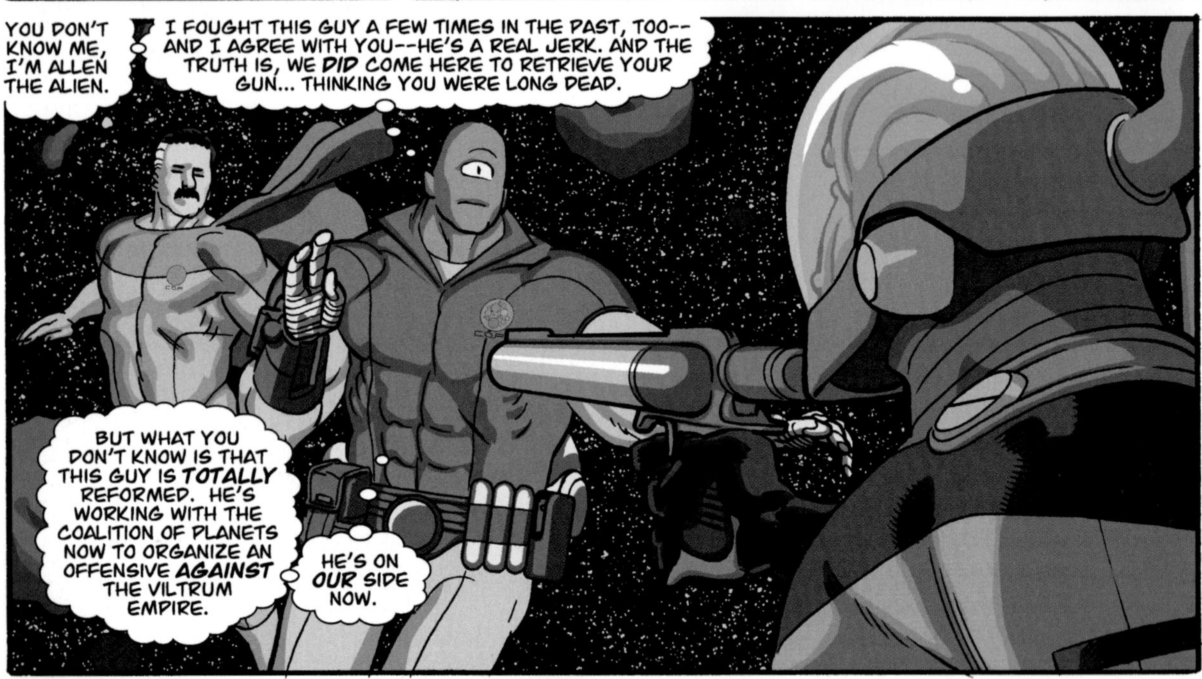
YOU DON'T KNOW ME, I'M ALLEN THE ALIEN.
I FOUGHT THIS GUY A FEW TIMES IN THE PAST, TOO--AND I AGREE WITH YOU--HE'S A REAL JERK. AND THE TRUTH IS, WE DID COME HERE TO RETRIEVE YOUR GUN... THINKING YOU WERE LONG DEAD.
BUT WHAT YOU DON'T KNOW IS THAT THIS GUY IS TOTALLY REFORMED. HE'S WORKING WITH THE COALITION OF PLANETS NOW TO ORGANIZE AN OFFENSIVE AGAINST THE VILTRUM EMPIRE.
HE'S ON OUR SIDE NOW.

ASSUMING YOU WERE ON OUR SIDE...

WHAT ALLEN IS SAYING IS TRUE. I AM REFORMED. I'VE TURNED AGAINST THE VILTRUMITES AND AM NOW TRYING TO DO MY PART IN ENDING THEIR REIGN.

I AM VERY SORRY FOR WHAT I'VE PUT YOU THROUGH--BUT PLEASE DON'T HOLD MY PAST ACTIONS AGAINST THE COALITION--THEY MAY BE THE UNIVERSE'S LAST BEST HOPE AGAINST THE VILTRUM EMPIRE.

IF YOU COULD PLEASE JUST ACCOMPANY US BACK TO THE COALITION HEADQUARTERS YOU COULD SEE THAT WE ARE INDEED FIGHTING AGAINST THE VILTRUMITES.
WE COULD PROVIDE YOU WITH WHATEVER ASSURANCES--

I HAVE BEEN BURIED UNDER THAT RUBBLE FOR NEARLY ONE-HUNDRED YEARS...

I KNOW AND MY ASSOCIATE HAS SAID HE'S VERY SORRY ABOUT THAT, AND--

DO YOU HAVE ANY FOOD?

SURE DO! JUST GIVE ME A SECOND...

EVER HEARD OF KANSLOK?

PASS.
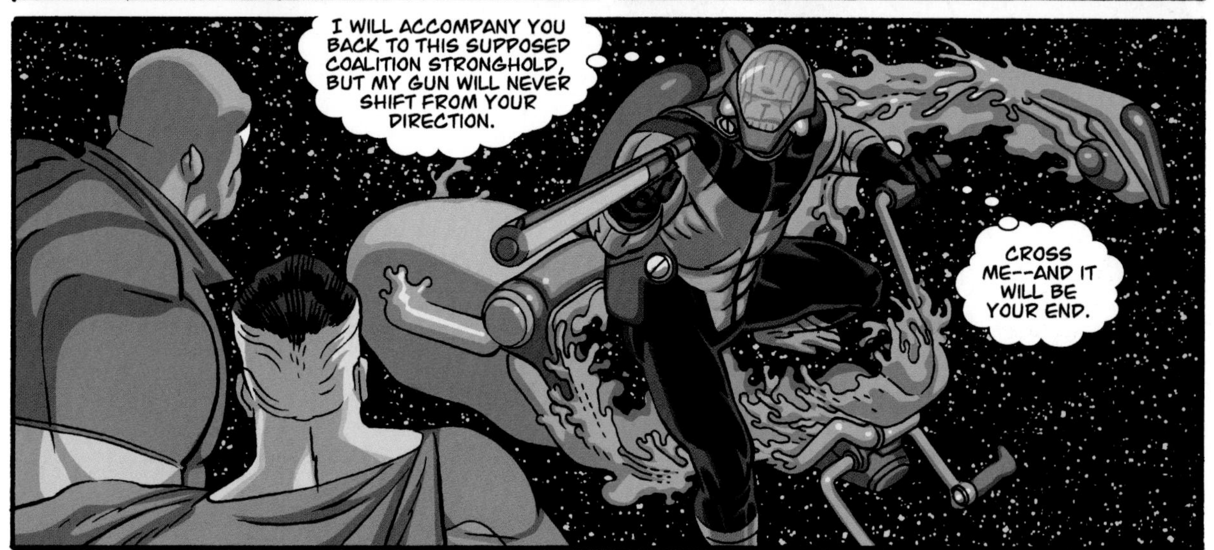
I WILL ACCOMPANY YOU BACK TO THIS SUPPOSED COALITION STRONGHOLD, BUT MY GUN WILL NEVER SHIFT FROM YOUR DIRECTION.
CROSS ME--AND IT WILL BE YOUR END.

OOH, SCARY.
HEH.

HIDDEN AMONG THE TOWERING SKYSCRAPERS OF TELESCRIA LIES THE CENTRAL BASE OF THE COALITION OF PLANETS.
HE'S STILL VERY CAUTIOUS ABOUT THIS SITUATION BUT I'M TOLD HE'S OPTIMISTIC ABOUT WORKING WITH US.
MY MEDICAL SPECIALISTS ARE EXAMINING HIM TO MAKE SURE HE'S IN GOOD PHYSICAL SHAPE. HIS METABOLISM IS ASTOUNDING.
THIS GUY IS GOING TO BE A HUGE HELP TO US. VERY WELL DONE, BOTH OF YOU.

THANK YOU, GREAT THAEDUS.
I'M GOING TO HEAD HOME WHILE YOUR TEAM ASSEMBLES FOR OUR NEXT MISSION. YOU SAY IT COULD BE TWO DAYS BEFORE THEY ARE READY?
C.O.P.

I WILL ALERT YOU BOTH AS SOON AS WE'RE READY TO GO.

WHERE SHOULD I--?
ARE YOU KIDDING? YOU'RE CRASHING AT MY PLACE, BUDDY!
C.O.P.

DUDE, WE'RE NOT KEEPING YOU UP, ARE WE?
NO.

OH, GOOD.
SEE YOU IN THE MORNING.

THE ROGNARR ARE VICIOUS, WE NEED TO BE CAREFUL. WHEN THE VILTRUMITES DISCOVERED THIS RACE OF MONSTERS, THEY SENT A FEW TEAMS HERE TO TRY AND DESTROY THEM-- TO DISASTROUS RESULTS. THESE THINGS ARE INDESTRUCTIBLE.
WITH ALL THIS ICE-- HOW ARE WE GOING TO FIND THEM?
FINALLY, I CAME UP WITH THE IDEA OF USING A SOLAR DISK TO BLOCK THEIR SUN-- FREEZING THEM. IF THESE THINGS THAW OUT WHILE WE'RE HERE-- WE'RE IN TROUBLE.
COP

YOU'RE RIGHT.
NOLAN TO BRIDGE. WE'RE GOING TO NEED TO PREPARE A TEAM TO TRANSPORT THESE THINGS TO THE CARGO HOLD BEFORE THEY COMPLETELY THAW OUT. THE ONLY WAY WE'RE GOING TO FIND THEM IS BY REMOVING THE SOLAR DISK.
WE CAN HANDLE THAT ON OUR OWN, THANK YOU VERY MUCH.
DOWNLOAD, FIRE AT WILL.

NO!!
WHAT? WHAT IS IT?

MORONS!

THIS ICE WILL BE MELTED IN A MATTER OF MINUTES... WE NEEDED TO *MOVE* THE DISK--NOT COMPLETELY *DESTROY* IT!
WE'VE GOT TO WORK FAST!

THERE! WE NEED TO GET THAT ONE UP TO THE SHIP BEFORE IT COMPLETELY THAWS OUT!
WE'RE ONLY GOING TO GET ONE SHOT AT THIS!

C'MON!
KRAKK!

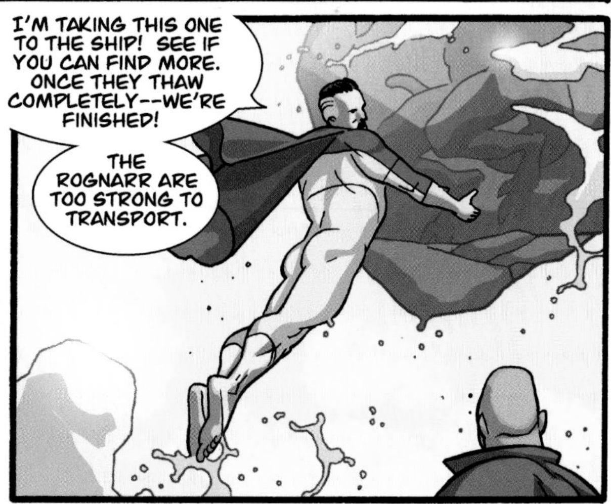
I'M TAKING THIS ONE TO THE SHIP! SEE IF YOU CAN FIND MORE. ONCE THEY THAW COMPLETELY--WE'RE FINISHED!
THE ROGNARR ARE TOO STRONG TO TRANSPORT.

SKRSSH!
CRAP!

AAAGH!

THE VILTRUMITE'S HEART RATE HAS MORE THAN DOUBLED, CAPTAIN. I THINK THEY'RE IN TROUBLE.

THESE CREATURES MAY BE THE THING WE NEED TO FINALLY TURN THE TIDE AGAINST THE VILTRUMITES! FAILURE IS NOT AN OPTION HERE!
WHAT IS GOING ON DOWN THERE?
REPORT!

WHAT'S GOING ON IS YOU MORONS SCREWED UP! THIS ICE IS ALMOST COMPLETELY MELTED--WE'RE SURROUNDED!
THIS MISSION IS BUST! I'M GETTING US OUT OF HERE NOW!

GO! JUST GET OUT OF HERE, *NOW!* I CAN TAKE CARE OF MYSELF!
I CAN HELP YOU!
NO! JUST--
THROMP!
ALLEN!

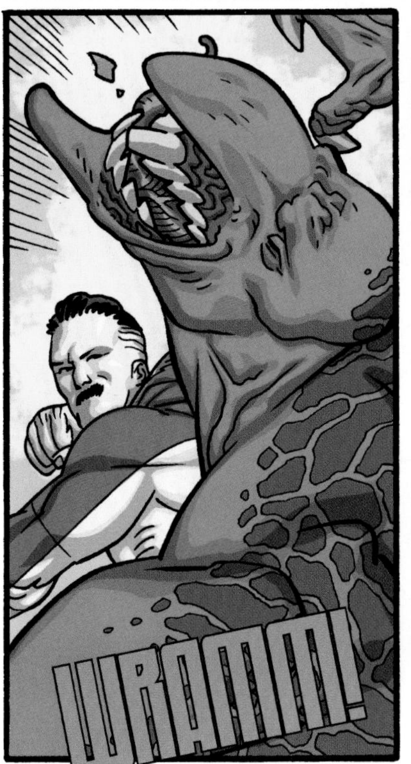
WRAMM!

I GOT THIS...
UNGH...

NO, YOU *DON'T!* THESE THINGS EAT VILTRUMITES ALIVE!
THE ONLY REASON WE'RE LASTING THIS LONG IS THAT THEY'RE STILL GROGGY FROM BEING FROZEN!

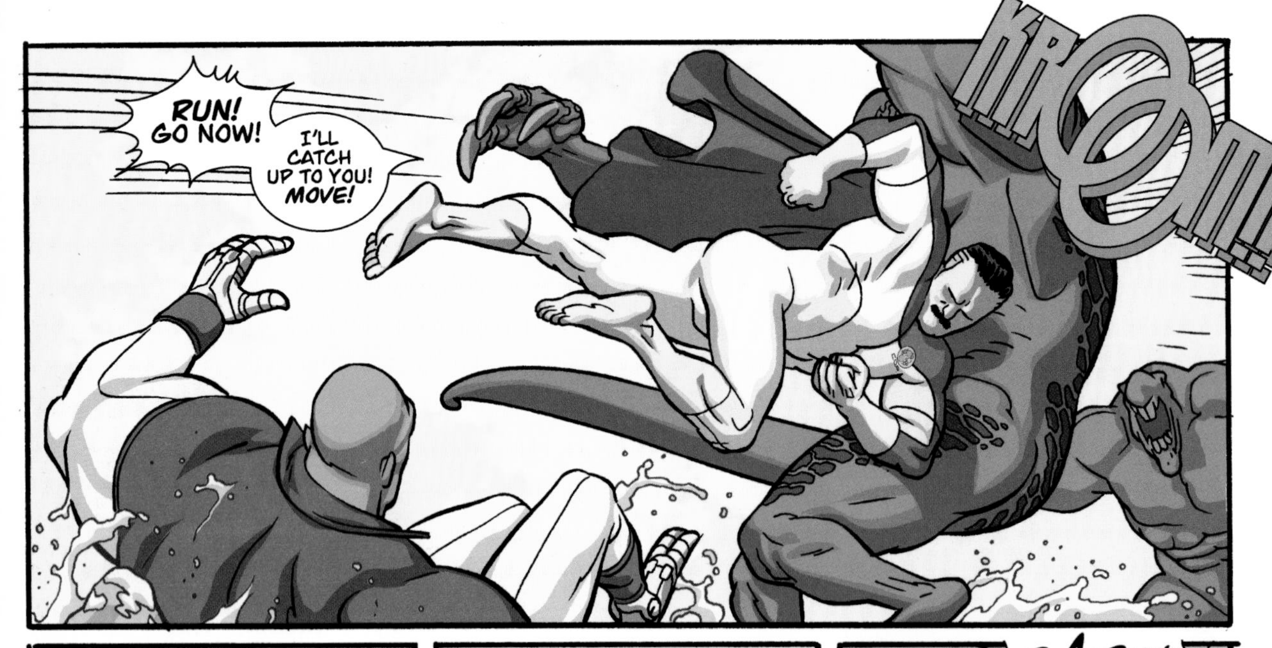
KROOM!
RUN! GO NOW!
I'LL CATCH UP TO YOU! MOVE!

GO FAST AND DON'T LOOK BACK! THESE THINGS CAN JUMP!

WHOA!
NO KIDDING!

RAARRGH!!
KROOM!

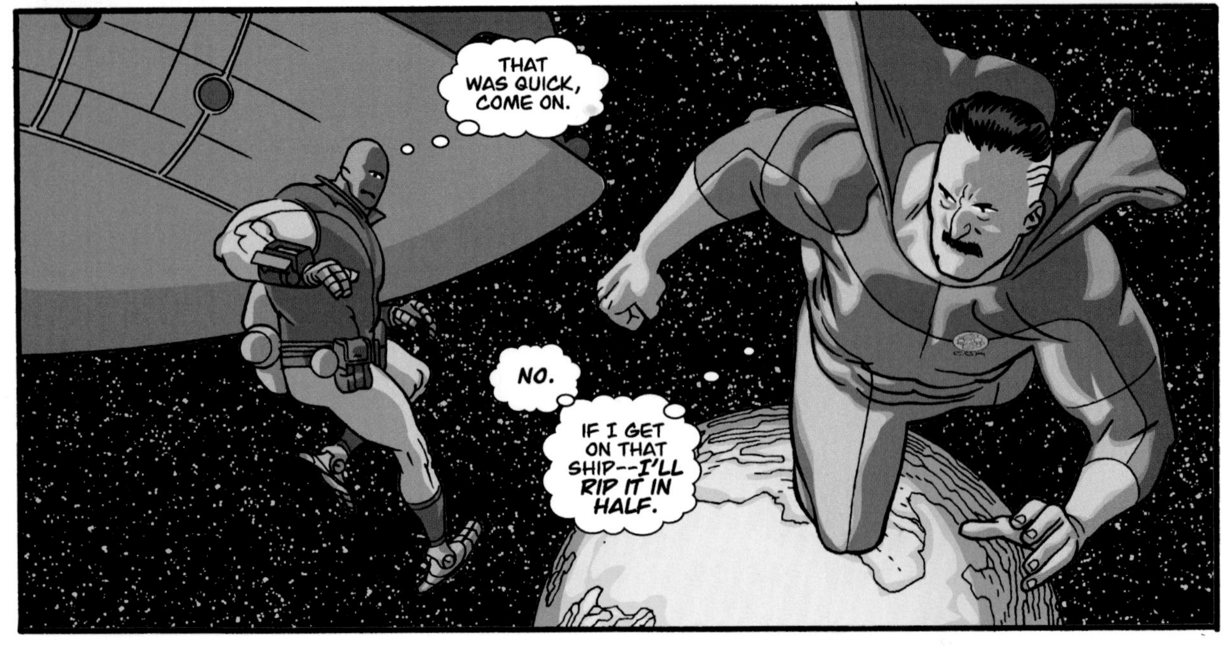
THAT WAS QUICK, COME ON.
NO.
IF I GET ON THAT SHIP--I'LL RIP IT IN HALF.

TELESCRIA, WHERE WE FIND THE HOME BASE OF THE COALITION OF PLANETS.

IT'S NOT A TOTAL LOSS. WE KNOW WHERE THEY ARE--AND THEY'RE ACTIVE AGAIN. WE COULD DISTRACT A SQUAD OF VILTRUMITES BY SENDING THEM THERE... AND I'M NOT COMPLETELY RULING OUT THE POSSIBILITY OF CAPTURING SOME TO TRAIN IN SOME WAY.
WE'LL FIGURE SOMETHING OUT.
WE'RE NOT GOING TO SUCCEED EVERY SINGLE TIME.

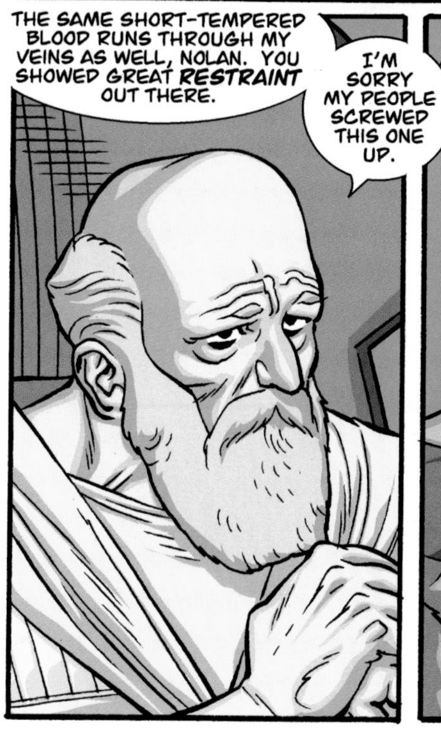
THE SAME SHORT-TEMPERED BLOOD RUNS THROUGH MY VEINS AS WELL, NOLAN. YOU SHOWED GREAT **RESTRAINT** OUT THERE.
I'M SORRY MY PEOPLE SCREWED THIS ONE UP.

BEST NOT TO BRING IT UP.
SERIOUSLY.
C.O.P.

THANKFULLY, THERE ARE FAR MORE POTENTIAL WEAPONS LISTED IN YOUR BOOKS... AND A FEW THINGS I'D LIKE YOU TO LOOK INTO THAT YOU DIDN'T WRITE ABOUT.
YOU HAVE A LONG ROAD AHEAD OF YOU.

THE KLAXUS PLANT IS POISONOUS TO VILTRUMITES. IT CAN'T KILL US--BUT IT WOULD MAKE US PRETTY EASY TO DEFEAT IN AN OTHERWISE EVENLY MATCHED FIGHT.
THE PROBLEM IS THE PLANT IS IMPOSSIBLE TO KEEP FROM GROWING. IT NEEDS VERY LITTLE WATER OR SUNLIGHT AND GROWS AT AN INSANELY RAPID RATE.
SO... WE INFESTED THIS PLANET WITH THESE SINLAK BEETLES, WHICH EAT THE PLANT FASTER THAN IT CAN GROW--AND ARE IMPOSSIBLE TO EXTERMINATE.
MAYBE WE CAN EXTRACT SOME OF THE POISON FROM PLANT MATERIAL INGESTED BY THE BEETLE...

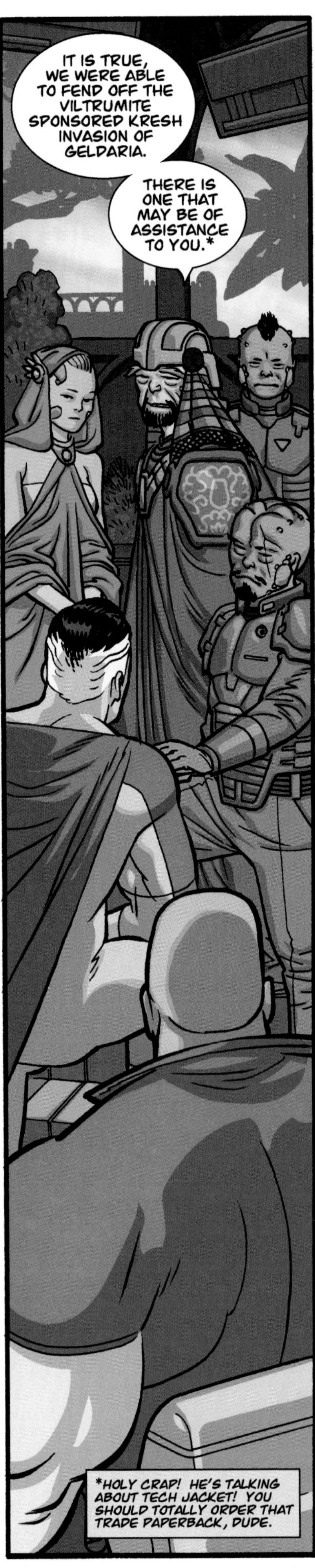
IT IS TRUE, WE WERE ABLE TO FEND OFF THE VILTRUMITE SPONSORED KRESH INVASION OF GELDARIA.
THERE IS ONE THAT MAY BE OF ASSISTANCE TO YOU.*
*HOLY CRAP! HE'S TALKING ABOUT TECH JACKET! YOU SHOULD TOTALLY ORDER THAT TRADE PAPERBACK, DUDE.

THEIR OLD MIGRATION PATHS CAME RIGHT THROUGH THIS SPOT ON THE STARMAPS.
IF WE COULD CATCH ONE OF THESE IT WOULD BE A HUGE HELP. SPACE SHARKS ARE BAD NEWS.

IF THIS THING IS STILL OUT HERE-- THIS BEACON WILL DETECT IT.
LET'S GO.
YIPE!

WE KNOW HIM AS BATTLE BEAST.
I KNOW OF THE ONE YOU SPEAK. MY PLANET'S FAVORITE SON... OUR WORLD'S PROTECTOR, HE BROUGHT US THIS UTOPIA.
BUT IN DOING SO, HE BECAME ADDICTED TO CONFLICT. INVULNERABLE AND IMMORTAL, HE LEFT OUR WORLD IN SEARCH OF CONFLICT WORTHY OF HIS UNIQUE ABILITIES.
I HAVE NEVER SEEN HIM, THERE ARE THOSE AMONG US WHO DO NOT BELIEVE HIM TO EXIST. I PRAY TO LIVE LONG ENOUGH TO SEE HIS RETURN. WE ALL DO.

GONE.
I FEAR I DID MY JOB TOO WELL.

HE'S SLEEPING!
THAT MAN WOULD SLEEP THROUGH ANYTHING! I STILL NEED TO TALK TO HIM. JUST--ASK HIM TOMORROW. WHEN IS HE GOING TO FINALLY MOVE OUT?
THIS IS RIDICULOUS. HE'S BEEN SLEEPING ON OUR COUCH FOR MONTHS!

YOU COULD HAVE ASKED ME INSTEAD OF LAUNCHING INTO THIS TIRADE. HE'S MOVING OUT NEXT WEEK.
WE'VE BEEN WORKING SO MUCH, IT'S BEEN DIFFICULT FOR HIM TO FIND A PLACE.
OH. I HAD NO IDEA.
OKAY.

NOW, CAN WE JUST GO TO BED?
AGAIN? OH, ALLEN-- YOU'RE SPOILING ME.

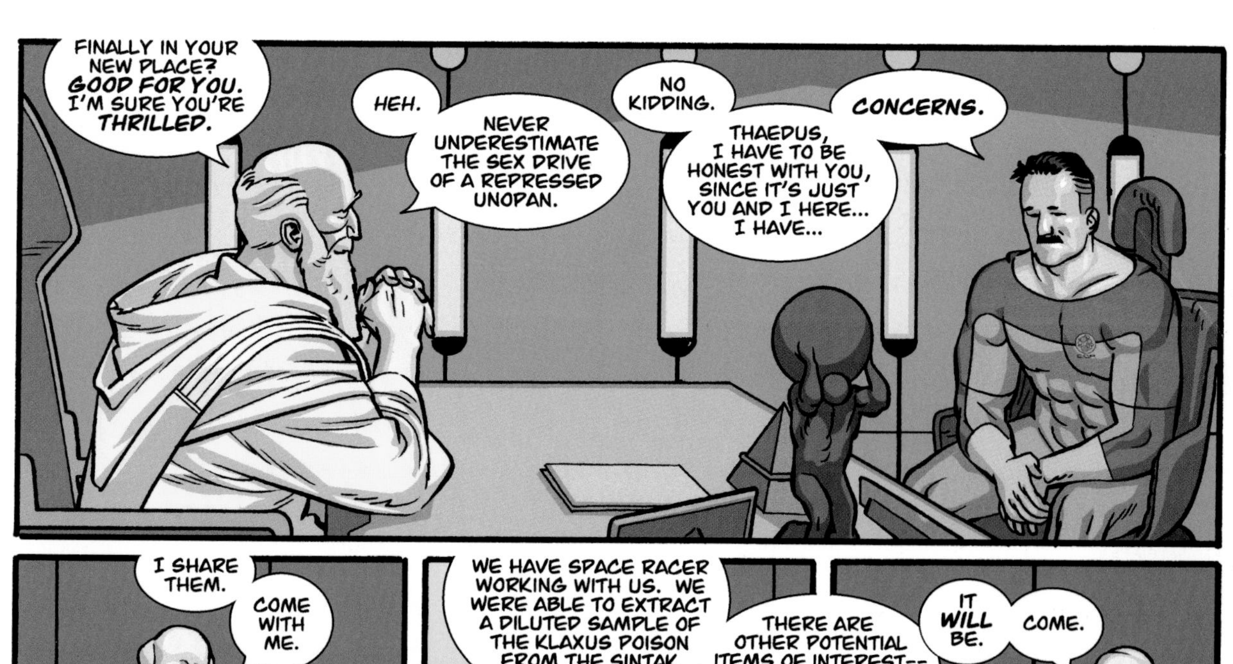
FINALLY IN YOUR NEW PLACE? **GOOD FOR YOU.** I'M SURE YOU'RE **THRILLED.**
HEH.
NEVER UNDERESTIMATE THE SEX DRIVE OF A REPRESSED UNOPAN.
NO KIDDING.
THAEDUS, I HAVE TO BE HONEST WITH YOU, SINCE IT'S JUST YOU AND I HERE... I HAVE...
CONCERNS.

I SHARE THEM.
COME WITH ME.

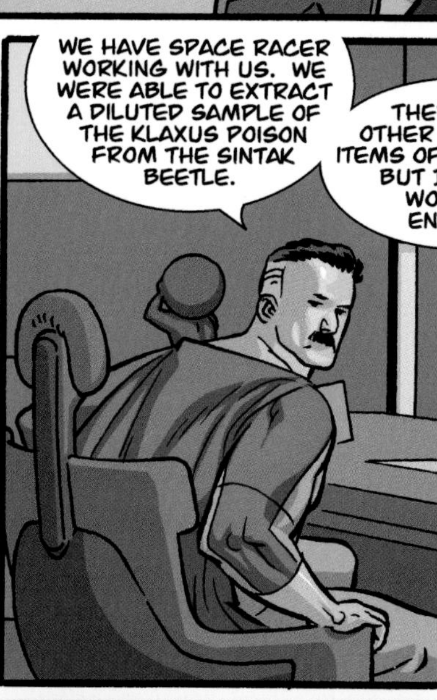
WE HAVE SPACE RACER WORKING WITH US. WE WERE ABLE TO EXTRACT A DILUTED SAMPLE OF THE KLAXUS POISON FROM THE SINTAK BEETLE.
THERE ARE OTHER POTENTIAL ITEMS OF INTEREST-- BUT I FEAR IT WON'T BE ENOUGH.

IT **WILL** BE.
COME.

THE TIME TO STRIKE IS **NOW.** YOU NEED TO GO TO EARTH.
GET YOUR SON AND THAT BOY WITH THE GELDARIAN WEAPON-- AND WHOEVER ELSE YOU THINK CAN HELP US.

WE WILL DO OUR BEST TO ARRANGE AS MANY THREATS TO THE VILTRUMITES AS WE CAN WHILE YOU ARE AWAY.
NOW...
...THERE IS SOMETHING I MUST REVEAL TO YOU.

WHEN YOU TOLD ME OF OUR PEOPLE'S GENOCIDE... I WASN'T COMPLETELY UNAWARE OF WHAT HAD TRANSPIRED.
I TURNED MY BACK ON MY PEOPLE BECAUSE I GREW TO BELIEVE THEIR ACTIONS TO BE, FOR LACK OF A BETTER WORD... EVIL. I HAVE DEDICATED MY LIFE TO BRINGING AN END TO THEIR TYRANNY.
I WILL STOP AT NOTHING TO BRING AN END TO THIS AGE OF VIOLENCE AND FEAR. BUT I NEVER KNEW... I WAS UNAWARE OF THE EXTENT OF THE DAMAGE I'D BROUGHT TO THE VILTRUMITES.
STEP THROUGH THIS DOOR.
THE WORST THING TO EVER HAPPEN TO OUR PEOPLE... IT WAS MY GENETIC SIGNATURE THAT MADE IT POSSIBLE...

THE SCOURGE VIRUS?
YES... AN IMPROVED STRAIN THAT WOULD CIRCUMVENT ANY IMMUNITY THAT HAS DEVELOPED...

AND ALTHOUGH IT COULD MEAN SUICIDE FOR US AND THE POTENTIAL EXTINCTION OF OUR PEOPLE...
...IF I BELIEVE OUR CAUSE TO BE LOST, I WON'T HESITATE TO USE IT AGAIN.

68

UNGH.
ALMOST THERE.
112

WRAMM!!
STOP!
CHOOM
ORTH

YOU DISRUPT THE NATURAL ORDER OF THINGS!
DO YOU HAVE ANY IDEA THE EVILS YOU HAVE SERVED?! HOW MUCH YOU HAVE DAMAGED CIVILIZATION WITH YOUR ACTIONS?!
DO YOU?!
El Madman's
TACOS
TACOS
DUDE... THE HECK--?!
TACOS...

YOU *DISGUST* ME, YOU NAIVE FOOL! YOU HAVE NO IDEA WHAT YOU'VE DONE. THE DEVASTATION WORLDWIDE--IN ALL THE MAJOR CITIES OF THE WORLD--WAS THE *BEST* THING THAT COULD HAVE HAPPENED TO US!
THE LACK OF FOOD AND SUPPLIES, THE SPREAD OF ILLNESS AMONG THE DISPLACED CITY DWELLERS WOULD HAVE STEMMED THE IMPENDING OVERPOPULATION CATASTROPHE.
THE DESTRUCTION OF THE DENSELY POPULATED CITY CENTERS WOULD HAVE LED TO A SUBSTANTIAL DECREASE IN CARBON EMISSIONS LEADING TO A POSSIBLE END TO GLOBAL CLIMATE CHANGE.

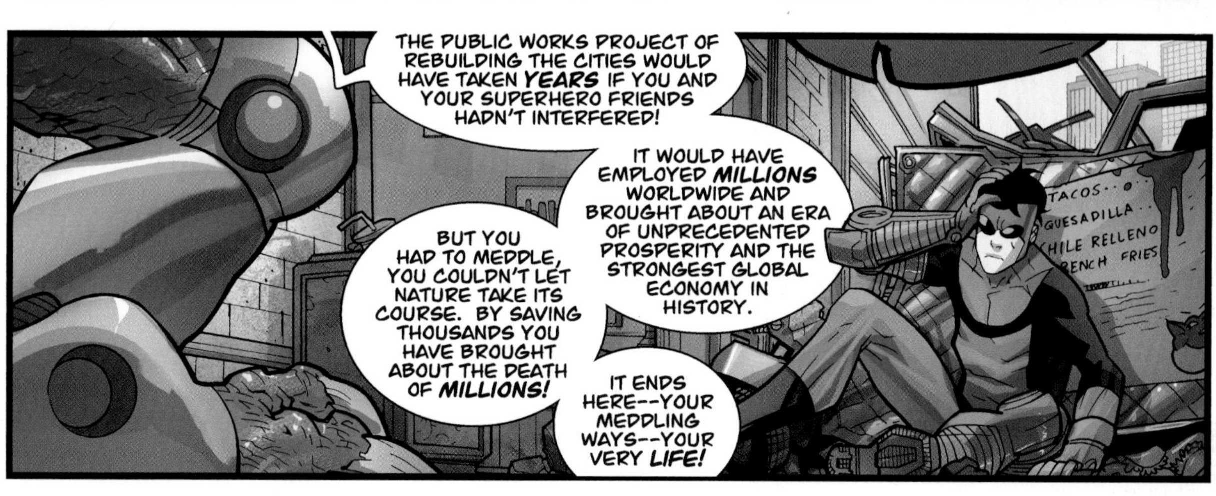
THE PUBLIC WORKS PROJECT OF REBUILDING THE CITIES WOULD HAVE TAKEN *YEARS* IF YOU AND YOUR SUPERHERO FRIENDS HADN'T INTERFERED!
IT WOULD HAVE EMPLOYED *MILLIONS* WORLDWIDE AND BROUGHT ABOUT AN ERA OF UNPRECEDENTED PROSPERITY AND THE STRONGEST GLOBAL ECONOMY IN HISTORY.
BUT YOU HAD TO MEDDLE, YOU COULDN'T LET NATURE TAKE ITS COURSE. BY SAVING THOUSANDS YOU HAVE BROUGHT ABOUT THE DEATH OF *MILLIONS!*
IT ENDS HERE--YOUR MEDDLING WAYS--YOUR VERY *LIFE!*
TACOS..
CHILE RELLENO

YOUR BOYFRIEND'S ON THE NEWS... JEEZ, IS THAT A *DINOSAUR?* LOOKS LIKE HE'LL BE LATE FOR DINNER TONIGHT.
NAH. HE'S GOT AN HOUR AND A HALF TO GET HERE. HE'LL MAKE IT, HE KNOWS HOW IMPORTANT IT IS TO ME.
DON'T KNOW WHO HE'S FIGHTING, THOUGH... AND HE'S HUGE...
GREAT, MOM--NOW YOU'VE GOT ME WORRIED.
FINALLY!
I THOUGHT YOU'D *NEVER* SHUT UP!
KROOM!

KRAKOOM!
CRAP!

ROBOT'S GOING TO BE PISSED. I'M SURE THESE THINGS AREN'T CHEAP.
OH, WELL-- I'M SURE I'M PLENTY HEALED BY NOW. I'VE BEEN WEARING THESE FOR--

AGH!
YOU'RE FAST!

HEY!
CHOMP!!
I STAND BEFORE YOU NOW TO SAY YOU ARE THE OLD WAY, INVINCIBLE!
I REPRESENT A NEW WORLD ORDER! TREMBLE BEFORE THE MIGHT OF DINOSAURUS!
AW, NUTS.
YOU'RE ACTUALLY A VIABLE THREAT.

OH, SHUT UP!
WRONMM!
WHUDD!
NO! NOT AGAIN!
WHAT THE--?!
BRO, YOU GOTTA DO SOMETHING. THAT THING IS LIKE-- AS EVIL AS IT IS SMART! I DON'T KNOW IF IT CAN BE STOPPED!
IT CAN RETURN AT ANY TIME... IT'S OUT OF CONTROL. IT MAKES ME HURT PEOPLE AND STUFF!
PLEASE, HELP ME!
WHOA! WHAT ARE YOU DOING, MAN?!

THE GUARDIANS OF THE GLOBE CAN TAKE IT FROM HERE, MY FRIEND.
WHAT A MESS. OUR WORK IS *NEVER* DONE.

INVINCIBLE, WHAT IS IT YOU WERE GOING TO DO TO HIM?
SURELY YOU WEREN'T...

I DIDN'T KNOW WHAT TO SAY.

"YEAH. I WAS GOING TO KILL HIM." WAS THE FIRST THING THAT POPPED INTO MY HEAD... AND HEARING IT PUT SO PLAINLY LIKE THAT...
IT JUST FELT SO... **WRONG.**
WERE YOU GOING TO KILL HIM? **COULD** YOU?

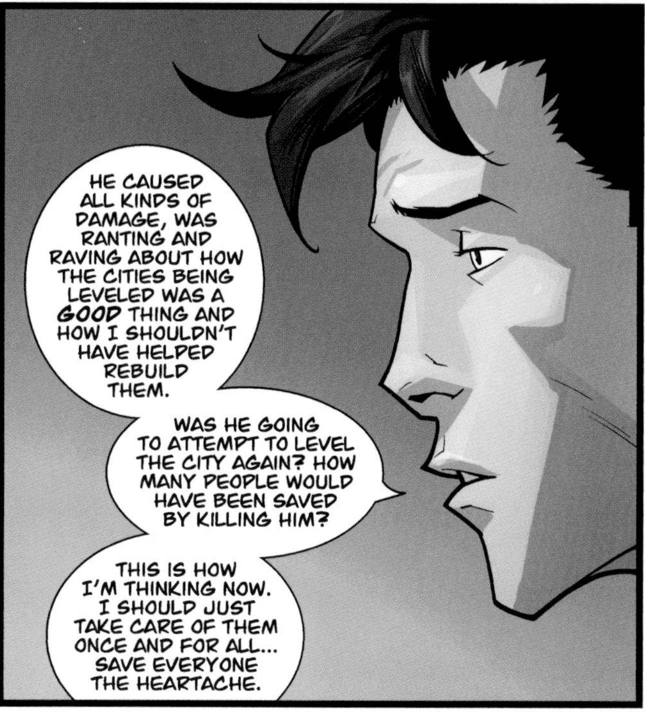
HE CAUSED ALL KINDS OF DAMAGE, WAS RANTING AND RAVING ABOUT HOW THE CITIES BEING LEVELED WAS A **GOOD** THING AND HOW I SHOULDN'T HAVE HELPED REBUILD THEM.
WAS HE GOING TO ATTEMPT TO LEVEL THE CITY AGAIN? HOW MANY PEOPLE WOULD HAVE BEEN SAVED BY KILLING HIM?
THIS IS HOW I'M THINKING NOW. I SHOULD JUST TAKE CARE OF THEM ONCE AND FOR ALL... SAVE EVERYONE THE HEARTACHE.

BUT **COULD** YOU?

I DON'T KNOW. CONQUEST... ANGSTROM... I HAD A PERSONAL STAKE IN THAT. I SNAPPED.
THIS GUY WAS JUST SOME IDIOT FRAT BOY. I FELT SORRY FOR HIM... BUT... I THINK I WAS GOING TO.
I DON'T KNOW.

THAT'S GOOD... I THINK THAT'S A GOOD THING... YOU NOT KNOWING.
LET'S GO EAT. MY PARENTS PROBABLY THINK WE'RE AVOIDING THEM.
THANKS FOR DOING THIS. THEY'RE EXCITED.

NO PROBLEM, EVE.
HOW BAD COULD IT BE?

...

WHAT DID I SAY?

SO, MARK... WHAT IS IT YOUR FATHER DOES?!

WELL... UH...

MOM!

WHAT?

DAMN IT, BETSY! HAVE YOU LOST YOUR *MIND?!*
THE BOY'S FATHER IS THE PSYCHO WHO TRIED TO TAKE OVER THE WORLD! DON'T YOU REMEMBER?!
OMNI-MAN!
THE BOY HAD TO FIGHT HIM--HIS OWN FATHER--TO SAVE THE PLANET! PROBABLY NOT HIS FAVORITE DINNER CONVERSATION, YOU DITZ!!

DAD!
STOP!

NO, IT'S OKAY. YOUR FATHER IS *RIGHT*. I WAS JUST TRYING TO MAKE CONVERSATION--BUT IT WAS A STUPID MISTAKE TO MAKE.
I'M VERY SORRY, MARK.

IT'S TOTALLY OKAY, REALLY.

WHY DO YOU LET HIM TREAT YOU LIKE THIS?

LET?! NOBODY "LETS" ME DO ANYTHING... NOT IN MY OWN HOME! I--

UM.

NEVER MIND.

SO, MR. WILKINS... ADAM...
YOU LIKE SPORTS?

JUST GOING TO LEAVE THEM WITH THE DISHES?
THEY LIKE IT. BONDING TIME. CIGAR?
NO, NO THANKS. WHAT DID YOU WANT TO TALK TO ME ABOUT?

I WANTED TO THANK YOU.
I KNOW THAT MY LITTLE ANGEL IS NO ANGEL. I CAUGHT HER ONE TIME, WITH THAT LONG-HAIRED BOY. THE ONE THAT DIED.
YOU KNOW SHE HAD HIM LIVING HERE FOR A WHILE? WE DIDN'T EVEN KNOW.
ANYWAY, I APPRECIATE YOU GIVING HER A CHANCE... KNOWING YOU'RE NOT HER FIRST.

SHE NEVER REALLY GOT JUST HOW IMPORTANT VIRGINITY IS TO A WOMAN.
MEN LIKE TO FEEL LIKE THEY'RE BREAKING NEW GROUND. THEY WANT TO BE THE TEACHERS... THEY WANT TO BE IN CHARGE.
HARD TO DO THAT IF THERE'S NO CORNERS LEFT UNEXPLORED, RIGHT?
BETSY WAS A VIRGIN WHEN WE GOT TOGETHER.
YOU CAN ALWAYS TELL WHEN YOU'RE WITH A VIRGIN. THEY JUST ACT DIFFERENTLY, THINK DIFFERENTLY... LESS CONFIDENCE. IT'S ATTRACTIVE.

DON'T KNOW IF I WOULD HAVE MARRIED BETSY, HAD THINGS BEEN... DIFFERENT.
I DON'T LIKE COMING IN SECOND... OR THIRD... OR... WHATEVER THE CASE MAY BE.
IT'S GOOD OF YOU TO LOOK PAST MY DAUGHTER'S OBVIOUS FLAWS. SHOWS CHARACTER. I RESPECT THAT.
OF COURSE, IT'S NOT THE END OF THE WORLD WHEN A WOMAN KNOWS A THING OR TWO, RIGHT? SO I GUESS THERE ARE POSITIVES AND NEGATIVES...

I TOLD YOU IT WOULD BE HORRIBLE.
WHAT WAS MY DAD SAYING TO YOU OUT THERE? YOU GUYS TALKED FOREVER.
NOTHING IMPORTANT.

WELL, THANKS FOR DOING THIS. I REALLY APPRECIATE IT. IT'S IMPORTANT TO ME THAT YOU HAVE A CHANCE TO DISLIKE MY PARENTS AS MUCH AS I DO.
MISSION ACCOMPLISHED?

SO, YOU WANT TO TALK ABOUT TOMORROW? ARE YOU READY?
I THINK I CAN DO ANYTHING, NOW.

STRONGHOLD PRISON.

I DO APPRECIATE THE VISIT. I JUST DON'T KNOW THAT IT'S GOING TO HELP THE SITUATION.
TOO LITTLE, TOO LATE.

WHILE IT'S NOT EXPRESSLY WRITTEN IN OUR AGREEMENT, I ASSUMED IT WOULD BE UNDERSTOOD THAT ANY WORLD-THREATENING EVENTS WOULD TAKE PRECEDENCE OVER OUR CLIENTS.
WHAT GOOD IS A SAFE PRISON IF THE WORLD AROUND IT IS DESTROYED-- RIGHT?

...
I SUPPOSE.
STILL, WE SUFFERED AN ESCAPE ATTEMPT SHORTLY AFTER THAT INVASION OF YOUR DOPPELGANGERS. YOU WERE FIGHTING THAT WHITE HAIRED MAN ON THE NEWS.
WILL YOU EVER BE AVAILABLE?

I'M AVAILABLE RIGHT NOW.
THIS IS GOING TO HAPPEN FROM TIME TO TIME. IT'S UNAVOIDABLE.

THE SERVICE IS STILL OF CONSIDERABLE VALUE IF HE PREVENTS ONLY ONE INCIDENT A YEAR. THIS WAS EXPLAINED TO YOU.

BEFORE THIS VISIT, I WAS CONSIDERING CANCELING ALTOGETHER. IT'S GOING TO TAKE A COMPLIMENTARY SIX MONTH PERIOD TO KEEP ME.
BOTTOM LINE.

OKAY--
THREE MONTHS, TAKE IT OR LEAVE IT. WE'LL SEE HOW OFTEN MY CLIENT OFFERS ASSISTANCE WHEN YOU'RE NOT IN THE ROTATION.

YOU DON'T SEEM TO COMPREHEND THE KIND OF REVOLUTIONARY SERVICE YOU'RE A PART OF.
SIGH
FINE.

OH, WOW! THAT WAS AWESOME! YOU WERE AMAZING IN THERE!
SOMEONE HAD TO BE. LORD, MARK--YOU'RE SUCH A PUSH OVER. YOU GIVE HIM SIX FREE MONTHS AND WE'LL NEVER HAVE OUR OWN PLACE!
SORRY.
YOU OKAY TO FLY? I MEAN, YOUR POWERS--?
I WOULDN'T BE FLYING SO HIGH IF YOU WEREN'T RIGHT HERE. I DON'T KNOW--THEY HAVEN'T ACTED UP IN A FEW DAYS... MAYBE THAT'S OVER.
ONE CAN ONLY HOPE...

SORRY I BROUGHT IT UP. DIDN'T MEAN TO UPSET YOU.
IT'S OKAY.
THE GOOD NEWS IS THAT I'VE GOTTEN SOME CALLS FROM A FEW POWER PLANTS INQUIRING ABOUT OUR SERVICE. THIS COULD BE HUGE.
DO YOU REALIZE HOW MUCH WE'LL BE MAKING IF WE GET SO MUCH AS SIX REGULAR CLIENTS?
NOPE... BUT AS LONG AS YOU KNOW, I'M COOL.

MIGHT NOT BE A BAD IDEA TO EXPAND OUR ROSTER A LITTLE... HAVE AT LEAST ONE RESERVE FOR WHEN YOU'RE TIED UP SOMEWHERE ELSE.
HOW DO YOU FEEL ABOUT MAYBE OLIVER HELPING OUT? I'M SURE HE NEEDS MONEY.

SPEAK OF THE DEVIL...

HEY GUYS-- YOU HEADED BACK TO THE HOUSE?
MOM'S OUT WITH PAUL TONIGHT. FIGURED YOU MIGHT... WELL... WANT TO KNOW YOU HAVE THE HOUSE ALL TO YOURSELF.
Y'KNOW... SEX.
CUTE.
WHOA, MAN--NICE COSTUME. I LIKE IT. WHAT BROUGHT THAT ON?
I JUST WENT A FEW ROUNDS WITH THE ELEPHANT. HE RIPPED MY COSTUME UP.
YOU FOUGHT HIM BEFORE, RIGHT?
SEEMS LIKE I HAVE... I DON'T REALLY REMEMBER. MAYBE ONCE.
WELL, ANYWAY, MY COSTUME GOT ALL RIPPED UP. I WENT TO ART FOR A FIX AND HE SAID "YOU'RE GETTING A LITTLE OLD FOR THE EXPOSED LEG BIT."
I AGREED-- AND THEN PRESTO CHANGO--
--YOUNG OMNI-MAN IS BORN!
WELL, I'M GOING BACK OUT ON PATROL--YOU GUYS HAVE FUN BACK AT THE HOUSE.
WINK.
RUDE.
EH... HE'S NOT WRONG, THOUGH.
HOUSE ALL TO OURSELVES-- WEE!

THE BLOCK. REMOTE GLOBAL DEFENSE AGENCY OUTPOST IN THE MOJAVE DESERT.

HNGH.

WHAT?
THE BOY LEFT ME ALIVE?
STUPID.

BREET
BREET

RUUUMMMMMBBLE!

RUUUMMMMMBBLE!

RAKOOM!

OH, FU--

OUR ARMY IS COMPLETE.
OUR GENERALS ARE IN PLACE.
THE SEQUID INVASION OF EARTH BEGINS *NOW!*

EVE? MY MOM'S GOING TO BE HOME SOON AND I'D RATHER IT NOT BE **OBVIOUS** WHAT WE'VE BEEN DOING.
I MEAN, I REALLY APPRECIATE THAT YOU'RE ALREADY COMFORTABLE ENOUGH IN OUR RELATIONSHIP TO SPEND SO MUCH TIME IN THE CAN--BUT YOU LEFT YOUR PANTS OUT HERE.
SENDS THE WRONG SIGNAL, Y'KNOW?
NOK! NOK!
EVE?

GO AWAY!

OKAY, UH... LET ME KNOW IF YOU NEED ANYTHING.

SORRY TO BOTHER YOU.

ONE STEP

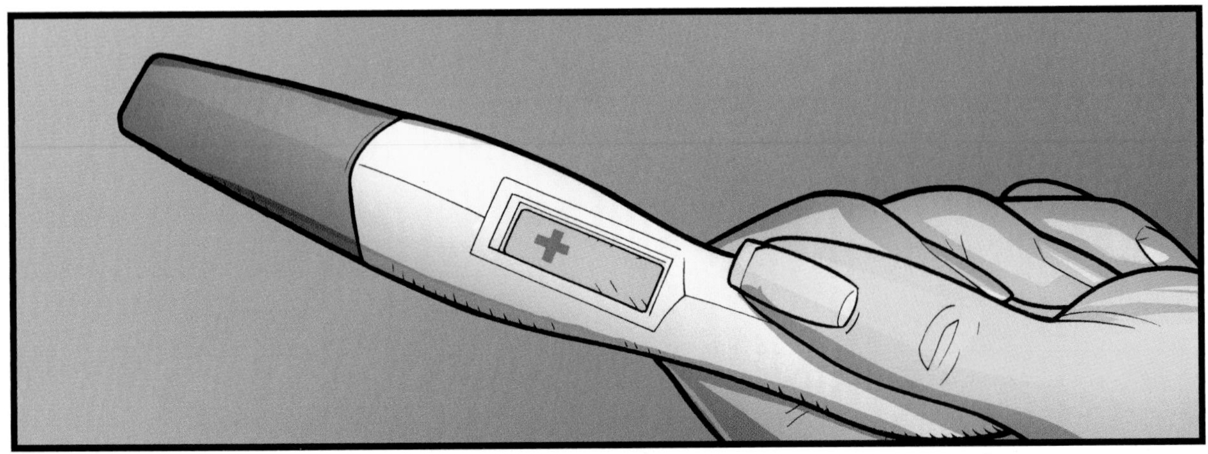

69

SHE IS UNIVERSA, WARRIOR QUEEN TO A FAR OFF WORLD.
SHE HAS TRAVELED COUNTLESS MILES TO THE PLANET EARTH. HER REASONS FOR DOING SO WILL PUT THE ENTIRE PLANET IN JEOPARDY.
SHE IS AS DEADLY AS SHE IS RELENTLESS.
SHE WILL NOT STOP-- WILL NOT REST UNTIL SHE GETS WHAT SHE HAS COME FOR.
THE POPULATION OF THIS PLANET IS IN GRAVE DANGER--THEY HAVE NO CONCEPT OF THE LEVEL OF THREAT COMING THEIR WAY.

BECAUSE THE PEOPLE OF EARTH HAVE FAR MORE PRESSING CONCERNS AT THE MOMENT.
KROOM!

HEAR ME, HUMAN RACE! IT IS TIME TO MEET YOUR NEW MASTERS!
TOGETHER WE WILL FORM A NEW RACE--A NEW CIVILIZATION. WE WILL LIVE TOGETHER AS ONE--A NEW COMBINED RACE OF HUMAN AND SEQUID!
EMBRACE US OR DIE!
CAFE
NG
THE PEOPLE OF EARTH DO NOT LIVE IN A CONSTANT STATE OF FEAR. WHILE THERE HAVE BEEN ALIEN INVASIONS, ENTIRE CITIES LEVELED AND VILLAINS WHO THREATEN ALL LIFE ON EARTH...
THESE ATTACKS ARE FEW AND FAR BETWEEN. THERE ARE DAYS, WEEKS, EVEN MONTHS OF PEACE.
AND EVEN ON DAYS WHEN THERE IS AN ATTACK OF SOME KIND, ON SOME LARGE SCALE, IT IS MOST OFTEN AN ISOLATED EVENT, AFFECTING ONE AREA, EASILY HANDLED BY ONE COSTUMED HERO.
IT IS A RARE OCCASION THAT TWO THREATS, OF SIMILAR MAGNITUDE, WOULD SOMEHOW OCCUR ON THE SAME DAY...

...BUT THIS IS ONE OF THOSE DAYS.
BROKKA-THOOM!!
THERE.

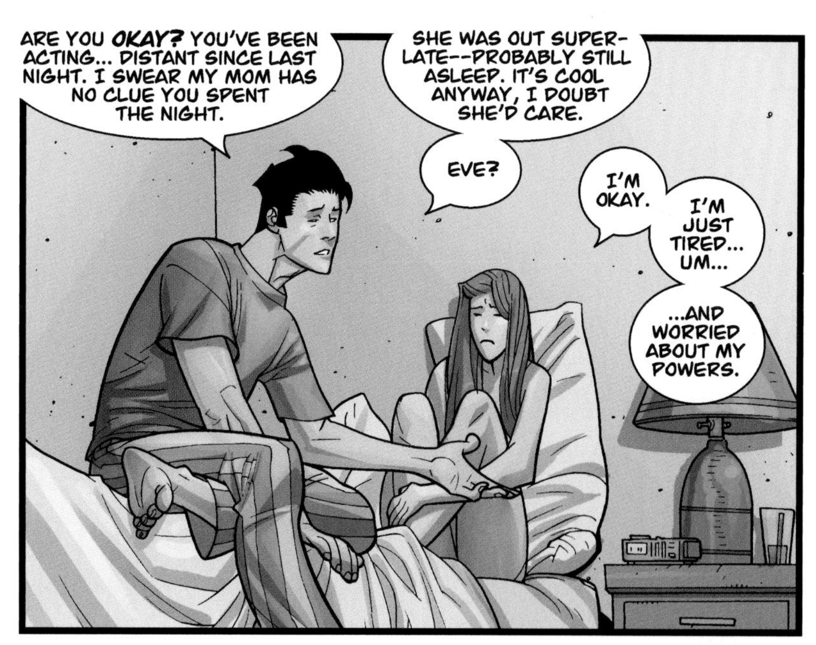
ARE YOU **OKAY?** YOU'VE BEEN ACTING... DISTANT SINCE LAST NIGHT. I SWEAR MY MOM HAS NO CLUE YOU SPENT THE NIGHT.
SHE WAS OUT SUPER-LATE--PROBABLY STILL ASLEEP. IT'S COOL ANYWAY, I DOUBT SHE'D CARE.
EVE?
I'M OKAY.
I'M JUST TIRED... UM...
...AND WORRIED ABOUT MY POWERS.

BUT YOU HAVEN'T HAD ANY MORE PROBLEMS WITH THEM, RIGHT? I THOUGHT IT MIGHT BE A ONE TIME THING.
DID SOMETHING ELSE--

BREET! BREET!
WHAT IS **THAT?**
I DON'T KNOW. WHERE IS IT COMING FROM?

WAIT!
CRAP!
CRAP!
CRAP!
HI--**INVINCIBLE INCORPORATED.** HOW MAY I HELP YOU?
RIGHT NOW?
OKAY. NO, WE CAN HANDLE THAT.
WE'RE ON OUR WAY.

WOW.
WHAT IS IT?

THAT WAS WESTERN POWER. THEY'VE GOT A NUCLEAR PLANT UNDER ATTACK--RIGHT NOW. THEY SAY IF WE CAN STOP WHOEVER IS ATTACKING THEY'LL SIGN A FIVE-YEAR CONTRACT.
HOW FAST CAN YOU GET--

--READY?
LET'S GO.

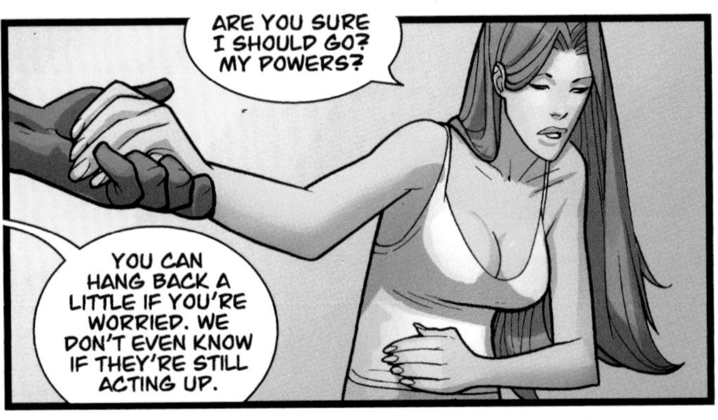
ARE YOU SURE I SHOULD GO? MY POWERS?
YOU CAN HANG BACK A LITTLE IF YOU'RE WORRIED. WE DON'T EVEN KNOW IF THEY'RE STILL ACTING UP.

YEAH.
YOU'RE RIGHT.

MARK!
ALIENS ARE ATTACKING HOUSTON--IT'S ALL OVER THE NEWS. I NEED TO--

SHOOT.

AAAGGH!
AAIIIEEE!!
60
SIXTY

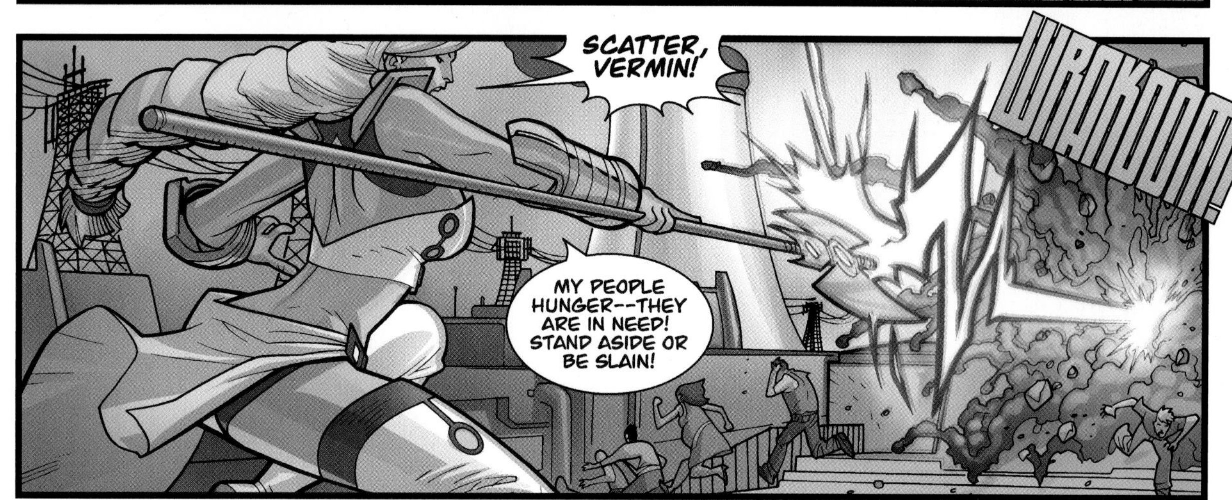
SCATTER, VERMIN!
WRAKOOM!
MY PEOPLE HUNGER--THEY ARE IN NEED! STAND ASIDE OR BE SLAIN!

I HAVE TRAVELLED VAST SPANS OF THE COSMOS TO ARRIVE HERE. YOU ARE A PLANET RICH WITH ENERGY.
I WANT IT!
I WANT IT ALL!

THE ENERGY GENERATED BY THIS PLANT-- IT'S SENT RIGHT INTO THE GRID-- WE DON'T *STORE* IT!
WE HAVE NO MEANS OF STORING IT AND GIVING IT TO YOU--WHAT YOU ASK FOR-- IT JUST ISN'T--
--PRACTICAL.
FOOL!
WRAMM!
I HAVE MY *OWN* MEANS OF STORING YOUR ENERGY.
DO NOT PRESUME TO TELL **UNIVERSA** HOW TO COMPLETE HER TASK!

CAN I PRESUME TO TELL UNIVERSA TO BE A LITTLE KINDER TO THE NATIVES?
SERIOUSLY.
UNCOOL.
I'LL CLEAR THE AREA--YOU DEAL WITH THE PRETTY, PRETTY PRINCESS.
I WILL LET NO ONE STAND IN MY WAY!
THRAKOOM!
OKAY, COOL-- LET'S DIVE RIGHT IN.
TALKING IS OVERRATED.

STILL, THOUGH--IF YOU DON'T MIND ME ASKING--WHAT IS IT YOU'RE AFTER?

HOW DARE YOU?!
WRAMM!

NONE BUT I CAN WIELD THE STAFF OF LEADERSHIP!
KROOM

STOP!
I DON'T **WANT** YOUR STUPID STAFF! I DON'T EVEN WANT TO FIGHT YOU!
ALL I WANT IS FOR YOU TO STOP HURTING PEOPLE!
YOU'RE IN A POWER PLANT--I GET IT. YOU'RE AFTER ENERGY--**GREAT!** DID YOU EVER THINK TO JUST **ASK** FOR HOWEVER MUCH YOU NEED?!
MAYBE WE CAN GIVE IT TO YOU--WOULDN'T **THAT** BE EASIER?

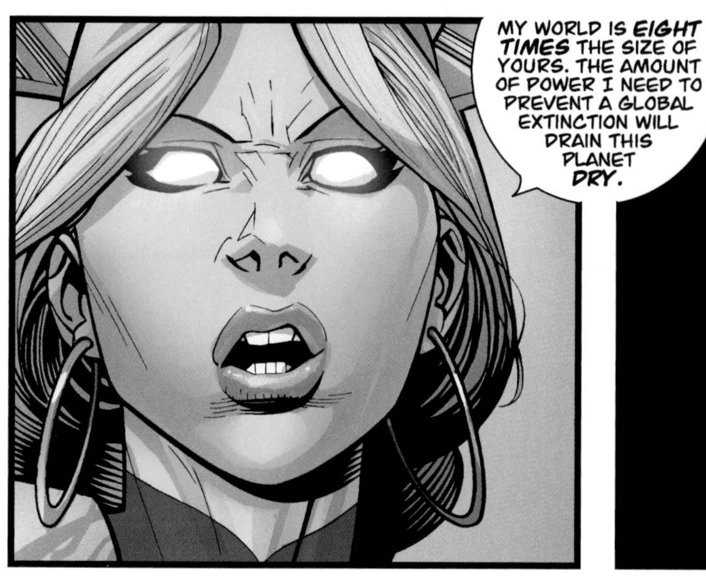
MY WORLD IS **EIGHT TIMES** THE SIZE OF YOURS. THE AMOUNT OF POWER I NEED TO PREVENT A GLOBAL EXTINCTION WILL DRAIN THIS PLANET **DRY**.

OKAY THEN...
WE CAN FIGHT NOW.

THERE IS NOWHERE FOR YOU TO RUN!
SOON, ALL CORNERS OF THIS PLANET WILL BE CRAWLING WITH MY BRETHREN! THERE IS NO ESCAPE FROM THE SEQUID INVASION!
YOU ONLY DELAY THE INEVITABLE!

ARE WE READY?
I WAS ONLY ABLE TO MAKE THREE DISRUPTER BRACELETS--THESE WILL CANCEL THE SEQUIDS' CONTROL OF THEIR HOST FOR A FEW SECONDS. LONG ENOUGH FOR A TELEPORT DART TO BE USED.
I'LL TRY TO MAKE MORE WHILE IN THE FIELD--WE'RE GOING TO NEED MORE.
IT'S IMPERATIVE THAT WE NOT HIT ANYONE ALREADY HOSTING A SEQUID WITH A TELEPORT DART. THAT WILL BREACH THE CONTAINMENT AREA.
UNDERSTOOD?

LOOK ALIVE, PEOPLE. BARRIER GOES LIVE IN FIVE, FOUR, THREE...

WHAT IS--?!

WE HAVE TO WORK FAST, PEOPLE!
PRIORITY ONE IS REMOVING PEOPLE FROM THE CONTAINMENT ZONE. HIT THEM WITH THE DARTS AND THEY'RE TELEPORTED AWAY. THERE ARE THOUSANDS OF PEOPLE LEFT UNDER THIS DOME--WE DON'T GET THEM ALL--THE SEQUIDS REMAIN LINKED.
AS LONG AS THEY HAVE AT LEAST ONE HOST TO ATTACH THEMSELVES TO THEIR MINDS REMAIN LINKED--NO HOST, AND THEY'RE MINDLESS DRONES.
I DON'T THINK I HAVE TO TELL YOU WHAT HAPPENS IF WE FAIL.

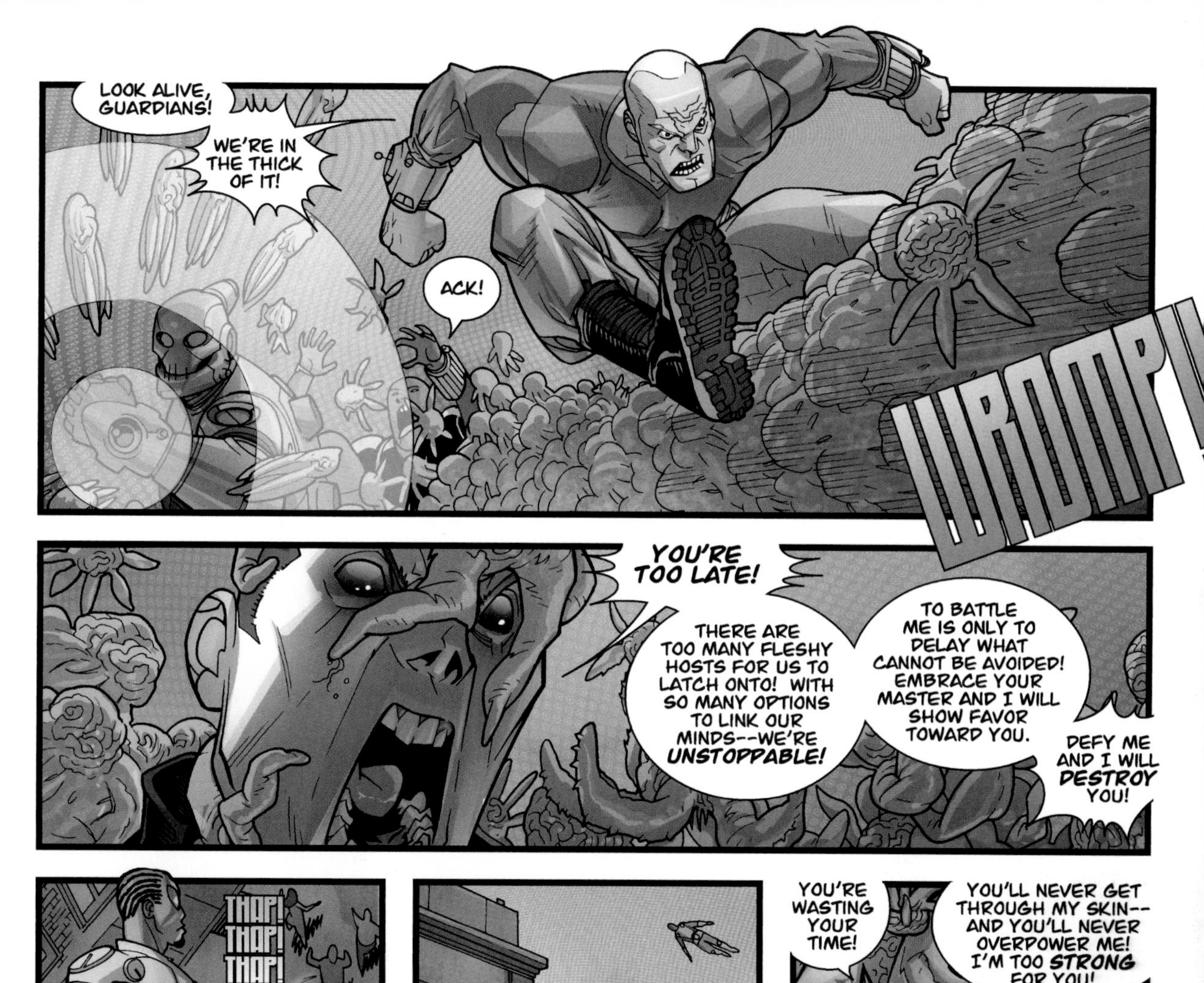
LOOK ALIVE, GUARDIANS!
WE'RE IN THE THICK OF IT!
ACK!
WROMP!
YOU'RE TOO LATE!
THERE ARE TOO MANY FLESHY HOSTS FOR US TO LATCH ONTO! WITH SO MANY OPTIONS TO LINK OUR MINDS--WE'RE UNSTOPPABLE!
TO BATTLE ME IS ONLY TO DELAY WHAT CANNOT BE AVOIDED! EMBRACE YOUR MASTER AND I WILL SHOW FAVOR TOWARD YOU.
DEFY ME AND I WILL DESTROY YOU!

THAP! THAP! THAP!
I HOPE THESE THINGS WORK--

AGH!
MY AR--!

YOU'RE WASTING YOUR TIME!
YOU'LL NEVER GET THROUGH MY SKIN--AND YOU'LL NEVER OVERPOWER ME! I'M TOO STRONG FOR YOU!

FOOLS!
YOU HAVE NO CLUE WHAT YOU'RE UP AGAINST!

WHOOM!
WHUDD!
OW!
SERIOUSLY...
OW.
SURRENDER YOUR PLANET'S ENERGY TO ME.
YOU ARE BEATEN.
BEATEN? I SAID "OW."
I NEVER SAID ANYTHING ABOUT BEING BEATEN.
SEE?
WRAMM!

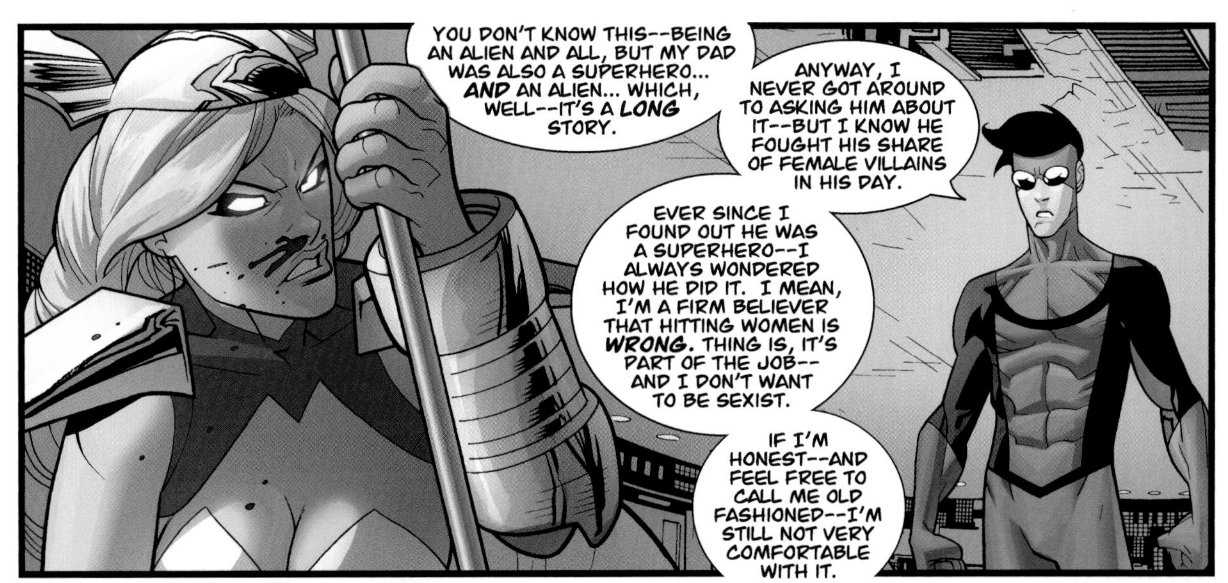
YOU DON'T KNOW THIS--BEING AN ALIEN AND ALL, BUT MY DAD WAS ALSO A SUPERHERO... ***AND*** AN ALIEN... WHICH, WELL--IT'S A ***LONG*** STORY.
ANYWAY, I NEVER GOT AROUND TO ASKING HIM ABOUT IT--BUT I KNOW HE FOUGHT HIS SHARE OF FEMALE VILLAINS IN HIS DAY.
EVER SINCE I FOUND OUT HE WAS A SUPERHERO--I ALWAYS WONDERED HOW HE DID IT. I MEAN, I'M A FIRM BELIEVER THAT HITTING WOMEN IS ***WRONG***. THING IS, IT'S PART OF THE JOB--AND I DON'T WANT TO BE SEXIST.
IF I'M HONEST--AND FEEL FREE TO CALL ME OLD FASHIONED--I'M STILL NOT VERY COMFORTABLE WITH IT.

VTOOM!
SILENCE!

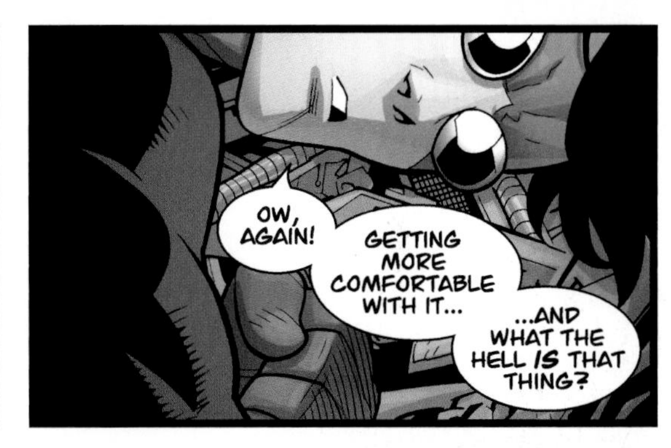
OW, AGAIN!
GETTING MORE COMFORTABLE WITH IT...
...AND WHAT THE HELL ***IS*** THAT THING?

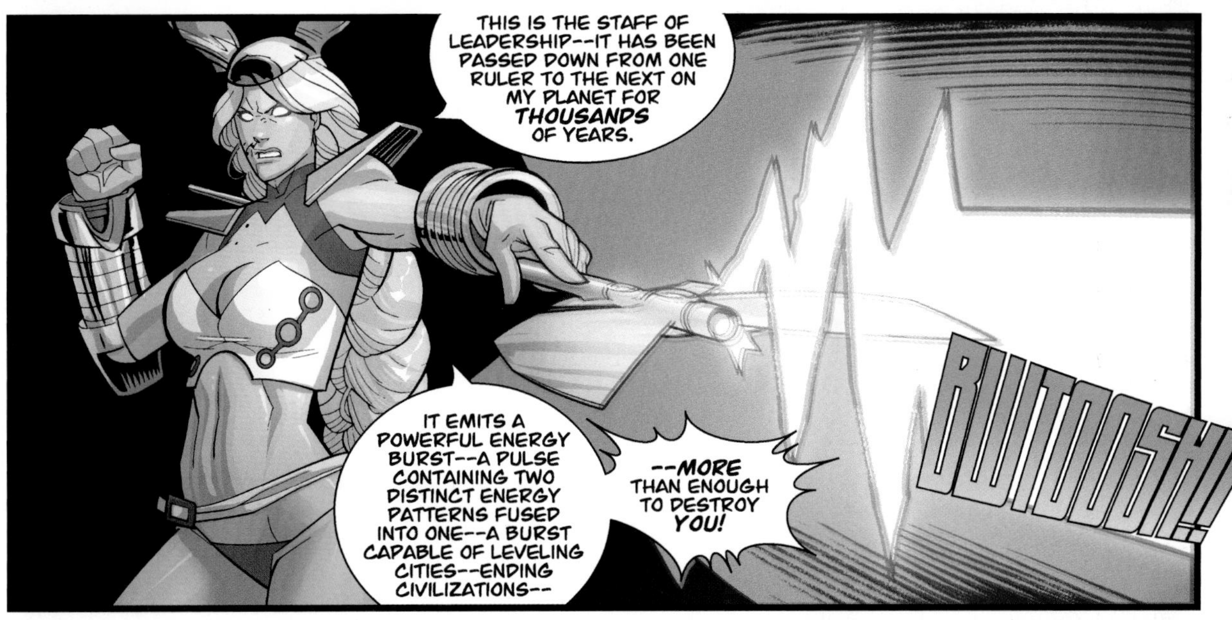
THIS IS THE STAFF OF LEADERSHIP--IT HAS BEEN PASSED DOWN FROM ONE RULER TO THE NEXT ON MY PLANET FOR ***THOUSANDS*** OF YEARS.
IT EMITS A POWERFUL ENERGY BURST--A PULSE CONTAINING TWO DISTINCT ENERGY PATTERNS FUSED INTO ONE--A BURST CAPABLE OF LEVELING CITIES--ENDING CIVILIZATIONS--
--***MORE*** THAN ENOUGH TO DESTROY ***YOU!***
BWOOSH!!

NNNGGH!
--CAN'T!

YOU WERE A FOOL TO OPPOSE--
AGH!
WRAMM!
BACK OFF HIM, LADY. I'M KIND OF IN LOVE WITH--
KROOM!
YOU DARE INTERFERE?!
THERE'S MORE WHERE THAT--
OH, NO--
CRAP!
BTWOOM!

POWERS NOT WORKING!
A LITTLE HELP HERE!
PLEASE!!

EVE?

EVE!

AAGH!!
BTWOKK!

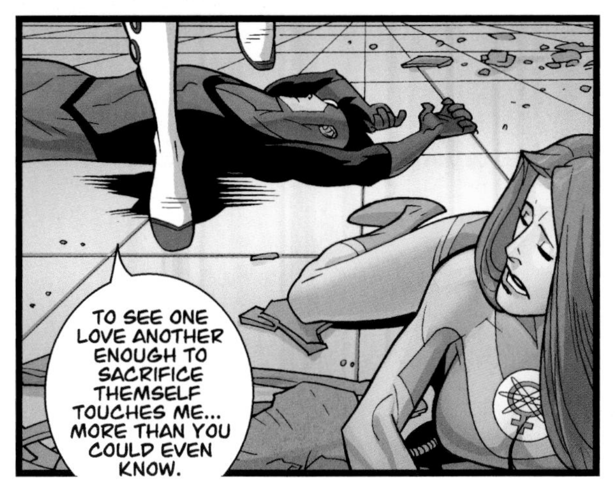
TO SEE ONE LOVE ANOTHER ENOUGH TO SACRIFICE THEMSELF TOUCHES ME... MORE THAN YOU COULD EVEN KNOW.

IT PAINS ME TO HAVE TO END YOUR LIFE--BUT THERE IS TOO MUCH AT STAKE. I CANNOT FAIL AND YOU WILL NOT YIELD TO ME.
YOU GIVE ME NO CHOICE...

GIVE ME THAT!
NO!
YEAAGH!!
BZZZKKCTT!
WHUDD!
NNG.
YOU FOOL, ONLY THOSE CHOSEN BY THE WORLD-GOD CAN WIELD THE STAFF OF LEADERSHIP.
YOU HAVE SEALED YOUR PLANET'S FATE.
HEY!

SHUT UP!
POW!

CRAP-- THAT WORKED!

POWER... WAS IN HER STAFF.

ARE YOU OKAY?
JUST... A LITTLE DAZED... I'M FINE.

WELL, THAT CERTAINLY TOOK LONG ENOUGH.
NOW THAT THAT CRISIS IS AVERTED-- I NEED YOU IN HOUSTON--RIGHT NOW!
THE GUARDIANS OF THE GLOBE ARE ON SITE, IT'S--
IF THEY'RE ALREADY THERE--WHY DO YOU NEED ME?

I DON'T KNOW HOW-- BUT THE SEQUIDS ARE BACK. WE'VE GOT THE CITY BLOCKED OFF, BUT WE DON'T KNOW HOW LONG THAT WILL HOLD.
HOW MANY-- HOW BAD IS IT?
I MEAN-- THE GUARDIANS HAVE IT PRETTY MUCH TAKEN CARE OF...
...RIGHT?

ALL TOO EASY!

70

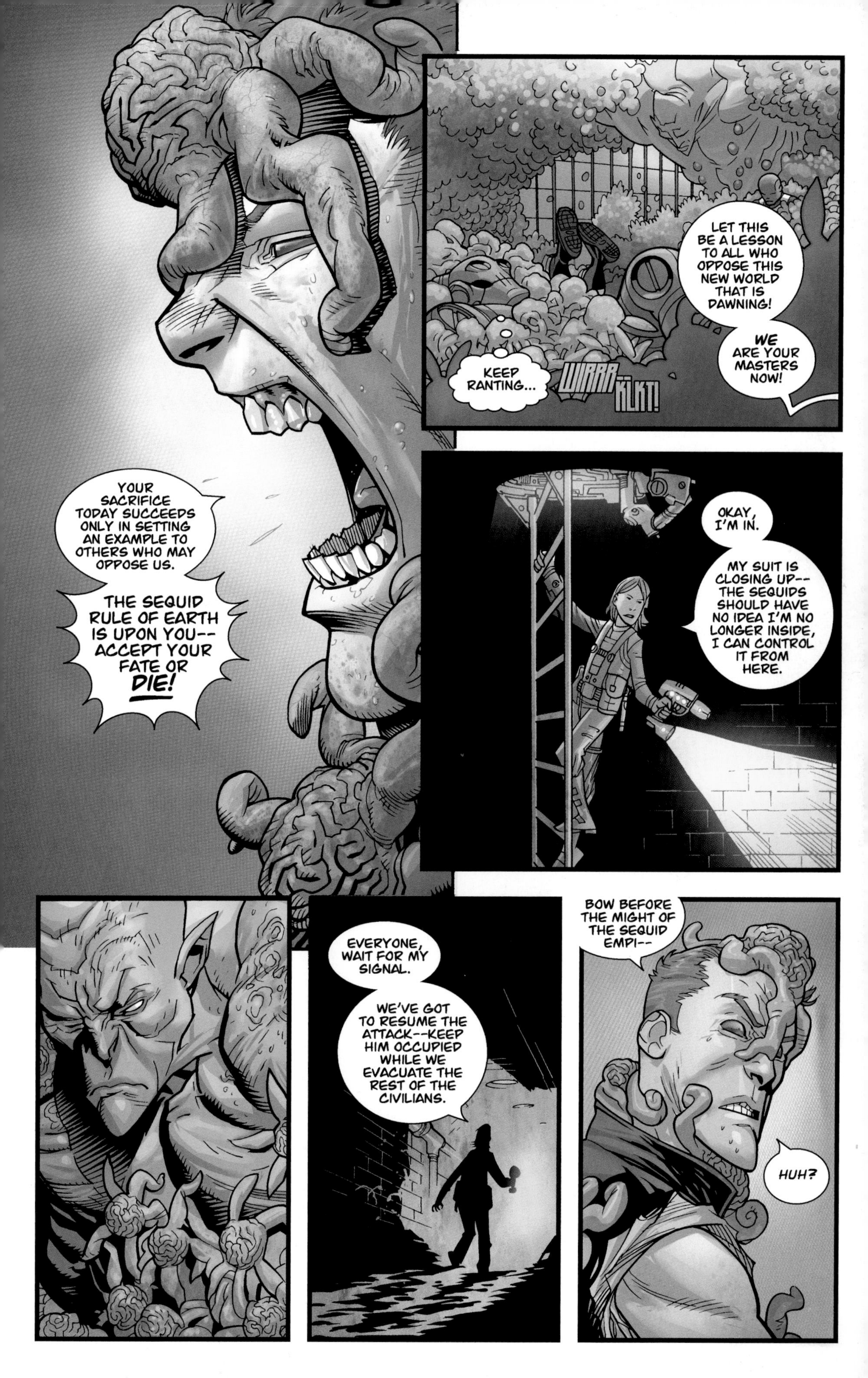
LET THIS BE A LESSON TO ALL WHO OPPOSE THIS NEW WORLD THAT IS DAWNING!
WE ARE YOUR MASTERS NOW!
KEEP RANTING...
WIRRR
KLKT!
YOUR SACRIFICE TODAY SUCCEEDS ONLY IN SETTING AN EXAMPLE TO OTHERS WHO MAY OPPOSE US.
THE SEQUID RULE OF EARTH IS UPON YOU-- ACCEPT YOUR FATE OR DIE!
OKAY, I'M IN.
MY SUIT IS CLOSING UP-- THE SEQUIDS SHOULD HAVE NO IDEA I'M NO LONGER INSIDE, I CAN CONTROL IT FROM HERE.
EVERYONE, WAIT FOR MY SIGNAL.
WE'VE GOT TO RESUME THE ATTACK--KEEP HIM OCCUPIED WHILE WE EVACUATE THE REST OF THE CIVILIANS.
BOW BEFORE THE MIGHT OF THE SEQUID EMPI--
HUH?

WRAMM!

HOW?!
HOW IN THE HECK ARE YOU BACK?!

CHOOM!

DID YOU **REALLY** THINK THAT WOULD HURT US?! IS THAT THE EXTENT OF YOUR PLAN?
A TACKLE?!
PATHETIC.

I WAS JUST TRYING TO GET YOUR ATTENTION.
THAT PLAN WORKED.
TO CONTINUE-- HOW ARE YOU HERE?! YOU WERE LEFT WITH THE MARTIANS, YOU HAD NO HOST-- THEY TOOK YOU BACK TO MARS.
RIGHT? I MEAN, OBVIOUSLY NOT... BUT WHAT HAPPENED? DID THE MARTIANS SEND YOU HERE? WAS IT AN ATTACK?
THIS ONE, THE BODY YOU SEE BEFORE YOU-- OUR ORIGINAL HOST. WE NEVER LEFT IT. **YOU** BROUGHT US HERE.

SO YOU'RE WANTING TO TAKE OVER THIS PLANET AND THEN ATTACK MARS... SOME KIND OF REVENGE THING?
COMBINING YOUR RACE WITH OURS--INCREASING YOUR NUMBER OF HOSTS TO A LEVEL THAT WOULD LEAD TO YOU NEVER BEING WITHOUT ONE...

...A NEW SYMBIOTIC RACE, ELIMINATING YOUR WEAKNESS ONCE AND FOR ALL, YOUR NEED TO LINK YOUR MINDS THROUGH THE CONNECTION OF AT LEAST ONE HOST.
VERY GOOD.
THAT IS OUR PLAN EXACTLY.

WELL, IT AIN'T GOING TO HAPPEN!

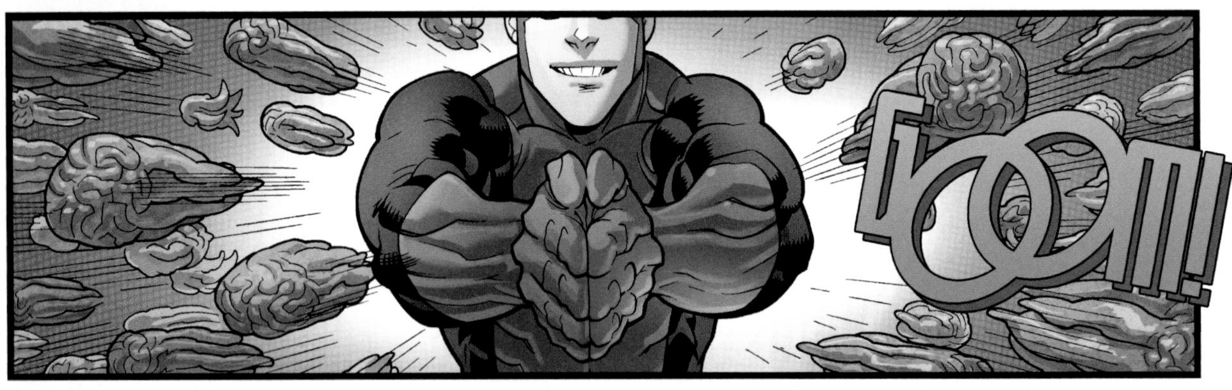
FOOM!

NOW!
LET'S BRING THIS ONE TO A CLOSE, GUARDIANS! I'M FED UP WITH THESE THINGS.

OH, COOL.
I HAD NO CLUE HOW I WAS GOING TO DO THIS ON MY OWN.
WHILE INVINCIBLE'S GOT HIM DISTRACTED, EVERYONE-- CLEAR OUT THE CIVILIANS!
VVMMMKK!
DON'T RISK USING THE DARTS WHEN WE'RE SURROUNDED LIKE THIS. BULLETPROOF-- THIS ONE'S CLEAR! GET HER OUT OF HERE!
WE DEFEATED YOU ONCE-- WHAT MAKES YOU THINK WE CAN'T DO IT AGAIN?
WROKK!
WHAT DO YOU THINK I'VE BEEN DOING ALL THIS TIME? YOU THINK I HAVEN'T PREPARED FOR THIS-- ANTICIPATED EVERY MOVE YOU COULD MAKE?
YOUR CAUSE IS LOST! THIS PLANET IS DOOMED!
IN A WAY--THIS IS ALL MY FAULT. I WAS PART OF A GROUP OF MARTIANS SYMPATHETIC TO THE SEQUIDS ENSLAVED ON MY PLANET.
KROOM!
I CAN'T BELIEVE HOW FOOLISH WE WERE TO PITY THEM.
I CAUSED THIS.
REGARDLESS OF HOW THIS SHAKES DOWN-- YOU'RE PROBABLY GOING TO WANT TO START KEEPING THAT TO YOURSELF.

SO FAR, SO GOOD.

NO, DAMN IT!
YOU HAVE NO IDEA WHAT I'VE HAD TO DEAL WITH LATELY.
I'M NOT PLAYING AROUND HERE!!

AND WE WERE STARTING TO SEE YOU AS SUCH A FORMIDABLE ADVERSARY.
WHAT YOU SEE BEFORE YOU IS NOT US. WE ARE MANY! HURTING THIS FORM WILL ONLY CAUSE US TO CHOOSE ANOTHER HOST--
YOU CANNOT DEFEAT US THIS WAY!

I WILL HURT YOU THE ONLY WAY I KNOW HOW-- AND I DON'T KNOW IF YOU'RE PAYING ATTENTION, BUT YOU'RE ALMOST OUT OF ALTERNATIVE HOSTS!
YOU'RE LOSING!!

ANOTHER ONE DOWN! MOVE-- GET HIM OUT OF HERE!
KEEP IT UP, PEOPLE! WE'RE ALMOST IN THE CLEAR! IT'S LIGHT AT THE END OF THE TUNNEL TIME.

YOU'RE NOT GOING TO SUCCEED! THESE PEOPLE ARE UNDER MY PROTECTION!
THEY HAVE ENDURED TOO MUCH! I WILL NOT ALLOW YOU TO HARM THEM!
YOU WILL NOT ENSLAVE THIS PLANET!
KROOM!!
MY PLANET!

MY--

...

KROOM!!

I KNEW IT! WHAT WE'RE FIGHTING ABOVE--IT'S LITTLE MORE THAN A DECOY!
EVEN IF WE WIN UP THERE--YOU'RE HERE, HIDING, WAITING FOR THE FORCEFIELD AROUND THE CITY TO BE DROPPED.
IT'S OVER!
NO.

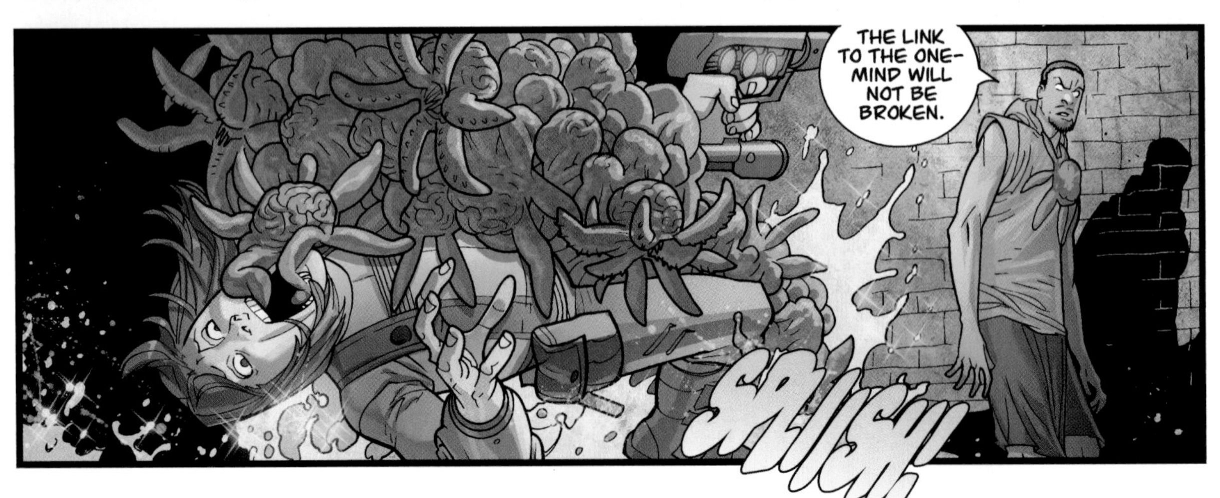
THE LINK TO THE ONE-MIND WILL NOT BE BROKEN.
SPLUSH!

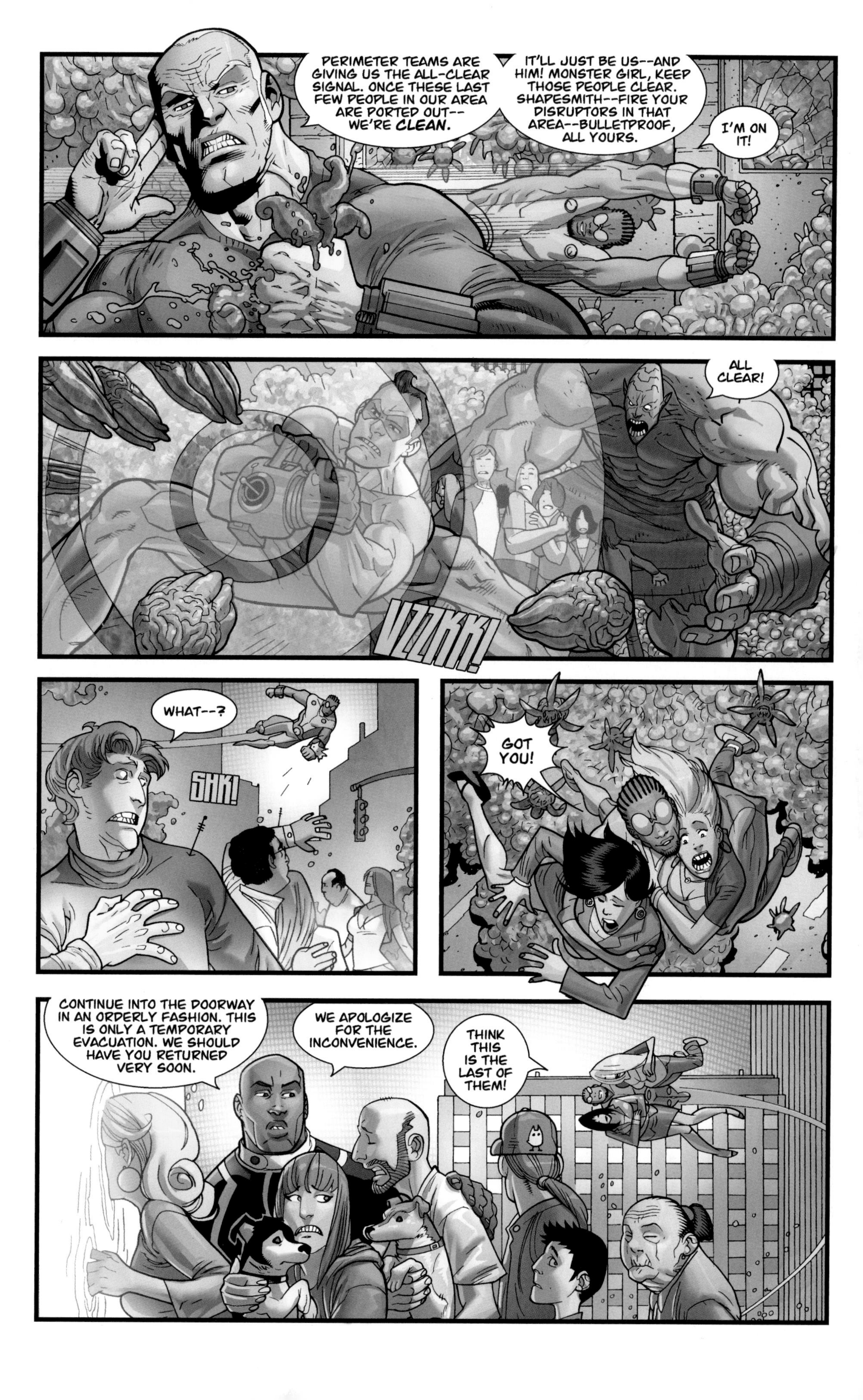
PERIMETER TEAMS ARE GIVING US THE ALL-CLEAR SIGNAL. ONCE THESE LAST FEW PEOPLE IN OUR AREA ARE PORTED OUT-- WE'RE CLEAN.
IT'LL JUST BE US--AND HIM! MONSTER GIRL, KEEP THOSE PEOPLE CLEAR. SHAPESMITH--FIRE YOUR DISRUPTORS IN THAT AREA--BULLETPROOF, ALL YOURS.
I'M ON IT!
ALL CLEAR!
VZZKK!
WHAT--?
SHK!
GOT YOU!
CONTINUE INTO THE DOORWAY IN AN ORDERLY FASHION. THIS IS ONLY A TEMPORARY EVACUATION. WE SHOULD HAVE YOU RETURNED VERY SOON.
WE APOLOGIZE FOR THE INCONVENIENCE.
THINK THIS IS THE LAST OF THEM!

SHKK!
VZZZKKK!

HOPE THIS--
THOK!

--WORKS.
WOW-- LOT OF PEOPLE.

OKAY, I GOT DISTRACTED--
DON'T GET COCKY!
THRAKK

COCKY?
WE WILL COMMAND YOUR PLANET. WE KNOW THIS TO BE FACT.
YOU CANNOT STOP US.
REALLY? HAH!
I DON'T THINK YOU'VE BEEN PAYING ATTENTION.
OKAY, GUARDIANS--LISTEN UP! IT'S JUST HIM AND US IN THE CITY--SO LET'S FOCUS ALL ATTENTION ON THIS GUY AND WRAP THIS UP.
I'D LIKE TO PUT BRIT JUNIOR TO BED MYSELF TONIGHT, GIVE THE LITTLE WOMAN A BREAK. I'VE BEEN WORKING TOO MANY NIGHTS LATELY.
SO LET'S TAKE THIS JERK DOWN!
HE HAD A HOST HIDDEN IN THE SEWERS, BUT I TOOK CARE OF HIM--I'M BACK AT THE HOLDING AREA NOW WITH THE REST OF THE REFUGEES.
LET'S BRING THESE PEOPLE HOME.
HEAR THAT, SEQUID MAN--OR WHATEVER YOU'RE CALLING YOURSELF...
...IT'S ONLY A MATTER OF TIME.
SKRAGG!
NOW WHO'S BEING COCKY?

KROOM!
MONSTER GIRL!

UGH.
WRAMMM!

VZZKKK!
MONSTER GIRL--SNAP OUT OF IT! NOW IS NOT THE TIME TO REVERT BACK TO HUMAN FORM!

GOT YOU! I'LL SEE YOU IN A SECOND. DON'T--
SKRKK!

TAKE THIS!
VZNKK!
THESE BANDS--THAT'S WHAT'S BEEN GIVING YOU THE UPPER HAND! THE SAME DEVICE YOU USED TO DEFEAT ME ON THE MARTIAN SHIP!
I REMEMBER IT WELL!
YOU MAY CONSIDER IT YOUR SAVING GRACE--I SEE IT FOR WHAT IT IS--A WEAK SPOT, SOMETHING YOU RELY TOO HEAVILY ON!

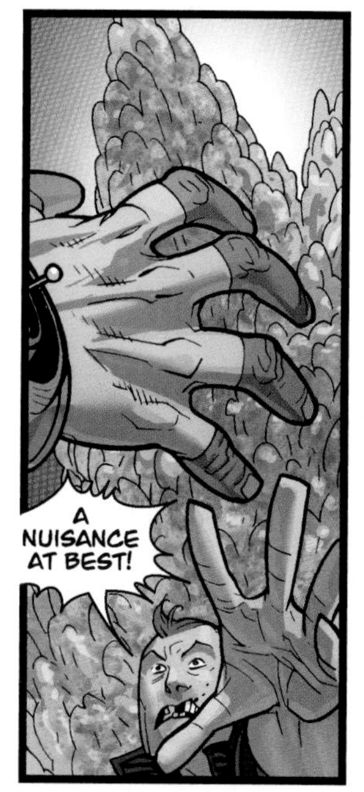
A NUISANCE AT BEST!

NO MORE!
KROOM!

CRAP!
SKRKK!!

SKROOM!
OOH-- SORRY!
MEANT TO SAVE THE BRACELET! I PANICKED!

OKAY, EVERYONE. NOW WE--
ACK!
NOW WE PROVIDE YOU WITH YOUR LAST CHANCE TO SUBMIT! BOW TO US AND WE WILL SPARE YOUR LIVES.
YOU HAVE NO WEAPON AGAINST US! WE OUTNUMBER YOU GREATLY! NO MATTER HOW STRONG YOU ARE, HOW POWERFUL YOU'VE BECOME--OR HOW TIGHT YOU BELIEVE YOUR DEFENSES TO BE--WE WILL OVERCOME ALL!
THE WORLD AS YOU KNEW IT IS ON THE BRINK OF COLLAPSE. YOU HAVE NO HOPE OF DEFEATING US NOW!

I KNOW.
I'VE BEEN HOLDING BACK--WAITING FOR THEM TO GET INTO POSITION, TO USE THEIR LITTLE DISRUPTOR THINGS.
I KNOW THE THREAT YOU POSE--YOU COULD ACTUALLY SUCCEED IN ENSLAVING THIS ENTIRE PLANET--AND I CAN'T LET THAT HAPPEN.
YOU'VE LEFT ME WITH NO CHOICE.

SPLAGCH!!

INVINCIBLE, WHAT HAVE YOU ***DONE?***
RUS LIVINGSTON WAS A ***HOST***, NOT THE THREAT. HE WAS ***INNOCENT***. WE COULD HAVE FOUND ANOTHER WAY... WE COULD HAVE MADE THIS WORK.
YOU DIDN'T HAVE TO KILL AN INNOCENT MAN.

...

UNITED STATES
PENTAGON
Parking in Rear

DID HE JUST KILL HIM?
I CAN'T BELIEVE--
I CAN. BOY'S HAD A LOT TO DEAL WITH RECENTLY. IT WOULD APPEAR THAT HE'S BEEN PUSHED OVER THE EDGE.
THAT IS DEFINITELY A MAJOR CONCERN.

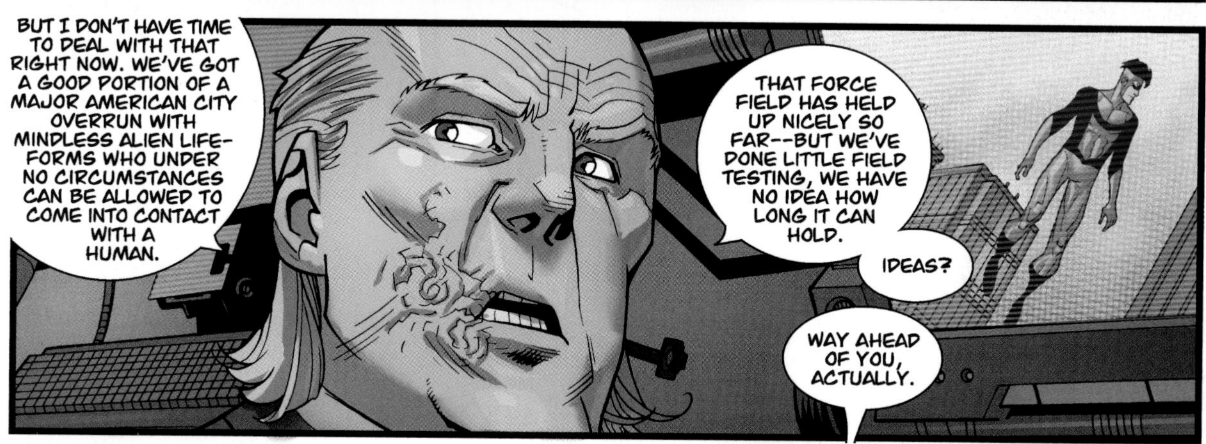
BUT I DON'T HAVE TIME TO DEAL WITH THAT RIGHT NOW. WE'VE GOT A GOOD PORTION OF A MAJOR AMERICAN CITY OVERRUN WITH MINDLESS ALIEN LIFE-FORMS WHO UNDER NO CIRCUMSTANCES CAN BE ALLOWED TO COME INTO CONTACT WITH A HUMAN.
THAT FORCE FIELD HAS HELD UP NICELY SO FAR--BUT WE'VE DONE LITTLE FIELD TESTING, WE HAVE NO IDEA HOW LONG IT CAN HOLD.
IDEAS?
WAY AHEAD OF YOU, ACTUALLY.

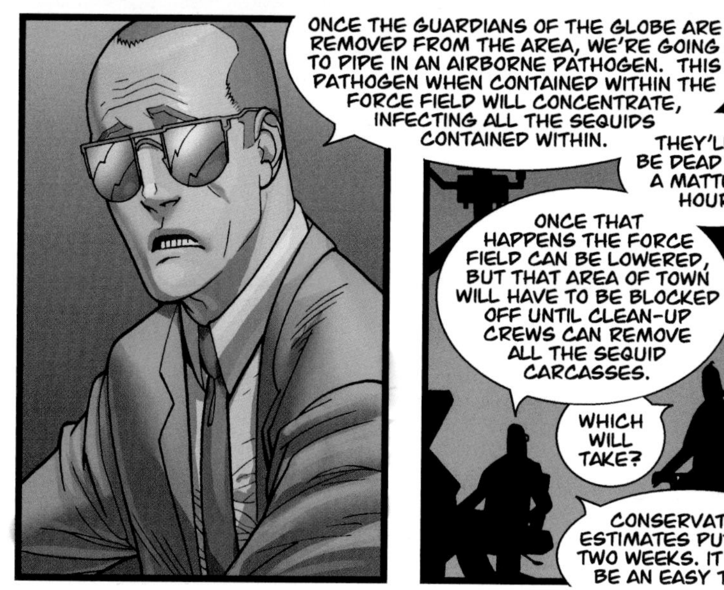

ONCE THE GUARDIANS OF THE GLOBE ARE REMOVED FROM THE AREA, WE'RE GOING TO PIPE IN AN AIRBORNE PATHOGEN. THIS PATHOGEN WHEN CONTAINED WITHIN THE FORCE FIELD WILL CONCENTRATE, INFECTING ALL THE SEQUIDS CONTAINED WITHIN.
THEY'LL ALL BE DEAD WITHIN A MATTER OF HOURS.
ONCE THAT HAPPENS THE FORCE FIELD CAN BE LOWERED, BUT THAT AREA OF TOWN WILL HAVE TO BE BLOCKED OFF UNTIL CLEAN-UP CREWS CAN REMOVE ALL THE SEQUID CARCASSES.
WHICH WILL TAKE?
CONSERVATIVE ESTIMATES PUT IT AT TWO WEEKS. IT WON'T BE AN EASY TASK.

INVINCIBLE IS TRYING TO LEAVE THE PROTECTED AREA, SIR.
LET HIM GO. I KNOW WHERE TO FIND HIM.

I TOLD YOU, APRIL. I ROCK.
WELL, THERE'S NO DISPUTING THAT NOW, OLIVER. THESE TEST SCORES ARE AMAZING. IT'S JUST... REMARKABLE HOW QUICKLY YOU'VE MASTERED THIS.
POSSIBLY LONGER... YOUR AGING IS SLOWING CONSIDERABLY.
WITH THE PURPLE HUE OF YOUR SKIN FADING AS YOU GET OLDER... IN A FEW MONTHS YOU COULD PROBABLY GO TO COLLEGE.

YOU THINK I'LL BE AN ADULT SOON? I'VE DONE SOME MATH, TRYING TO EXTRAPOLATE THE RATE AT WHICH I'LL HIT CERTAIN AGES, BUT WITH MY PROGRESSION SLOWING AT SUCH AN ABRUPT RATE...
MY DATA IS KIND OF USELESS.
IT'S HARD TO SAY. WHEN YOU FIRST ARRIVED, THERE WERE CHANGES DAILY... I COULD LITERALLY WATCH YOU GROWING OLDER.
THEN IT WAS WEEKS BEFORE I'D NOTICE A DIFFERENCE.
NOW MONTHS.
YOUR BROTHER'S POWERS DIDN'T EMERGE UNTIL LATE PUBERTY... MAYBE YOU'RE TRANSITIONING CLOSER TO VILTRUMITE AGE PROGRESSION.
AT BIRTH, YOU WERE AGING AT THE SAME RATE AS YOUR MOTHER'S PEOPLE...I DON'T BELIEVE YOU'LL EVER SLOW TO THE POINT OF VILTRUM AGING RATES... BUT YOU MAY SOON SEE YOURSELF AGING AS SLOW AS HUMANS, OR CLOSE TO IT.

YOU'VE GONE FROM AGING A MONTH EVERY THREE DAYS, TO... SOMETHING CONSIDERABLY LOWER.

YOU APPEAR TO BE FOURTEEN, MAYBE FIFTEEN NOW. IT COULD BE A YEAR OR EVEN TWO BEFORE YOU REACH ADULTHOOD.
CRUD.

WELL, I GUESS YOU ACTUALLY DIDN'T NEED MY HELP, THEN?
I'LL BE IN MY ROOM.

WHAT WAS THAT? YOU GUYS AREN'T FIGHTING AGAIN, ARE YOU?
NO. WHO KNOWS WHAT'S WRONG... IT'S ALWAYS SOMETHING WITH HIM.
DRAMA, DRAMA, DRAMA.

I'VE KNOWN INVINCIBLE FOR A LONG TIME. I FEAR HE'S GONE TOO FAR THIS TIME. HE *MURDERED* THAT MAN.
I WATCHED HIM.
I--I COULDN'T BELIEVE IT.
IT'S IN CECIL'S HANDS NOW. HE'LL KNOW WHAT TO DO. SHADY AS THAT MAN IS, HE KNOWS WHAT HE'S DOING.
KNOWS HOW TO PUSH OUR BUTTONS.

I HOPE THE TELEPORTATION WASN'T TOO JARRING FOR YOU. I WAS SO WORRIED ABOUT YOU.
IT--

TO BE CONTINUED...
YOU REEK OF SEWER. GO SHOWER-- **NOW.**
OKAY, MESSAGE RECEIVED LOUD AND CLEAR...

QUICK SHOWER...
ANYTHING FOR MY--

KOFF!
HUURK!

HLWAGG!!

NO! NO WAY!

YOU'RE DONE! THIS IS OVER!

OVER!
SQUIPP!

SCHLOGG
SCHLOGG
SCHLOGG

OKAY...
LOOKS LIKE IT FINALLY IS, AT LONG LAST... OVER.

SO... YOU TOOK CARE OF IT? IS EVERYTHING OKAY? THOSE ALIEN THINGS ARE DONE?
I KILLED HIM.

I DIDN'T HAVE A CHOICE--I HAD TO. THERE WERE LIVES AT STAKE--PEOPLE IN DANGER.
THERE WAS NO OTHER WAY.
I HAD TO KILL HIM.

IT'S OKAY.

IT'S GOING TO BE OKAY.

I DON'T THINK IT IS.
IT'S TOO MUCH--IT'S BEEN TOO MUCH. I JUST CAN'T HOLD BACK... I'M LETTING GO... I'M LOSING CONTROL.

I DON'T THINK IT WILL EVER BE OKAY AGAIN.
I CAN'T STOP--

LOOK, MARK...
I KNOW WE'VE HAD OUR DIFFERENCES IN THE PAST, BUT IN LIGHT OF YOUR RECENT ACTIONS... WE REALLY NEED TO TALK.

RETURNS
1

DEEP BELOW THE PENTAGON, THE SECRET HEADQUARTERS OF THE GLOBAL DEFENSE AGENCY, LED BY CECIL STEDMAN.
UNITED STATES PENTAGON
Parking in Rear

OKAY, CECIL. WE'RE HERE... AND I HAVE A GOOD IDEA WHAT YOU WANT TO TALK ABOUT. START YOUR LECTURE.
MY, WHAT A DIFFERENCE A FEW MONTHS MAKE. REMEMBER BEFORE? WE WERE WORKING TOGETHER SO WELL AND THEN YOU FOUND OUT THAT I WAS REFORMING CRIMINALS--TAKING "MURDERING SCUM" AND TURNING THEM TO OUR SIDE, USING THEM FOR GOOD CAUSES.
YOU JUST COULDN'T HANDLE IT--THE THOUGHT OF ME GIVING KILLERS A SECOND CHANCE.
NOW LOOK AT YOU. YOUR BROTHER KILLED THE MAULER TWINS AND YOU SIMPLY LOOK THE OTHER WAY. YOU MURDERED CONQUEST. THEN THERE'S THE CASE OF COMPLETELY INNOCENT FORMER ASTRONAUT RUS LIVINGSTON...
...ALSO MURDERED.

OLIVER ISN'T FROM THIS PLANET, HIS PEOPLE HAVE DIFFERENT VIEWS OF LIFE AND DEATH. WHAT HE DID TO THE MAULER TWINS... IT WASN'T HIS FAULT.
CONQUEST WAS TRYING TO TAKE OVER THE WORLD. I'D DO IT AGAIN WITHOUT HESITATION.
AND RUS... THE SEQUIDS WERE GOING TO DEFEAT US. I HAD NO CHOICE.

I'M GOING TO LEVEL WITH YOU, MARK.
THE TRUTH IS... I'M TERRIFIED OF YOU.

THE DISAGREEMENT THAT ENDED OUR RELATIONSHIP STEMMED FROM YOUR UNYIELDING SENSE OF RIGHT AND WRONG. ONCE YOU MAKE UP YOUR MIND, THAT'S *IT*--YOU'LL FIGHT YOUR OWN BEST FRIEND IF YOU THINK YOU'RE RIGHT.
YOU DISAGREED WITH YOUR OWN FATHER WHEN HE REVEALED HIS PLANS TO CONQUER THIS PLANET. YOU **IMMEDIATELY** CHOSE TO FIGHT HIM--PUTTING AT RISK A LIFELONG RELATIONSHIP.
I ADMIRE YOUR ABILITY TO STAND UP FOR WHAT YOU BELIEVE IN--NO MATTER THE COST. BUT NOW YOU'RE DISPLAYING AN ABILITY TO **CHANGE** WHAT YOU BELIEVE IN, TO ADJUST YOUR STANCE AT WILL.
WHAT HAPPENS WHEN YOU DECIDE **YOU'RE** THE ONLY ONE FIT TO RULE THIS PLANET?

YOU'RE MAKING A LEAP IN LOGIC THERE. REALIZING THAT CERTAIN ENEMIES POSE A THREAT SO GREAT THAT IT JUSTIFIES EXTREME ACTION IS A FAR CRY FROM SEEKING WORLD DOMINATION.
I MEAN... **REALLY?**

HOLD THAT THOUGHT. SINCLAIR, ARE YOU READY TO RECEIVE US?

GIVE ME ANOTHER THIRTY SECONDS AND WE'LL BE CLEAR.
WHY DOES HE WANT **ME** HERE FOR THIS?
I HAVE NO IDEA. HELP ME GET THESE CANISTERS CLOSED. HE WANTS THEM HIDDEN FOR SOME REASON.

YOUR TEMPER GETS THE BETTER OF YOU MORE TIMES THAN I WOULD LIKE. IT'S BRED INTO YOU--IN YOUR BLOOD.
YOU ARE A **VILTRUMITE,** THAT APPEARS TO COME WITH A GOOD DEAL OF BUILT-IN AGGRESSION.
WE'VE DISCUSSED THIS, I KNOW THIS IS A CONCERN YOU SHARE.

THAT'S NOT WHAT THIS IS ABOUT. ANGSTROM LEVY CAME BACK, HE KILLED THOUSANDS--DO YOU HEAR ME? **THOUSANDS** OF PEOPLE.
IF I HAD ACTUALLY KILLED HIM THE FIRST TIME, SOMETHING I INITIALLY REGRETTED, THOSE PEOPLE WOULD BE ALIVE.
HE NEEDED TO DIE--AND HE'S STILL OUT THERE SOMEWHERE. IF I EVER HAVE A CHANCE, I WILL KILL HIM.

IN THAT PARTICULAR CASE, I CAN'T ARGUE WITH YOU.
THE PROBLEM IS, YOU'RE NOT ALWAYS EQUIPPED TO MAKE SUCH A CLEAR JUDGMENT CALL.
YOU CAN'T **ALWAYS** BE RIGHT WHEN CHOOSING WHO LIVES OR DIES.

HERE'S ONE OF THE TIMES YOU WOULD HAVE BEEN WRONG.
HELLO, INVINCIBLE.
WHAT? WHY ARE YOU BRINGING ME HERE? WHAT PURPOSE WILL THIS SERVE, CECIL?

THIS IS A LEARNING EXPERIENCE. D.A. SINCLAIR, HE WAS DEVELOPING HIS REANIMEN TECHNOLOGY WHILE ATTENDING UPSTATE UNIVERSITY. HE EXPERIMENTED ON THE HOMELESS PEOPLE IN THE AREA--EVEN A FEW STUDENTS.
HORRIFIC THINGS WERE DONE TO THOSE MEN, WE ALL AGREE ON THAT, BUT NO ONE LISTENED TO SINCLAIR, NO ONE BELIEVED HIS THEORIES AT FIRST. HE HAD TO PUT THEM INTO PRACTICE TO PROVE HIMSELF.
NOW THAT THE TECHNOLOGY IS IN USE, THE REANIMEN TROOPS ARE SAVING COUNTLESS LIVES. BUILT ON CADAVERS NOW, THEY EACH TAKE THE PLACE OF TWENTY FOOT SOLDIERS.
THEY'RE MAKING THIS WORLD A BETTER PLACE.

I'M HAPPY TO REPORT, SINCLAIR HIMSELF IS NOW COMPLETELY REFORMED. HE'S DEVELOPING NEW TECHNOLOGY WITH THE FULL SUPPORT OF THE GLOBAL DEFENSE AGENCY. HE'S MAKING MY-- AND YOUR JOB EASIER.
AND HE'S ENGAGED TO BE MARRIED TO JUSTINE, ONE OF OUR OTHER SCIENTISTS. ALSO, I'VE JUST LEARNED THAT THEY'RE EXPECTING THEIR FIRST CHILD.
HI.

I'M NOT A BAD PERSON. DRIVEN--ALMOST DRIVEN MAD BY MY WORK, BUT ONLY BECAUSE I KNEW WHAT I WAS DOING WAS RIGHT--THAT THE ENDS JUSTIFIED THE MEANS.
I REGRET WHAT I HAD TO DO, BUT I FIND COMFORT IN THE KNOWLEDGE THAT IT HAD TO BE DONE--IN THE END, I WAS RIGHT.
THANK YOU FOR YOUR TIME, D.A.
YEAH... THANKS--AND CONGRATULATIONS.

SOUND FAMILIAR? THE ENDS JUSTIFY THE MEANS? DID YOU KNOW DARKWING SACRIFICED HIMSELF TO SAVE THE REST OF HIS TEAM? ARE YOU STARTING TO SEE THAT--
YEAH, I KNOW... I GET IT, OKAY? I WAS STARTING TO GET IT BEFORE YOU BROUGHT ME HERE. KILLING RUS, IT FELT WRONG. I HAD TO FORCE MYSELF TO DO IT, BECAUSE I THOUGHT IT WAS THE RIGHT THING TO DO.
BUT IT FEELS HORRIBLE. LIKE MAYBE I WAS JUST TAKING THE EASY WAY OUT--KILLING HIM SO I DIDN'T HAVE TO FIGURE SOMETHING ELSE OUT.

I GET WHAT YOU'RE SAYING, KILLING IS ALMOST NEVER JUSTIFIED. OTHERWISE, I'M JUST LIKE ALL THE OTHER VILTRUMITES. YOU KNOW I DON'T WANT THAT.
THESE LAST FEW MONTHS HAVE BEEN HARD ON ME--IT'S GOT ME ALL TURNED AROUND. I'LL BE THE FIRST TO ADMIT I LOST MY WAY.
THANK YOU FOR ADMITTING THAT. LOOK, I KNOW THIS ISN'T GOING TO REPAIR OUR RELATIONSHIP OVERNIGHT, BUT IF--

WE'VE GOT A SITUATION IN NEW YORK. LOOKS LIKE WE'RE GOING TO NEED TO SEND SOMEONE IN.

INVINCIBLE, COULD YOU--FOR OLD TIMES' SAKE?

...

VOOSH!

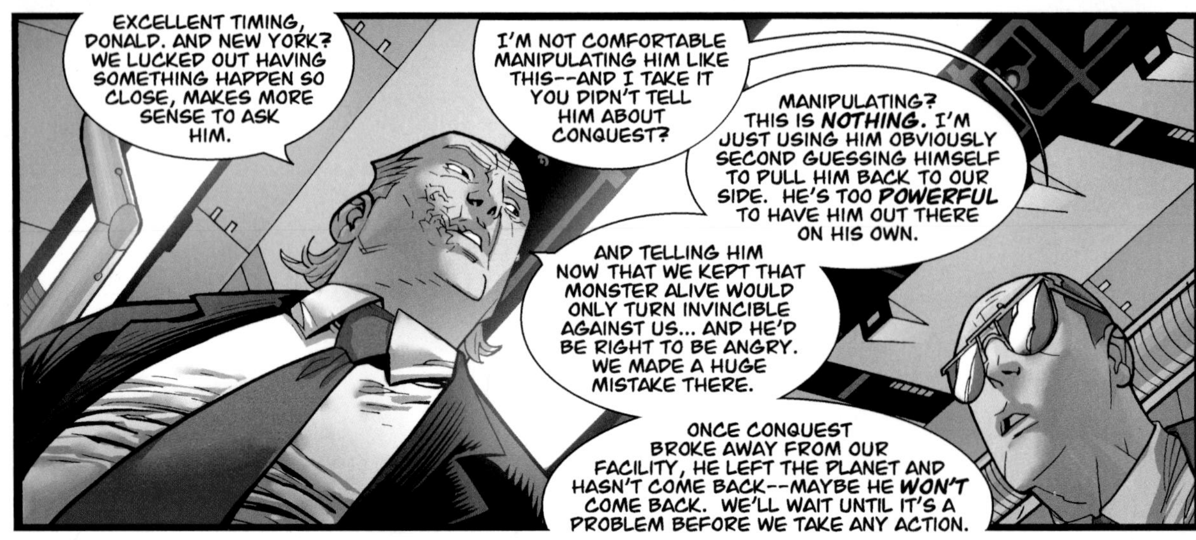
EXCELLENT TIMING, DONALD. AND NEW YORK? WE LUCKED OUT HAVING SOMETHING HAPPEN SO CLOSE, MAKES MORE SENSE TO ASK HIM.
I'M NOT COMFORTABLE MANIPULATING HIM LIKE THIS--AND I TAKE IT YOU DIDN'T TELL HIM ABOUT CONQUEST?
MANIPULATING? THIS IS NOTHING. I'M JUST USING HIM OBVIOUSLY SECOND GUESSING HIMSELF TO PULL HIM BACK TO OUR SIDE. HE'S TOO POWERFUL TO HAVE HIM OUT THERE ON HIS OWN.
AND TELLING HIM NOW THAT WE KEPT THAT MONSTER ALIVE WOULD ONLY TURN INVINCIBLE AGAINST US... AND HE'D BE RIGHT TO BE ANGRY. WE MADE A HUGE MISTAKE THERE.
ONCE CONQUEST BROKE AWAY FROM OUR FACILITY, HE LEFT THE PLANET AND HASN'T COME BACK--MAYBE HE WON'T COME BACK. WE'LL WAIT UNTIL IT'S A PROBLEM BEFORE WE TAKE ANY ACTION.

SIRE, IF YOU'LL JUST ALLOW ME A MOMENT TO EXPLAIN--

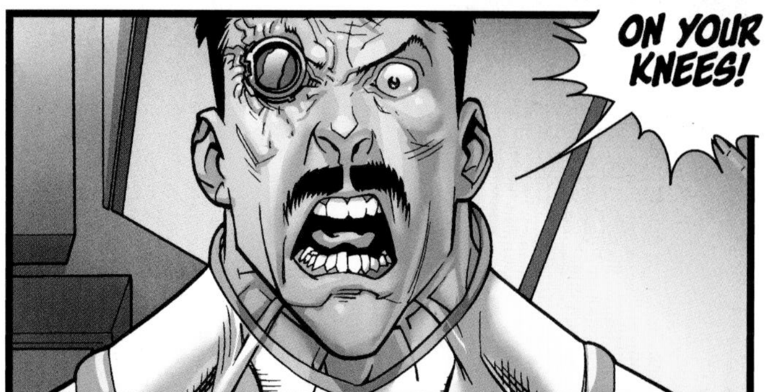
ON YOUR KNEES!

NONE MAY ADDRESS GRAND REGENT THRAGG WITHOUT SUBMISSION!
BOW YOUR HEAD!

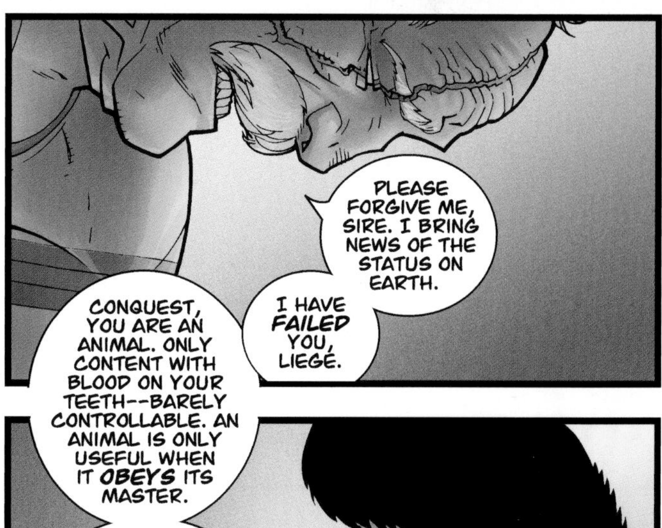
PLEASE FORGIVE ME, SIRE. I BRING NEWS OF THE STATUS ON EARTH.
I HAVE FAILED YOU, LIEGE.

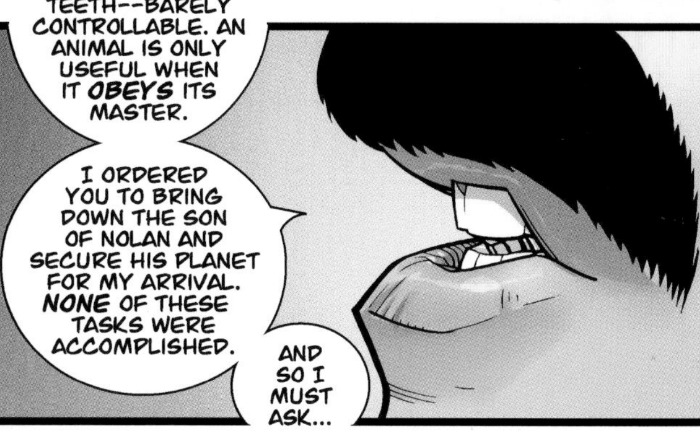
CONQUEST, YOU ARE AN ANIMAL. ONLY CONTENT WITH BLOOD ON YOUR TEETH--BARELY CONTROLLABLE. AN ANIMAL IS ONLY USEFUL WHEN IT OBEYS ITS MASTER.
I ORDERED YOU TO BRING DOWN THE SON OF NOLAN AND SECURE HIS PLANET FOR MY ARRIVAL. NONE OF THESE TASKS WERE ACCOMPLISHED.
AND SO I MUST ASK...

...OF WHAT FURTHER USE COULD YOU BE TO ME?
I UNDERESTIMATED THE BOY. I TOYED WITH HIM FAR TOO LONG, I GAVE HIM TIME TO GAIN AN ADVANTAGE.
I HAVE SERVED YOU WELL FOR MANY YEARS. PLEASE FORGIVE MY CARELESSNESS AND SPARE ME.

I BEG YOU...
WE HAVE LEARNED OF A TEAM SENT TO EARTH TO RETRIEVE NOLAN'S SON AND BRING HIM INTO DIRECT CONFLICT WITH US.
I DOUBT YOU HAVE TIME TO PREVENT THIS, BUT GO, CATCH THEM ON THEIR RETURN AND ENSURE NONE OF THEM ARE ABLE TO JOIN THE FIGHT.
LEAVE NONE ALIVE.
DO NOT FAIL ME AGAIN.

UH, CONGRATULATIONS THEN?

DON'T SAY THAT! I DON'T WANT CONGRATULATIONS! THIS ISN'T SOMETHING TO BE HAPPY ABOUT.
I DON'T WANT A BABY!

...
ARE YOU OKAY?

THAT'S THE FIRST TIME I'VE SAID IT OUT LOUD...
BABY.

WHAT IS THERE TO BE UPSET ABOUT? YOU AND MARK LOVE EACH OTHER.
YOU COULD MAKE THIS WORK.

I'M TOO YOUNG TO BE A MOTHER-- AND WE'RE NOT EVEN MARRIED. WE HAVEN'T EVEN TALKED ABOUT MARRIAGE.
I'M NOT READY TO HAVE A BABY NOW.

WELL, MAYBE THE TWO OF YOU SHOULDN'T HAVE BEEN--

HEH, UH... FORGET I SAID ANYTHING.

I WANT TO HAVE CHILDREN SOME DAY... WITH MARK. IT'S ALL EXACTLY WHAT I WANT...
...BUT RIGHT NOW?

MY POWERS ARE ACTING UP AND MARK IS... ALL OVER THE PLACE. HE'S FIGHTING SOME NEW THREAT EVERY DAY AND THERE'S BEEN SO MUCH GOING ON LATELY.
HOW COULD I EXPECT HIM TO BE THERE FOR ME AND A CHILD? WHAT KIND OF FATHER WOULD HE BE?
IT'S NOT LIKE HE CAN JUST STOP DOING WHAT HE'S DOING. I SEE HIM A LOT--BUT HE'S ALWAYS GETTING PULLED AWAY.
HE'D BE TOO UNRELIABLE.

WHY ARE YOU TELLING ME ABOUT THIS?
I MEAN, NOT THAT I MIND, IT'S JUST--WHY ME?

WITH ALL THAT'S GOING ON, I CAN'T TELL MARK. NOT YET... AND I HAD TO TELL SOMEONE. I DON'T HAVE ANY--
SIGH
HOW SAD IS IT THAT YOU'RE THE CLOSEST THING I HAVE TO A FRIEND?

UH...
...THANKS?

EATING AGAIN? MY WORD, OLIVER.
HUNGRY.
STARVING, ACTUALLY. ARE YOU GOING OUT SOON? WE'RE ALMOST OUT OF CEREAL.

I'M GOING OUT WITH PAUL LATER, BUT I DON'T PLAN ON HAVING THE TIME TO GET YOU MORE CEREAL.
WHY DON'T YOU FLY YOUR LITTLE BUTT OVER TO THE STORE AND GET SOME YOURSELF?

I'M LAZY.
HOW ARE THINGS BETWEEN YOU AND PAUL? YOU'VE BEEN SEEING HIM FOR A WHILE. IS THAT GETTING SERIOUS?

SERIOUS? I DON'T KNOW IF I'D GO THAT FAR. HE'S A GOOD COMPANION. WE GET ALONG. I ENJOY SPENDING TIME WITH HIM.
DEEP DOWN, I DON'T KNOW HOW I FEEL. I HAVEN'T REALLY THOUGHT IT OUT VERY--

I'M NOT TALKING TO YOU ABOUT THIS! DON'T YOU HAVE HOMEWORK OR SOMETHING TO BE DOING?
DON'T YOU THINK MARK NEEDS HELP SOMEWHERE?

OH... UH... I SHOULDN'T HAVE SAID ANYTHING...

I'M SORRY... COME HERE, YOU.

OLIVER, KID...
I SURE AM GLAD YOU CAME ALONG.

NOW GET OUT OF THE HOUSE. I'M SURE YOUR BROTHER COULD USE HELP OF SOME KIND.

HELP DOING WHAT? HE'S PROBABLY OFF SOMEWHERE SPENDING TIME WITH ATOM EVE.
NEAR AS I CAN TELL THAT'S ALL HE DOES THESE DAYS.

I CAN'T **BELIEVE** IT! I CAN'T BELIEVE THIS IS HAPPENING **AGAIN!**
RELAX!
NOBODY ASKED YOU TO GET INVOLVED!
KROOM!
3M TA3

OKAY, BOYS-- LET'S EARN THAT PAY!
FWOOSH!

THAT SHOULD KEEP HIM BUSY.
GOOD-- YOU'LL HAVE TIME TO GIVE ME ANSWERS!

THAT THING ATTACKED BOTH OF US AT STRONGHOLD PRISON A WHILE BACK. WHAT IS IT?! WHY IS IT AFTER YOU?
THIS IS SIMPLY A DISPUTE OVER MY TERRITORY. YOU DON'T WANT TO GET INVOLVED. THE LESS YOU KNOW, THE BETTER. TRUST ME.

THAT'S JUST NOT GOING TO CUT IT--
--TALK!
KROK!

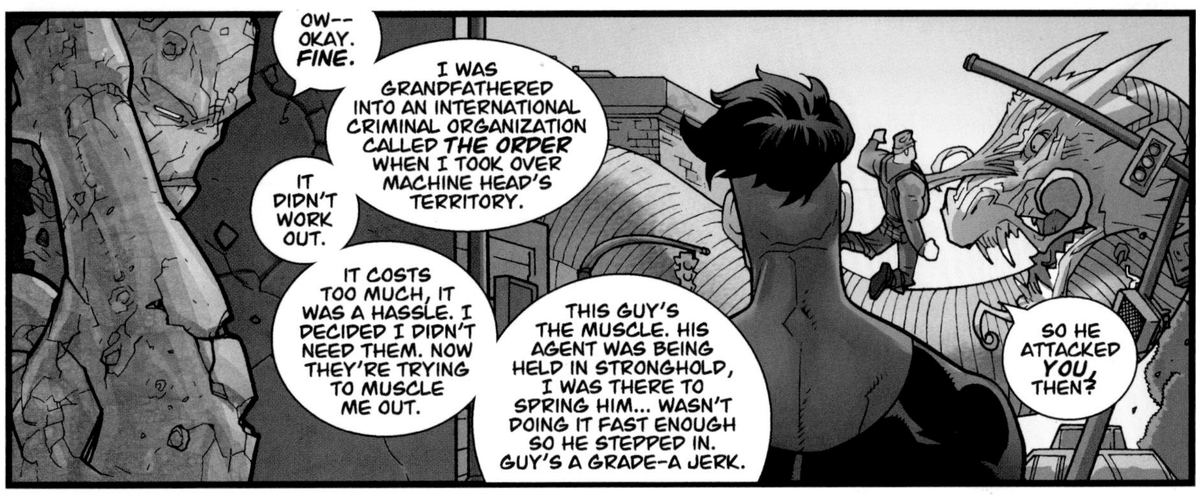
OW-- OKAY. FINE.
I WAS GRANDFATHERED INTO AN INTERNATIONAL CRIMINAL ORGANIZATION CALLED THE ORDER WHEN I TOOK OVER MACHINE HEAD'S TERRITORY.
IT DIDN'T WORK OUT.
IT COSTS TOO MUCH, IT WAS A HASSLE. I DECIDED I DIDN'T NEED THEM. NOW THEY'RE TRYING TO MUSCLE ME OUT.
THIS GUY'S THE MUSCLE. HIS AGENT WAS BEING HELD IN STRONGHOLD, I WAS THERE TO SPRING HIM... WASN'T DOING IT FAST ENOUGH SO HE STEPPED IN. GUY'S A GRADE-A JERK.
SO HE ATTACKED YOU, THEN?

DOES HE HAVE ANY WEAKNESSES YOU KNOW OF?
I FOUND HIM. COME ON.
SORRY, THIS IS MY STOP.
WHAT THE-- ARE YOU KIDDING ME?!
WHAT A BUNCH OF CRAP.
WRAKOOM!

WHERE ARE YOU GOING?! I THOUGHT YOU WERE GOING TO HELP?!
FEH.
VILLAINS.

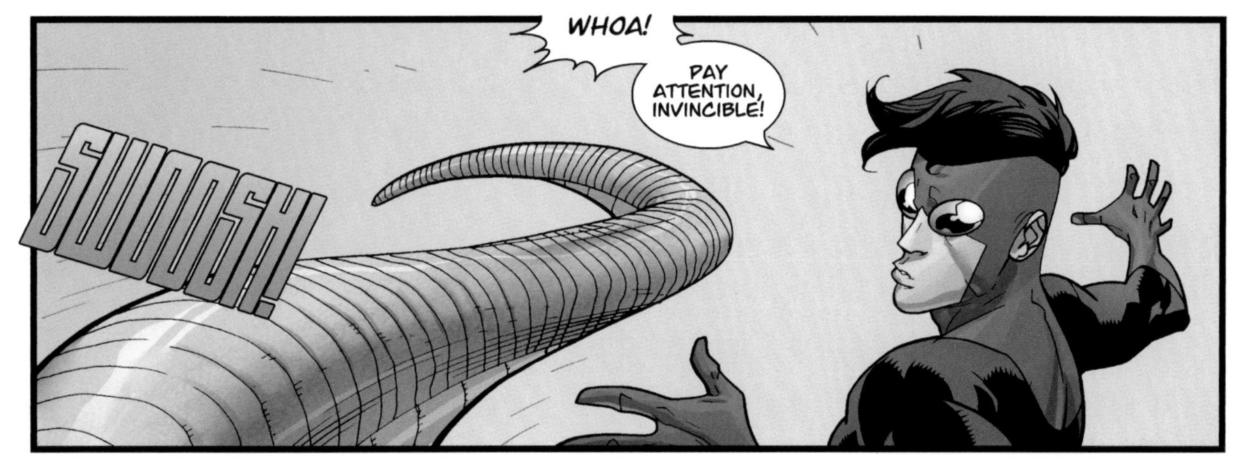
WHOA!
PAY ATTENTION, INVINCIBLE!
SWOOSH!

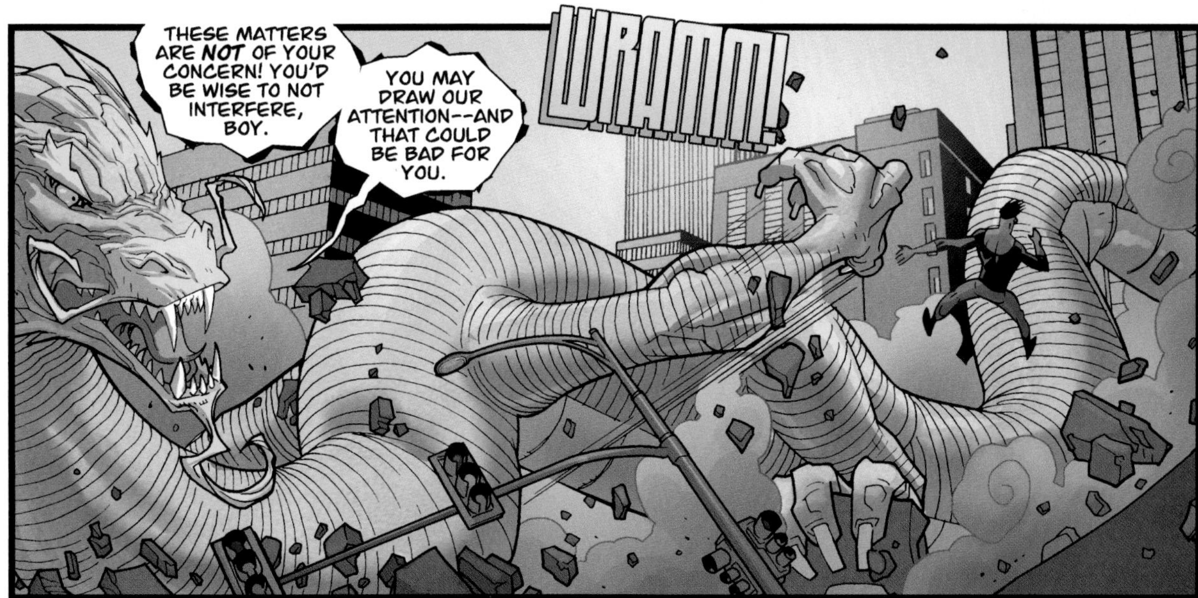
THESE MATTERS ARE NOT OF YOUR CONCERN! YOU'D BE WISE TO NOT INTERFERE, BOY.
YOU MAY DRAW OUR ATTENTION--AND THAT COULD BE BAD FOR YOU.
WRAMM!

SORRY, BUT I DON'T SCARE THAT EASY.
IF ANYTHING THAT'S JUST GOING TO MAKE ME WANT--

HUH?!

WHERE'D IT GO?

WROKK!!
WRAMM!
NOT SO TOUGH NOW, ARE YOU?

WHUD!
WHAT IS GOING ON HERE?!

LUCKY YOU. HE FOUND US.
BYE BYE.

GOOD TIMING.

WHAT IS THIS?! NOW YOU'VE GOT YOUR PEOPLE KILLING OLD MEN?!
THAT'S HIM! THE ONE WHO ATTACKED ME. THE DRAGON IS SOME KIND OF SOUL PROJECTION-- THE BIG GUY PROTECTS HIS BODY WHILE HE'S OUT.
HE'S NOT SOME SWEET OLD MAN!

YOU THINK I'M GOING TO LET YOU KILL HIM BECAUSE I LET YOU TRICK ME INTO HELPING YOU TAKE DOWN MACHINE HEAD?!
I THOUGHT YOU WERE A GOOD GUY! THOUGHT YOU WOULD MAKE THINGS BETTER-- CLEAN UP YOUR ACT!
LOOK AT WHAT YOU'VE DONE! LOOK AT ALL THE DAMAGE!
CAN'T--
BREATHE--

YOU--!
INVINCIBLE, STOP!
WE'LL TAKE IT FROM HERE...

BUT HE--IF WE--
WE CAN'T--

ART ROSENBAUM'S TAILOR SHOP.
TAILOR shoppe

OKAY, THEN... JUST LET YOURSELF IN.
I DON'T MIND.

MARK?
EVERYTHING **OKAY?**

I'M SORRY TO SHOW UP LIKE THIS, ART. IT'S JUST BEEN SO LONG SINCE WE'VE TALKED, AND YOU'VE ALWAYS BEEN SOMEONE WILLING TO LISTEN TO ME, AND...
NO. **NOT AT ALL.**
...I'VE BEEN THROUGH-- SEEN SO MUCH RECENTLY. I WORRY IT'S **CHANGED** ME. MADE ME MORE LIKE **HIM.**
YOU KNOW HOW I FEEL ABOUT YOUR FATHER, MARK. HE'S A GOOD MAN. THE BAD STUFF IS THE ACT, HIM TRYING TO BE SOMETHING HE FEELS LIKE HE SHOULD BE, BUT ISN'T.
YOU BEING LIKE HIM **ISN'T** A BAD THING.

I'M NOT TALKING ABOUT THE **GOOD** PARTS. SOMETIMES I THINK, AND I KNOW THIS SOUNDS CRAZY...
IT'S ALMOST LIKE THIS COSTUME IS A **CURSE.**

I'VE SEEN THE MAJOR CITIES OF THE WORLD LEVELED, I SPENT **MONTHS** DIGGING OUT BODIES... PARTS OF BODIES.
I'VE SEEN MORE DEATH THAN I CAN BEAR.

CONQUEST CAME, MADE THINGS EVEN WORSE. I SAW THE DEATH OF MY GIRLFRIEND... EVEN THOUGH SHE DIDN'T ACTUALLY DIE...
I STILL HAD TO **SEE** THAT... FEEL WHAT IT WOULD HAVE BEEN LIKE.

IT'S LIKE--NOW THAT I KNOW WHAT'S REALLY AT STAKE, I'M WILLING TO GO TO EXTREMES.
I **KILLED** A MAN.

...

I DID IT TO PREVENT MORE DEATHS... BUT IT STILL FELT SO WRONG.
AND I...

I ALMOST DID IT AGAIN, TODAY.

NOW THAT I'VE OPENED THAT DOOR, I DON'T KNOW IF I CAN CLOSE IT. MY TEMPER GETS THE BEST OF ME...
...IT'S HARD TO HOLD BACK.

I CAN'T EVEN **LOOK** AT MYSELF ANYMORE. I CAN'T STAND THE SIGHT OF MYSELF.
I FEEL LIKE I CAN'T WEAR THIS COSTUME ANY MORE. LIKE THIS WHOLE THING WAS A MISTAKE, BEING INVINCIBLE...
NONSENSE. THE FACT THAT YOU'RE SITTING HERE, QUESTIONING YOUR ACTIONS, **PROVES** THAT YOU'RE A GOOD MAN.
YOU'VE STRAYED, MAYBE CROSSED A LINE OR TWO, BUT YOU RECOGNIZE THAT. SO MANY OTHERS **DON'T**. I'VE SEEN IT TOO MANY TIMES.

WHAT YOU DO COMES WITH AN ENORMOUS AMOUNT OF PRESSURE. IT **WEARS** ON YOU.
YOU'RE HANDLING IT BETTER THAN MOST--AND YOU'VE SEEN THE WORST THIS JOB HAS TO OFFER.

IF YOU FEEL LIKE YOU CAN'T WEAR **THAT** COSTUME ANYMORE... THEN DON'T WEAR THAT COSTUME ANYMORE.
I CAN'T GO BACK IN TIME, I CAN'T **UNDO** WHAT YOU'VE DONE.

BUT IF YOU'RE READY TO GO BACK TO THE MAN YOU **WERE**, IF THAT'S REALLY WHO YOU WANT TO BE... I CAN MAKE SURE YOU **LOOK** THE PART.

IT WAS A JUSTIFIED LECTURE. HE'S WORRIED ABOUT MY RECENT ACTIONS, WHAT IT COULD MEAN FOR ME.

WHAT WE WERE TALKING ABOUT WHEN HE SHOWED UP.

AND?

I THINK THAT'S FOR THE BEST.
LOOK AT YOU... IT'S ALMOST LIKE YOU ARE BACK TO YOUR OLD SELF AGAIN.
HAH.
YEAH.

IT SOUNDS STUPID, BUT IT DOES FEEL DIFFERENT.
IT FEELS GOOD.

AND I SEE ART JUST CAN'T HELP BUT KEEP MAKING LITTLE TWEAKS.
I LIKE THE CHANGES.

YEAH, ART ISN'T BIG ON LOOKING BACK. I'M STILL ON THE FENCE-- BUT I DON'T MIND IT.

YOU WANT TO GET SOME DINNER? I COULD REALLY USE A NICE QUIET EVENING.

YEAH. THAT'D BE NICE.

I REALLY DO NEED TO TALK TO YOU ABOUT--
UM...

WHAT IS IT?
EVE?

OH.

IT IS TIME, SON. YOU ARE NEEDED.
THE TIME FOR WAR IS UPON US.

LATER.
Crocket

WE DIDN'T HAVE TO DO THIS. I KNOW YOUR MIND IS ELSEWHERE. I MEAN, CRAP, MARK. YOUR DAD JUST CAME BACK TO EARTH.
NO, I WANTED TO DO THIS. WHEN'S THE LAST TIME WE WENT ON AN ACTUAL DATE?

AREN'T THERE OTHER THINGS YOU SHOULD BE DOING BEFORE YOU LEAVE?
NOLAN AND ALLEN WENT OFF TO FIND SOMEONE CALLED TECH JACKET. THEY'RE GOING TO BE OUT FOR A WHILE. I'VE GOT TIME.
AND THIS IS THE ENTIRETY OF WHAT I NEED TO DO BEFORE I LEAVE. I WANT TO SPEND EVERY WAKING MOMENT WITH YOU. I'M GOING TO MISS YOU.
I KNOW. I WISH I COULD COME WITH YOU, BUT WITH MY POWERS ACTING UP, AND...

WHAT? YOU KEEP ACTING LIKE YOU WANT TO SAY SOMETHING--AND THEN DON'T. WHAT IS IT?

NOTHING. IT'S...
NOTHING.
I'M JUST WORRIED ABOUT YOU.

WAS IT WEIRD SEEING YOUR FATHER AGAIN?

"YOU MEAN BECAUSE HE TRIED TO KILL ME ONCE?
"OR IS IT THE FACT THAT BEFORE DOING SO, HE REVEALED TO ME AFTER BEING A COMPLETELY NORMAL, ALBEIT SUPERHERO DAD ALL MY LIFE THAT HE WAS ACTUALLY A MEMBER OF AN ALIEN RACE OUT TO CONQUER THE UNIVERSE AND HE WANTED MY HELP TAKING OVER EARTH?
"OR IS IT THAT HE TOLD ME DURING THE FIGHT THAT HE WAS COMPLETELY PREPARED TO KILL ME, WAS INDIFFERENT ABOUT THAT, AND CONSIDERED MY MOTHER TO BE LITTLE MORE THAN A PET?
"OR, WELL... ALL OF THE ABOVE?"

PRETTY MUCH, YEAH.
I MEAN, THAT'S ALL WEIRD, RIGHT?
IS WEIRD THE RIGHT WORD?

WEIRD WORKS... IT WAS EXTREMELY DIFFICULT, TOO. UPSETTING. SCARRING.
THIS ISN'T THE FIRST TIME I'VE SEEN MY FATHER SINCE OUR FIGHT OVER THIS PLANET. THAT WAS ON THE ALIEN PLANET THRAXA WHERE HE CONCEIVED OLIVER WITH ANDRESSA.
SOUNDS WEIRD JUST LAYING IT ALL OUT LIKE THAT.
DON'T KNOW WHERE MY MIND WAS. I KNEW ALL ABOUT THAT.
WE WEREN'T DATING AT THE TIME. YOU TOLD ME ALL ABOUT IT WHEN YOU CAME TO VISIT WITH... AMBER.
YOU AND YOUR FATHER FOUGHT OTHER VILTRUMITES WHILE YOU WERE THERE, DIDN'T YOU?

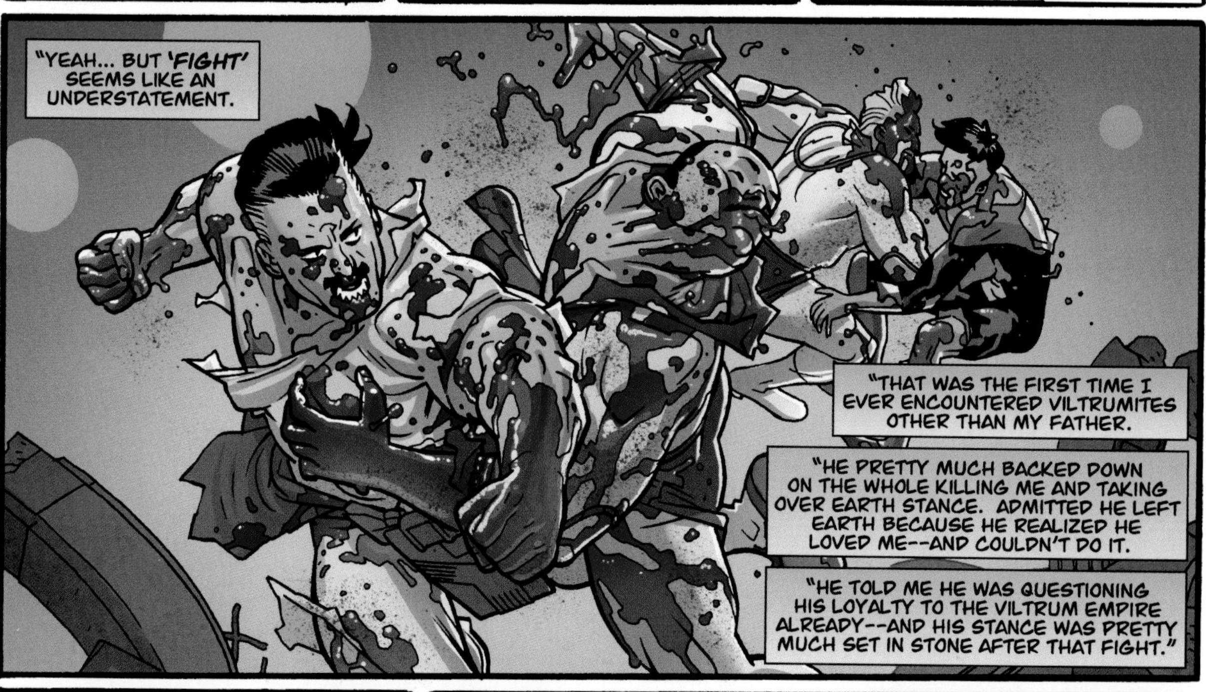
"YEAH... BUT 'FIGHT' SEEMS LIKE AN UNDERSTATEMENT.
"THAT WAS THE FIRST TIME I EVER ENCOUNTERED VILTRUMITES OTHER THAN MY FATHER.
"HE PRETTY MUCH BACKED DOWN ON THE WHOLE KILLING ME AND TAKING OVER EARTH STANCE. ADMITTED HE LEFT EARTH BECAUSE HE REALIZED HE LOVED ME--AND COULDN'T DO IT.
"HE TOLD ME HE WAS QUESTIONING HIS LOYALTY TO THE VILTRUM EMPIRE ALREADY--AND HIS STANCE WAS PRETTY MUCH SET IN STONE AFTER THAT FIGHT."

REFRESH YOUR BEVERAGE, SIR?
UH... OKAY.

NOT THE BEST ATMOSPHERE FOR THIS CONVERSATION...
MAYBE WE SHOULD GO?

OKAY, SO NOW THAT WE'RE OUT OF THERE AND CAN SPEAK FREELY--YOU SHOULD KNOW THAT I KNOW NEXT TO NOTHING ABOUT VILTRUMITES. IT'S THIS LOOMING THREAT THAT HANGS OVER YOUR HEAD EVERY SECOND OF EVERY DAY AND YOU NEXT TO NEVER TALK ABOUT IT.
OH, WHATEVER. YOU HAVE TO KNOW SOMETHING ABOUT THEM.
I'M UP TO SPEED ON EVERYTHING BETWEEN YOU AND YOUR DAD AND EVERYTHING THAT HAPPENED WITH... CONQUEST.
IT'S ALL THE BETWEEN STUFF THAT I'M IN THE DARK ABOUT.
CAN YOU JUST TELL ME EVERYTHING--EVEN IF YOU THINK I ALREADY KNOW SOME OF IT?
EVERYTHING I KNOW ABOUT VILTRUMITES?
THIS SHOULD TAKE TWO MINUTES.
I'VE HAD BRIEF ENCOUNTERS HERE AND THERE, BUT I REALLY KNOW NEXT TO NOTHING ABOUT THE VILTRUM EMPIRE.
I DON'T EVEN KNOW WHO THEIR LEADER IS.
WELL, YOU KNOW MORE THAN I DO, WHICH ISN'T COOL.
I PROMISE I WORRY ABOUT THIS STUFF MUCH MORE THAN YOU DO.
I TRY NOT TO THINK ABOUT IT. IT'S TOO OVERWHELMING.
SO MUCH HAS HAPPENED. I THOUGHT MY DAD WAS DEAD. HE WAS SCHEDULED FOR EXECUTION.
I KNOW, IF IT'S TOO HARD TO TALK ABOUT, I UNDERSTAND.
NO, YOU'RE RIGHT. I DON'T WANT YOU FEELING LEFT IN THE DARK. THIS IS TOO BIG.

"A GOOD EXAMPLE OF ME NOT KNOWING ANYTHING ABOUT VILTRUMITES... THERE WAS THIS GUY ON THRAXA, I HEARD SOMEONE CALL HIM GENERAL KREGG. HE TOLD ME I'D BEEN MADE THE VILTRUMITE AGENT STATIONED ON EARTH, THAT IT WAS MY RESPONSIBILITY TO PREPARE IT FOR VILTRUMITE INVASION.
"THIS WAS SHORTLY AFTER THEY TOOK MY FATHER AWAY TO BE EXECUTED."
DIDN'T KNOW WHO HE WAS, HE COULD BE THEIR LEADER FOR ALL I KNOW. HE NEVER REALLY SAID ANYTHING ELSE TO ME--AND HAVING JUST BEEN TOLD MY FATHER WAS GOING TO BE EXECUTED, I WAS A LITTLE SHAKEN.
AND I WAS BADLY BEATEN UP... SO MUCH SO THAT I JUST LAID THERE, HALF CONSCIOUS FOR THE REST OF THE NIGHT.
THEY JUST TOOK HIM AND LEFT. IT WAS SO WEIRD.
"YOU'RE IN CHARGE OF EARTH, KID. NOW IF YOU'LL EXCUSE US, WE'RE GOING TO GO KILL YOUR DAD."
WHY WOULD THEY PUT ME IN CHARGE OF EARTH? THAT MAKES NO SENSE! THAT'S LIKE APPOINTING YOU TO BE IN CHARGE OF MY LAUNDRY OR SOMETHING-- YOU NEVER SIGNED UP FOR THAT. IT'S SOMETHING I KNOW YOU DON'T WANT TO DO.
BUT YOUR DAD'S OKAY... AND HE'S TOTALLY GONE "GOOD GUY" NOW. HE'S FIGHTING FOR THIS COALITION OF PLANETS THING?
THAT'S COOL.
I'M CURIOUS, THOUGH? HOW DID YOUR DAD ESCAPE?
HIS SPINE WAS BROKEN ON THRAXA. THERE'S SOME CREEPY VILTRUMITE LAW WHERE YOU CAN'T BE EXECUTED UNLESS YOU'RE COMPLETELY WHOLE... IN PERFECT CONDITION.
THESE ARE MY PEOPLE.
IN THE TIME IT TOOK HIM TO HEAL, ALLEN FOUND HIS WAY TO HIM AND HELPED HIM ESCAPE.
THEY'RE LIKE BEST FRIENDS NOW.

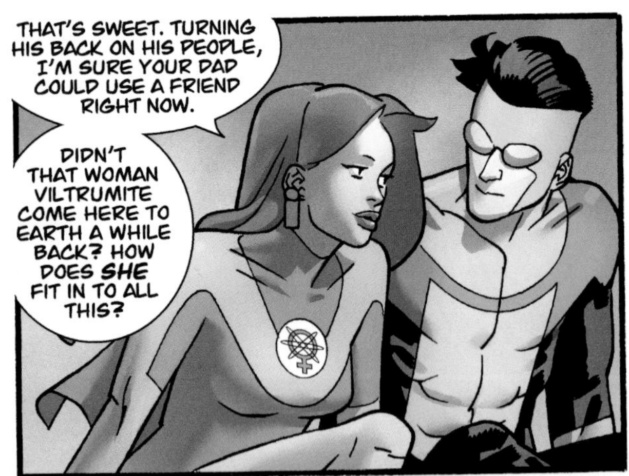
THAT'S SWEET. TURNING HIS BACK ON HIS PEOPLE, I'M SURE YOUR DAD COULD USE A FRIEND RIGHT NOW.
DIDN'T THAT WOMAN VILTRUMITE COME HERE TO EARTH A WHILE BACK? HOW DOES SHE FIT IN TO ALL THIS?

ANISSA. YEAH.
THAT WAS WEIRD.
SHE WAS SENT HERE TO CHECK ON MY PROGRESS, OF WHICH, THERE WAS NONE.

"THAT DIDN'T MAKE HER HAPPY.
"WE FOUGHT A LITTLE BIT. THINKING BACK, SHE WAS CLEARLY GOING EASY ON ME. JUST HERE TO WARN ME, REALLY."

SHE HAD SOME NONSENSE STORY ABOUT VILTRUMITES MAKING EARTH A BETTER PLACE. SHARING THEIR TECHNOLOGY AND HELPING OUR CIVILIZATION GROW.
NO MORE DISEASE, NO MORE WAR, BLAH BLAH BLAH.
IT WAS ALL BULL.

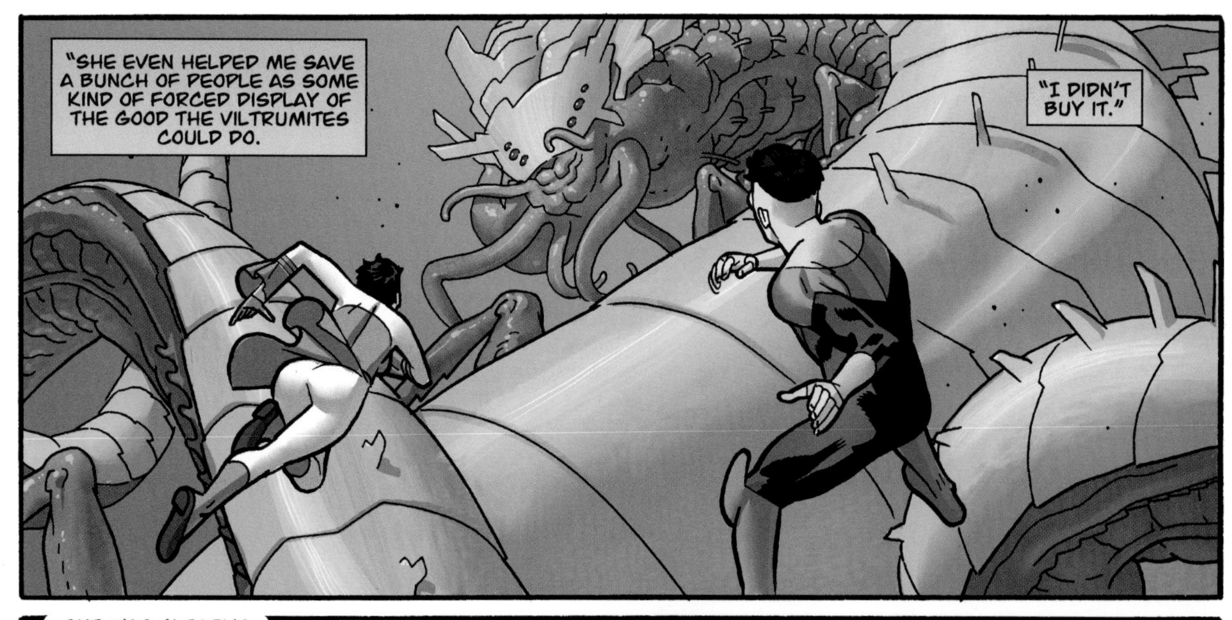
"SHE EVEN HELPED ME SAVE A BUNCH OF PEOPLE AS SOME KIND OF FORCED DISPLAY OF THE GOOD THE VILTRUMITES COULD DO.
"I DIDN'T BUY IT."

SHE WAS CLEARLY SOME KIND OF LAST DITCH EFFORT TO WIN ME OVER. IT ALL SEEMED LIKE A TRICK.
IN HINDSIGHT, SHE WAS CLEARLY THE HONEY, SOON TO BE FOLLOWED BY THE VINEGAR.
I KNEW A BIT ABOUT THE VILTRUMITES ALREADY. WORLD CONQUERORS, ALIEN ENSLAVERS, GENERALLY BAD PEOPLE... I WASN'T BUYING HER KINDER, GENTLER VILTRUMITES ACT.

SHE WARNED ME. TOLD ME I BETTER START MY WORK, PREPARING EARTH FOR TAKEOVER--THAT IT WOULD BE BETTER FOR EVERYONE IF I DID IT PEACEFULLY.
BECAUSE THEY WOULD NOT.
AND SHE SAID THE NEXT AGENT THEY'D SEND WOULDN'T BE AS REASONABLE AS SHE WAS.
CONQUEST.

YEAH.. CONQUEST.
NO NEED TO GO THERE, MARK. REALLY.
THE LESS SAID ABOUT HIM THE BETTER.

MY DAD TELLS ME THEIR NUMBERS ARE ASTONISHINGLY LOW. SOME VIRUS HAS DWINDLED THEIR POPULATION DOWN TO NEXT TO NOTHING.
SO THE BATTLE, ACCORDING TO THE COALITION OF PLANETS, IS VERY WINNABLE.
MY DAD HAS BEEN WORKING WITH ALLEN THE ALIEN, GATHERING THE THINGS LISTED IN HIS BOOKS THAT CAN BE USED AGAINST THE VILTRUM EMPIRE.
HE SAYS NOW IS THE TIME TO STRIKE.

WHAT DO YOU THINK?
THEY'VE SINGLED OUT EARTH BECAUSE OF OUR COMPATIBLE DNA... THAT'S THE RESOURCE THEY WANT FROM US. WE'RE A WAY FOR THEM TO RESTORE THEIR POPULATION.
I WAS ALWAYS GOING TO BE IN THIS BATTLE. I'M JUST GLAD MY FATHER IS ON MY SIDE.

DO YOU TRUST HIM?

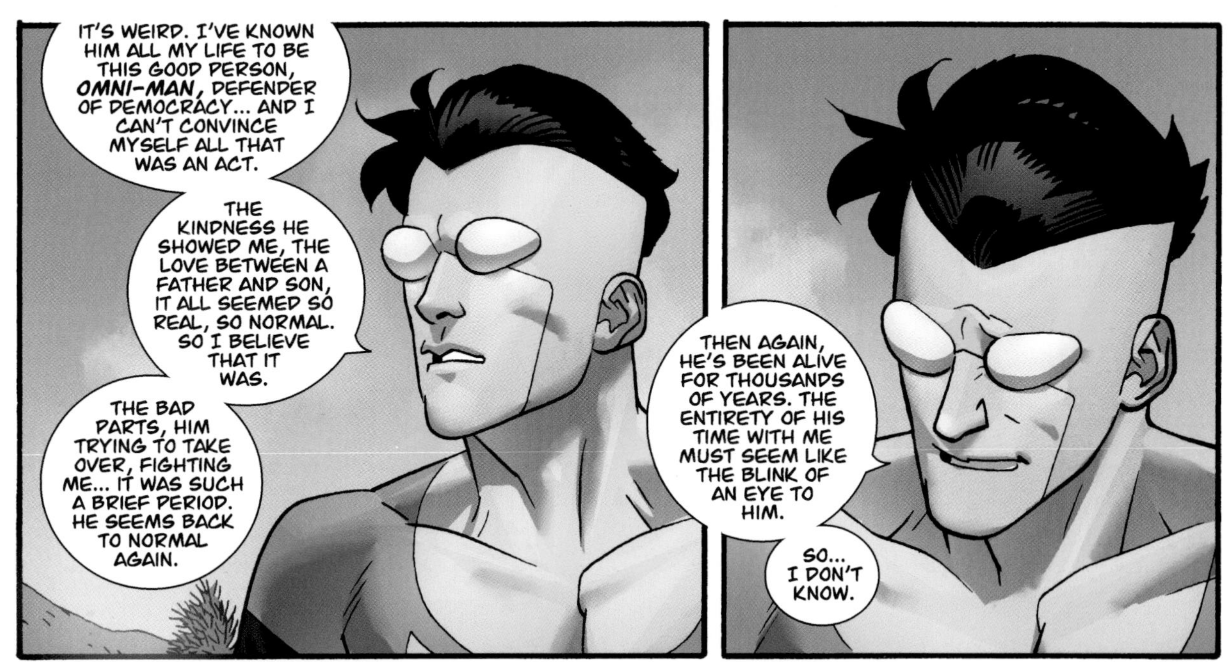
IT'S WEIRD. I'VE KNOWN HIM ALL MY LIFE TO BE THIS GOOD PERSON, OMNI-MAN, DEFENDER OF DEMOCRACY... AND I CAN'T CONVINCE MYSELF ALL THAT WAS AN ACT.
THE KINDNESS HE SHOWED ME, THE LOVE BETWEEN A FATHER AND SON, IT ALL SEEMED SO REAL, SO NORMAL. SO I BELIEVE THAT IT WAS.
THE BAD PARTS, HIM TRYING TO TAKE OVER, FIGHTING ME... IT WAS SUCH A BRIEF PERIOD. HE SEEMS BACK TO NORMAL AGAIN.
THEN AGAIN, HE'S BEEN ALIVE FOR THOUSANDS OF YEARS. THE ENTIRETY OF HIS TIME WITH ME MUST SEEM LIKE THE BLINK OF AN EYE TO HIM.
SO... I DON'T KNOW.

WHAT CHOICE DO I HAVE? ALLEN TRUSTS HIM. THE COALITION TRUSTS HIM.
HE'S DONE NOTHING BUT REVEAL THE WEAKNESSES OF HIS PEOPLE SINCE HE BEGAN WORKING WITH THEM. I DON'T SEE HOW THAT COULD BE PART OF A LARGER PLAN...
BUT WHAT DO I KNOW?

WE'RE SUPPOSED TO LEAVE TOMORROW. I DON'T KNOW HOW LONG I'LL BE GONE AND I WON'T HAVE ANY CONTACT WITH EARTH.
BUT THIS IS SOMETHING I HAVE TO DO-- FOR THE SAKE OF THE WHOLE PLANET.

I KNOW. I UNDERSTAND.
I--
I'LL HOLD DOWN THE FORT WHILE YOU'RE GONE.

ARE YOU SCARED?
YES.

BUT NOT FOR WHAT MIGHT HAPPEN TO ME, OR EVEN THE OUTCOME OF THE WAR... NOT MOSTLY, AT LEAST.
AFTER EVERYTHING THAT'S HAPPENED, EVERYTHING I'VE DONE... HOW I'VE CHANGED...
VILTRUMITE BLOOD COURSES THROUGH THESE VEINS. I'M WORRIED ABOUT WHAT THIS WAR WILL BRING OUT OF ME...

...WHAT IT COULD MAKE ME BECOME.

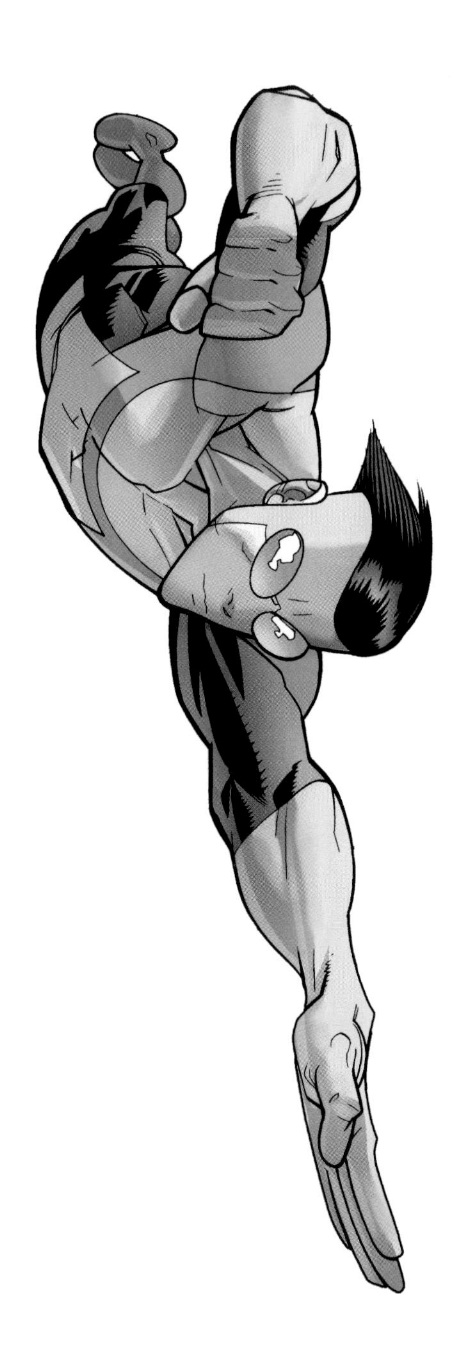

Kirkman: So, y'know... these sketchbook sections usually start with a process piece of the cover, a sketch or rough design, something to kick things off with a bang. So why, you ask are we looking at an AWESOME con-sketch of Allen that Ryan drew for a fan? Well... maybe Ryan can answer that for us. Ryan?

Ottley: I am sorry. I have failed each and every one of you readers that care about the sketchbook section of Invincible. Normally I scan my layouts and sketches to show the progress of the cover, unfortunately for this Hard Cover you are holding I did not. I think all I did was take a photo with my phone and texted it to Robert and said "Hey dood, iz this drawing good enuff fer you?!?LOLz!!1". So that means it was never scanned and I fear I threw it out. I also didn't get a scan of the pencils since I went straight to inks without stopping to scan. I have failed you all. Here is a con sketch instead. I'll make sure to scan everything from now on, no phone photos! I'm turning over a new leaf, starting anew, I feel rejuvenated, indefatigable. Thank you!

Kirkman: Likely story. I'll let it slide this time, Mr. Ottley... but only this once! Over on the right there, you'll see the inks for said cover. Ain't they sweet?!

SKETCHBOOK

ROBERT KIRKMAN: The volume 12 cover is my new favorite TPB cover. I just love it. Great stuff by Ryan as always. On this page you'll find his sketch for the cover, which was awesome, but I'm a stickler for consistency and thought it deviated from your paneled cover theme a bit too much. So the panel scheme was worked in, as you can see on the following page.

RYAN OTTLEY: Cough. I just walked home in the rain. All I want is to curl up in front of the TV, but this is fine too. I guess. Sigh. No I like the panels added in too. It was a good idea. I can't wait to draw those alternate Invincible guys again, bring back Angstrom and tha boys!

KIRKMAN: On the following two pages you'll see various stages of the cover to Invincible 50, which was four pages wide. That's pretty cool. As I recall it was extremely easy to draw and took no time at all--right Ryan?

OTTLEY: You are mean to me. Your big ideas that take a split second to conjure up always take me weeks to create. I think this bastard took me two weeks total(well, 9-10 days). I pencilled it all the way to finished tight pencils hoping to get an inker. It didn't happen. But that's ok, it's nice doing something like this while the regular series gets more and more late. ;) Heh.

KIRKMAN: And on these two pages you'll see Ryan's inks for this cover. I tell you, every so often in this series there's a cover that comes along that makes this book seem way more awesome than I ever thought possible. I mean, look at this thing. I can't believe we got clearance to use all these characters. It's so cool to see them all together, awesome stuff.

OTTLEY: I loved drawing all these guys. I was an uber geek fan of Spawn, Pitt, Cyberforce, and others and all their creators. It's odd and a bit masochistic of me but a part of me wants to draw this cover all over again. Not just because I enjoyed it, but to draw them a little differently than I did here. I guess I always see past art and I just wish I could do it all over and make it better. Kinda weird. It's the only job where I've felt this way. I never felt like doing inventory over again when I worked in a warehouse. Hmm.

KIRKMAN: Here are the inks for the cover to 61. I believe this is the first finished drawing of Conquest, what fun that guy is. Great cover, perfect set up for the Conquest story. Lots of mystery to it.

***OTTLEY:** Count the dead bodies in the rubble. Win a pony.*

KIRKMAN: This cover was a bear. I wasn't thrilled with the figures because it looked, to me, like they were dancing instead of fighting. Ryan, prince that he is, changed them, but not before sending over a version to show me what dancing actually looks like. What a talented man you are, Ryan.

OTTLEY: I must be terrible at drawing people fighting sometimes because, every once in a while, Robert will say, "Re-draw it, looks like they're dancing." To which I say "NOOOOOOOOOO it does NOT!?! WTF is WRONG with you!?! ARRGH...ok fine." It's funny because the drawing where I was actually TRYING to show them dancing looks like Mark is getting bopped on the head! Man I can't do nothin right!

KIRKMAN: The cover to Invincible 63. You gotta love that exposed bone. I asked for a shot of Mark beat up more than he'd ever been beat up before in the comic--man, did Ryan deliver.

OTTLEY: You said exposed bone. Sorry.

KIRKMAN: The cover to 65, which, like most of Ryan's covers, is awesome. And was a cool call back to the cover to issue 8 by mister Cory Walker.

OTTLEY: I have a hard time when asked to re-draw something, especially when Cory initially drew it. There's no way I can come close to the way Cory does his work, he has such a solid foundation and a great design aspect to everything that makes his work so perfectly original. I tried to do a nice call back but it wasn't near as good.

KIRKMAN: Some pages. And yes, I did have Ryan remove the torch from Lady Liberty's butt. Sorry. Also, a splash from issue 61 and a spread from issue 63. Beautiful stuff.

OTTLEY: I imagined the mohawked alternative Invincible would be someone who liked not only to destroy things but to desecrate them as well. So I thought the torch up the statue's buttocks was completely acceptable and I still do. It added a bit more depth to the character. Robert thought it was silly, I thought it was awesome, and I know firsthand that Mohawk Invincible found it extremely amusing.

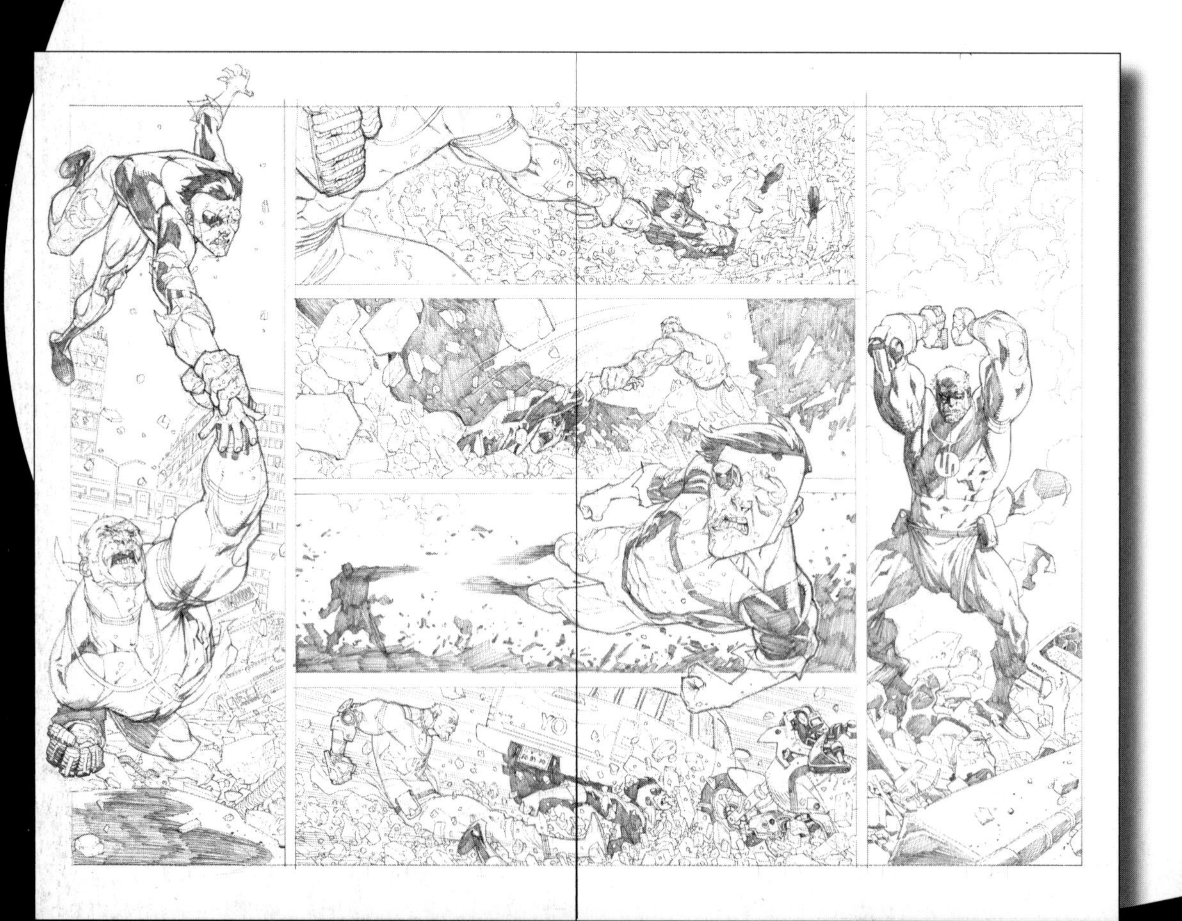

KIRKMAN: Ah, the two-page spread of a head. I went through a period where I tried to write as many of these possible, because they're awesome. I believe I bought all the originals. Check my books, this happened a lot to do one of these in Astounding Wolf-Man... oh, wait--I just thought of the perfect place. Check out issue 24 that book. Oh, and also on this page you'll see the two-page spread of Invincible smashing Conquest's robot Amazing stuff, should have probably talked about that spread more. Ryan?

OTTLEY: Can we please have one or two of the close-ups on heads double-page spreads in every issue? I know I loved drawing it. And of course the punching INTO Conquest's arm page was great fun as well. Visualizing Mark's hand going inside that robot arm was interesting. Like Mark's fist went into the robot hand and the robot fingers curled inward and everything else burst outward. Good times.

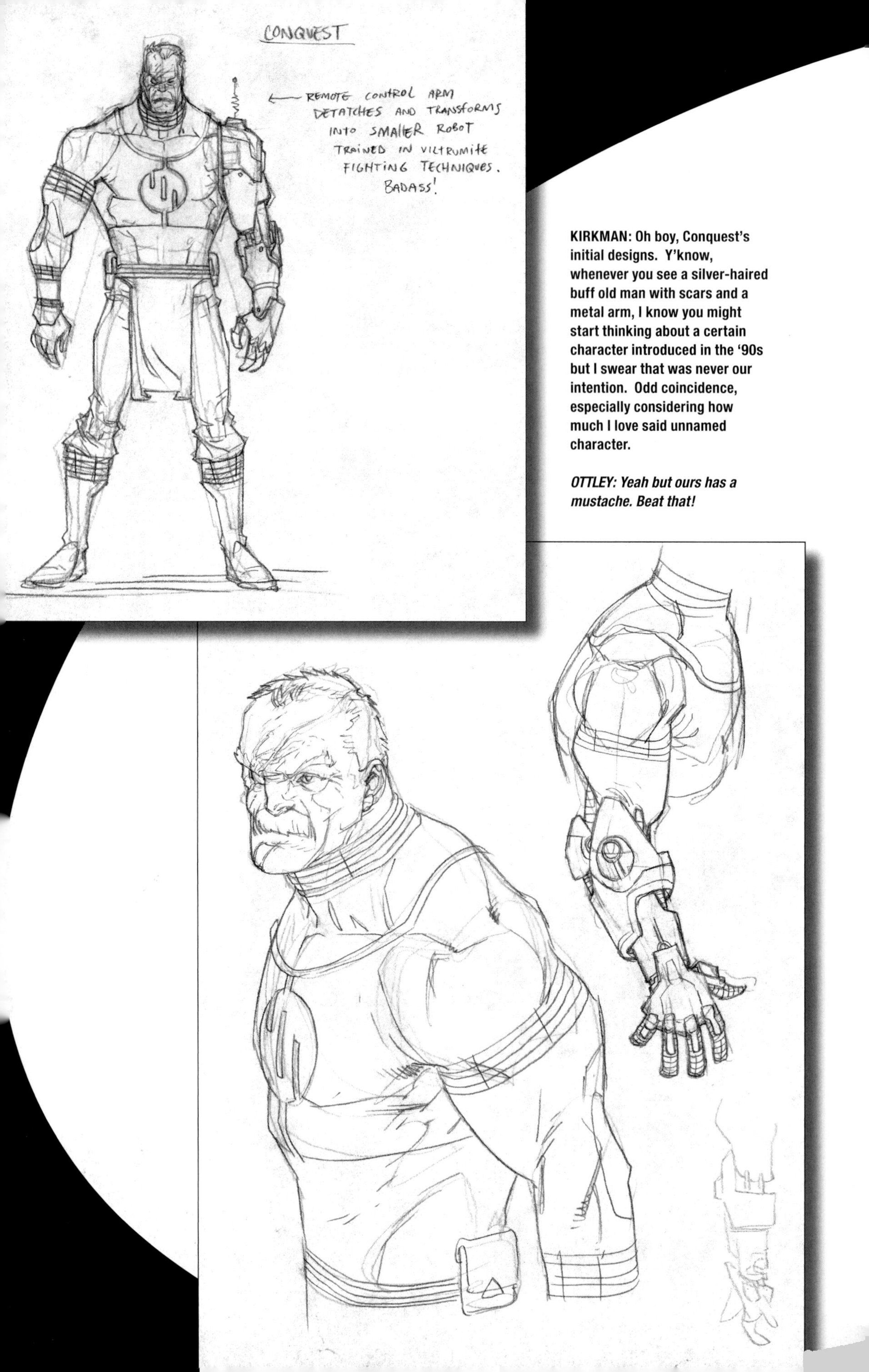

KIRKMAN: Oh boy, Conquest's initial designs. Y'know, whenever you see a silver-haired buff old man with scars and a metal arm, I know you might start thinking about a certain character introduced in the '90s but I swear that was never our intention. Odd coincidence, especially considering how much I love said unnamed character.

OTTLEY: Yeah but ours has a mustache. Beat that!

KIRKMAN: This, I think, is the best drawing Ryan has ever done. This pencil-shaded Conquest drawing is just amazing. I love it.

OTTLEY: I gotta find time to do more stuff like this. I was doing a lot of life drawing sessions at this time and was having fun with the rendering, one day I decided to break out the pencils and do up this Conquest. I'll do more as soon as I find time.

KIRKMAN: Convention sketches of Atom Eve. Whoever sees Ryan at a convention should really pay him lots of money for sketches like these--because you'll get awesome sketches, like these.

OTTLEY: Or even not like these! Whatever you wants!

KIRKMAN: Conquest convention sketches. Some fan asked for Eve punching a hole in Conquest-- and it's just awesome. I wish I owned that sketch. Brilliant stuff. Way to go, fan of this comic!

OTTLEY: HA! Yeah fans always give me some great ideas at conventions. Way too much fun.

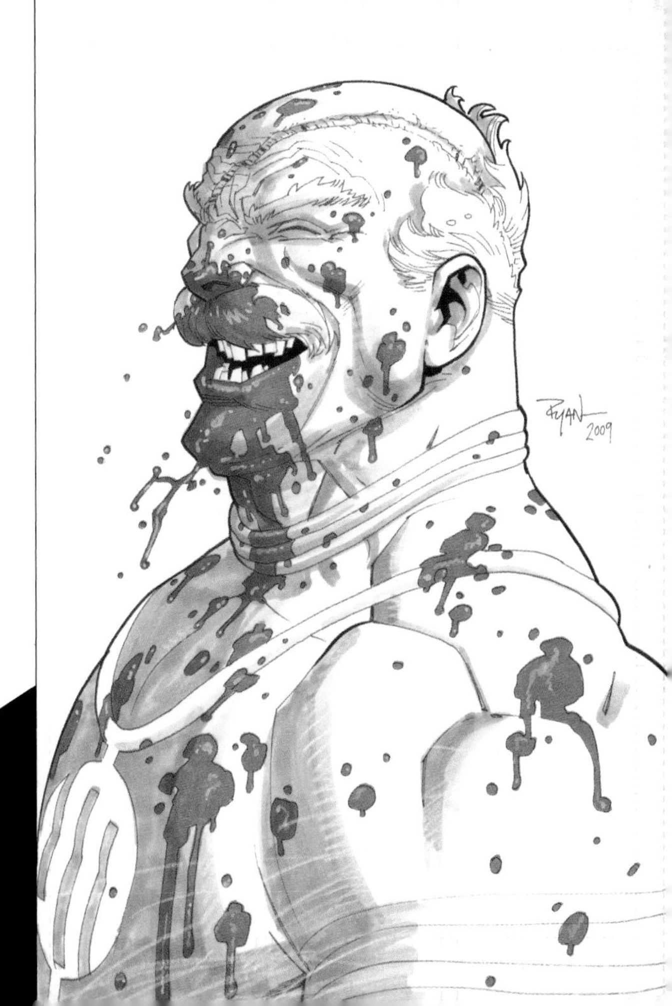

KIRKMAN: Sketches of Invincible and Atom Eve, so romantic. No doubt, these sketches were requested by girls, right Ryan?

OTTLEY: Actually no, guys like romance too, Robert.

KIRKMAN: Eve versus an awesome monster (need to do more stuff like that in the book) and Invincible versus some character I don't recognize... S-Man? Something like that.

OTTLEY: I've honestly never even heard of the character before. But that's what the guy asked for. The monster one with the tiny Atom Eve was great, no one has ever asked for a TINY drawing of Eve before. I've always had fun with monsters. Fun fact: I didn't read comics until I was 15. So what was I drawing for all those years before I knew anything about superheroes? Tons of weird faces and monsters, and lots of violence. My red crayons were always the shortest.

KIRKMAN: Another brilliant fan asked for a shot of the alternate Invincible who mentioned that he'd killed Spawn doing exactly that. Neat.

OTTLEY: I liked the idea. Let's not show Todd though. His noogies always hurt the worst.

KIRKMAN: And now for a magnificent drawing of Omni-Man. What a steal this art-buyer got, no matter what he paid. Neat stuff.

OTTLEY: Thanks Robert! Until next time, Stay coo.

ROBERT KIRKMAN: Look at that, there's another awesome trade paper back cover by ye olde Ryan Ottley. I think this might possibly be the last time that Ryan will ever draw the Sequids, I mean, I've got no plans to bring them back at this point, but who knows. What do you think, Ryan? Should we bring them back--do you miss drawing those little pink things?

RYAN OTTLEY: I hate to admit this in front of everyone, but yes I do miss them. The reason is that I can use them to cover up a lot of background. Mindless noodling is much easier than drawing cars and buildings and stuff. So yeah, if you ever want to bring them back, I won't complain.

KIRKMAN: So the plan to have Invincible co-creator Cory Walker come back to do a couple issues, focusing on Allen the Alien, had been in the works for a good long time. If I recall, we began talking about this before issue 50, when the Viltrumite War was originally planned to begin (before I ran out of room). These cover sketches were done back then when we first decided to do these issues.

CORY WALKER: The two versions of that cover that feature only Allen were done in 2006, I think.

OTTLEY: Well I want Cory to come back and do MORE issues, I loved having him do these two. So please, Cory, come back and do an issue every once in a while. It looks awesome AND it gives me a break. Win-win I say.

KIRKMAN: Later, when it finally came time to do these issues, I decided to change the story up a little and have it feature Nolan as well as Allen. So the cover had to be adjusted somewhat before it became what we know and love as the cover to issue 66.

WALKER: I'm pretty pleased with how this cover turned out. Upside-down is the new black.

OTTLEY: Yeah I remember drawing the cover to 46, the one with Immortal and Allen fighting on the moon, that was Robert's idea to do the upside-down cover, he hesitated because he wasn't sure if he wanted to interfere with Cory's upside down cover. As if Cory had a copyright on upside downness. It all worked out though, and I love the hell out of Cory's covers.

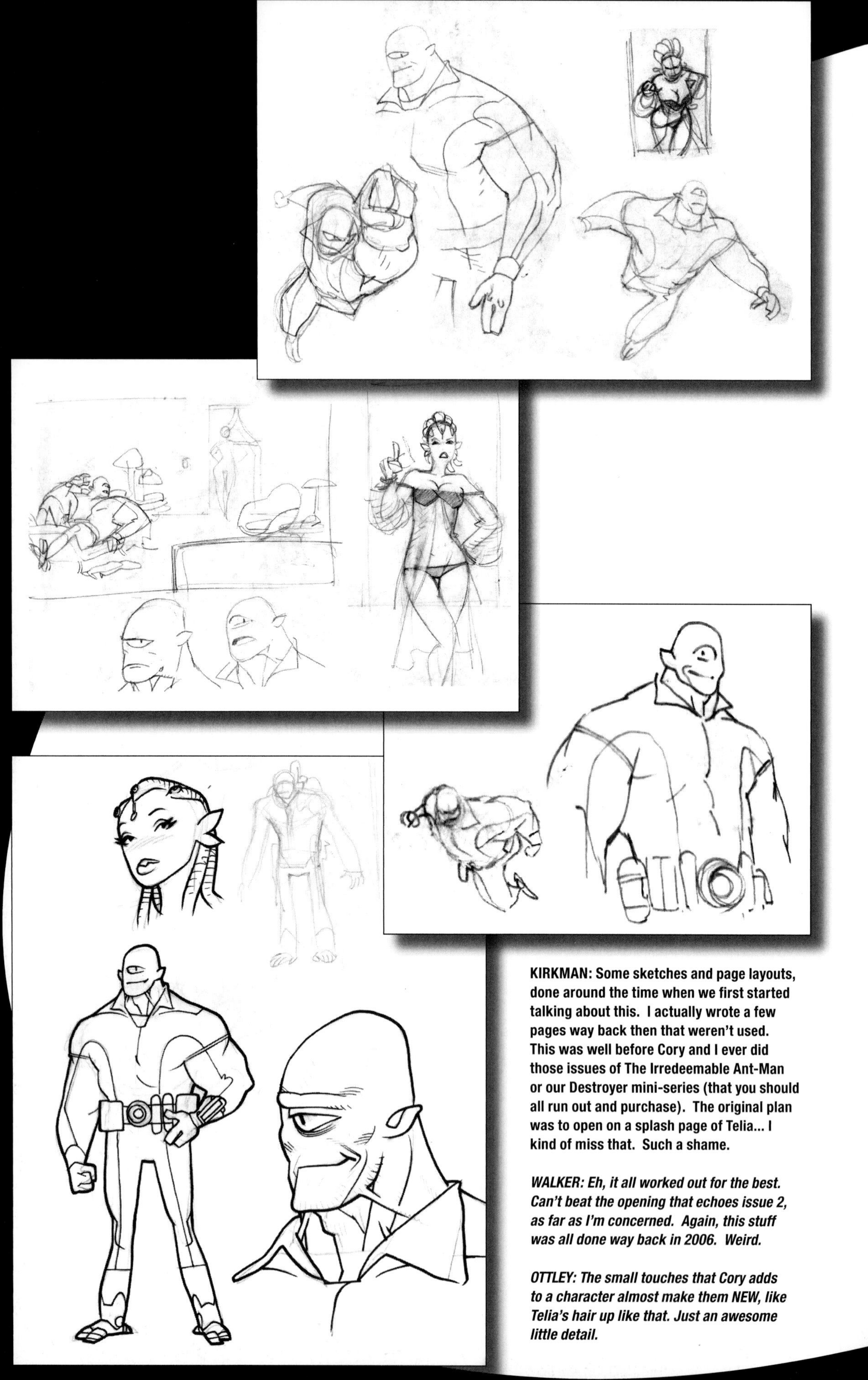

KIRKMAN: Some sketches and page layouts, done around the time when we first started talking about this. I actually wrote a few pages way back then that weren't used. This was well before Cory and I ever did those issues of The Irredeemable Ant-Man or our Destroyer mini-series (that you should all run out and purchase). The original plan was to open on a splash page of Telia... I kind of miss that. Such a shame.

WALKER: Eh, it all worked out for the best. Can't beat the opening that echoes issue 2, as far as I'm concerned. Again, this stuff was all done way back in 2006. Weird.

OTTLEY: The small touches that Cory adds to a character almost make them NEW, like Telia's hair up like that. Just an awesome little detail.

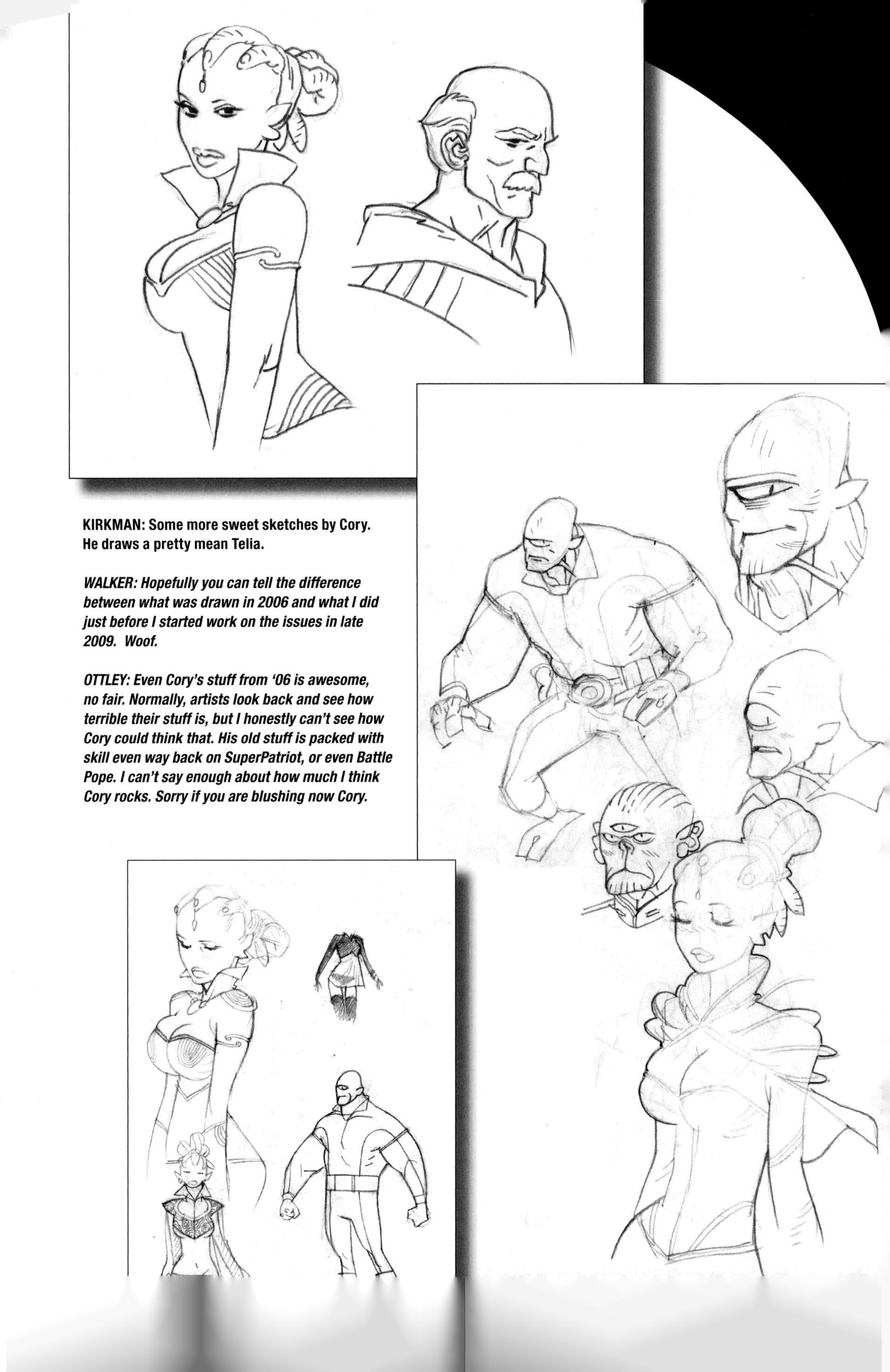

KIRKMAN: Some more sweet sketches by Cory. He draws a pretty mean Telia.

WALKER: Hopefully you can tell the difference between what was drawn in 2006 and what I did just before I started work on the issues in late 2009. Woof.

OTTLEY: Even Cory's stuff from '06 is awesome, no fair. Normally, artists look back and see how terrible their stuff is, but I honestly can't see how Cory could think that. His old stuff is packed with skill even way back on SuperPatriot, or even Battle Pope. I can't say enough about how much I think Cory rocks. Sorry if you are blushing now Cory.

KIRKMAN: More awesome sketches from Cory. Not really anything to add other than that Cory is great. He's such a master of the human form. Great looking stuff.

WALKER: I work out.

OTTLEY: He does, I watch him.

KIRKMAN: Here are Cory's designs for SPACE RACER which were done way back when the character first appeared in issue 35 of this series, when he was called Space Rider, but we'll pay no attention to that... that was just because Nolan changed the name for his book, you see. Wakka wakka. Move along.

WALKER: Space Racer is pretty cool. I wish I had made him a little less humanoid, but whatever. I'm no Nate Bellegarde.

OTTLEY: FUN FACT: Robert wanted me to change Cory's design a little bit, instead of feet, he wanted hands. Ok so maybe that fact wasn't fun at all. I should've just called it a semi-interesting fact? I don't know.

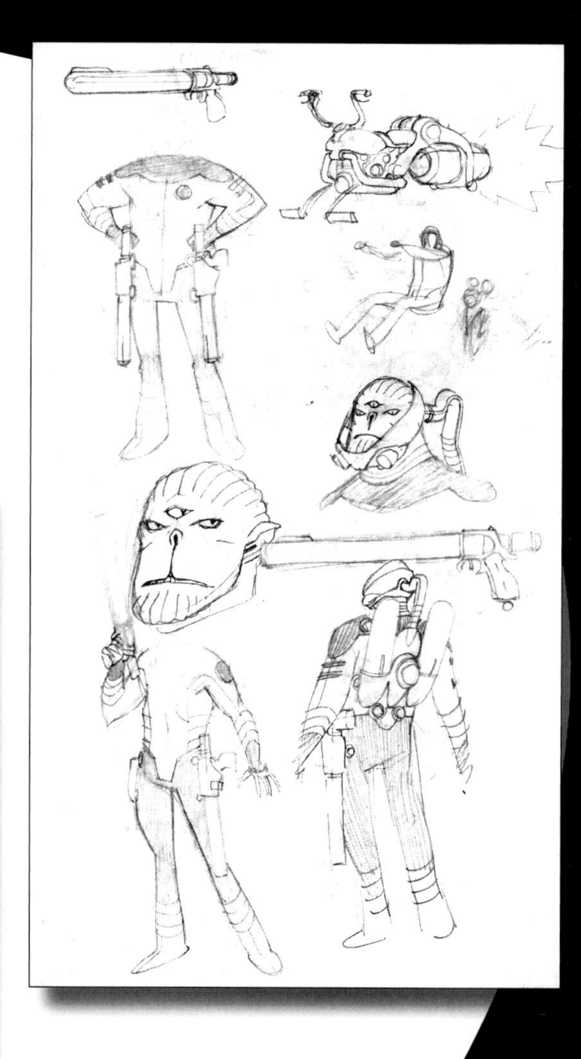

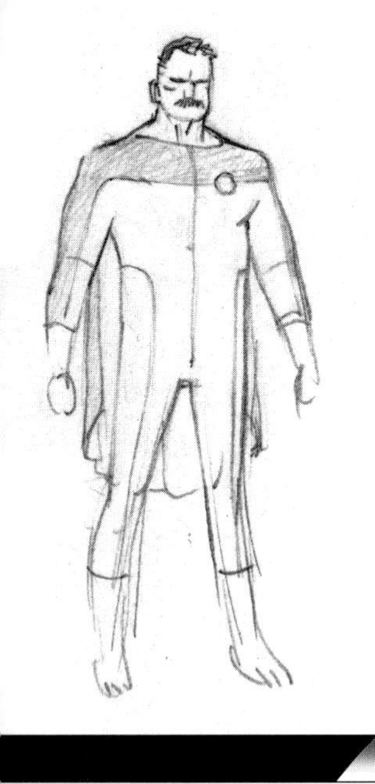

KIRKMAN: Some variations of Nolan's costume that Cory did. I don't remember which one we picked... and have no idea how I'd go about trying to figure that out in a definitive way.

WALKER: The colors, Duke, the colors! To be honest, I really quite liked the blue one, but I'm glad we went with the color scheme that we did.

OTTLEY: He could use shoes.

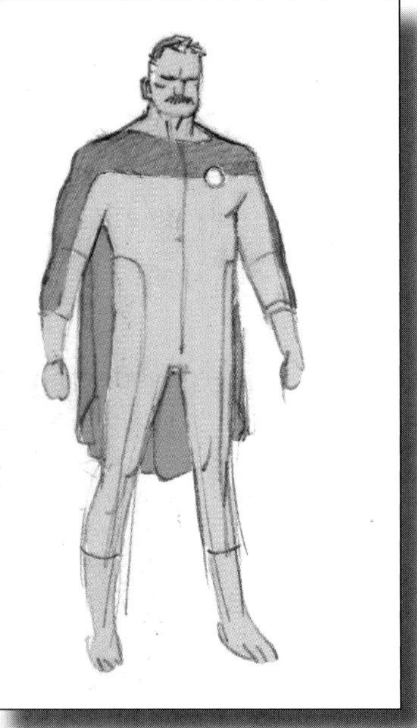

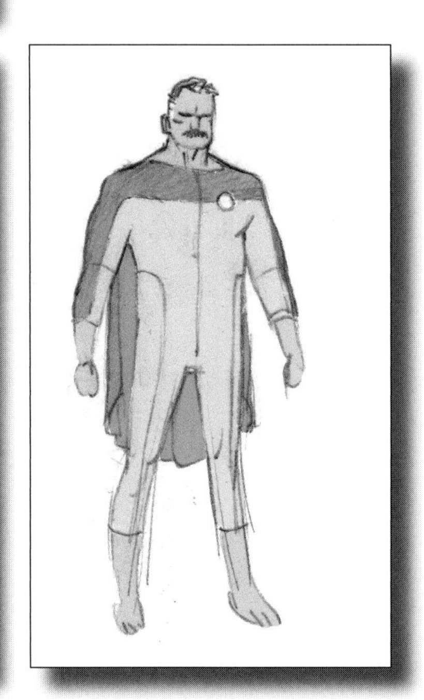

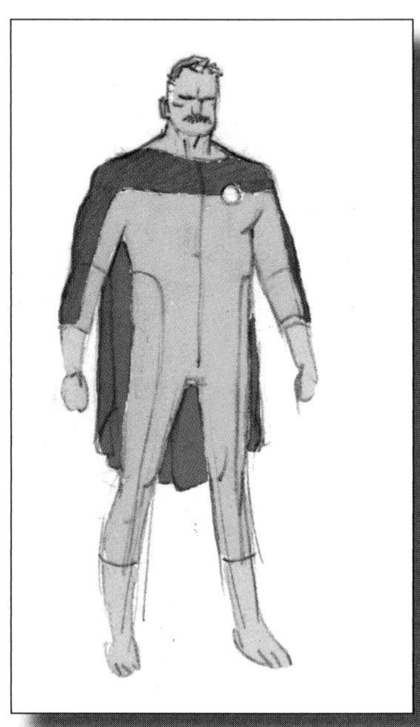

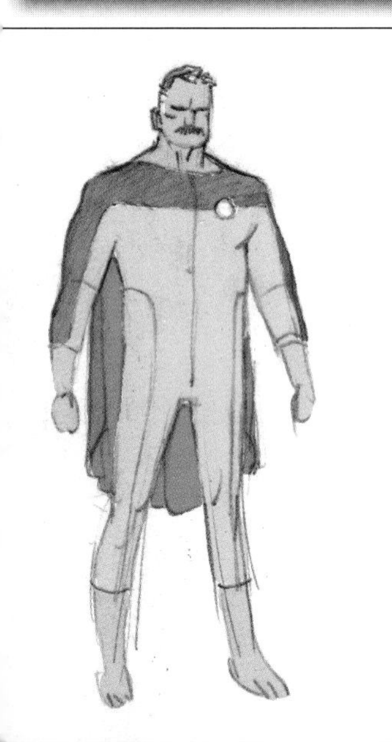

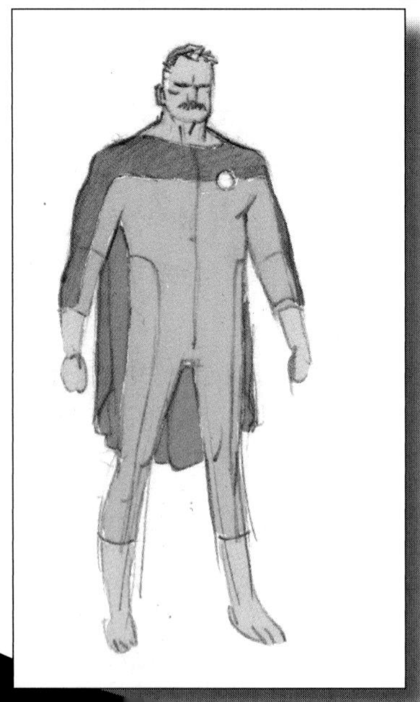

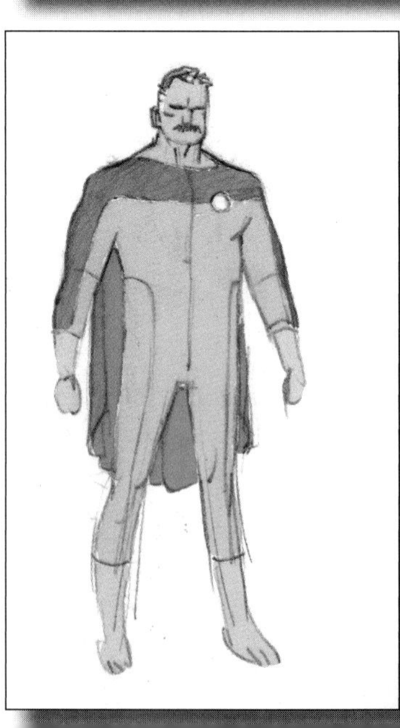

KIRKMAN: Some cool colored sketches by Cory.

WALKER: Pretty cool, right? Pretty cool bare feet, right?

OTTLEY: Bare feet are all right. We could get into WHY he would want bare feet but we could probably fill up pages talking about what benefits bare feet would have: is it a comfort thing, is he sick of wearing boots like the Viltrumites, is it simply because he's so strong that boots would not act as protection? Like goggles on Invincible? Like metal gloves on Allen's hands and feet? so on.

KIRKMAN: Page layouts for issue 66. I'm going to keep writing that page of Nolan talking over and over because it's great. This is what... the fourth time? Enjoy!

WALKER: Look, ladies, you can see a bit of the process used to do the first page of issue 66. Any time there's a large figure on a page, or in this instance, an enormous head, I thumbnail the drawing, then resize it for the page and lightbox it. That's what happened here.

OTTLEY: Yeah I do that too, but Cory has this uncanny ability to draw amazing detail SO small. It's pretty mind-blowing to see the actual size of Cory's thumbnail layouts and how CLEAN they are.

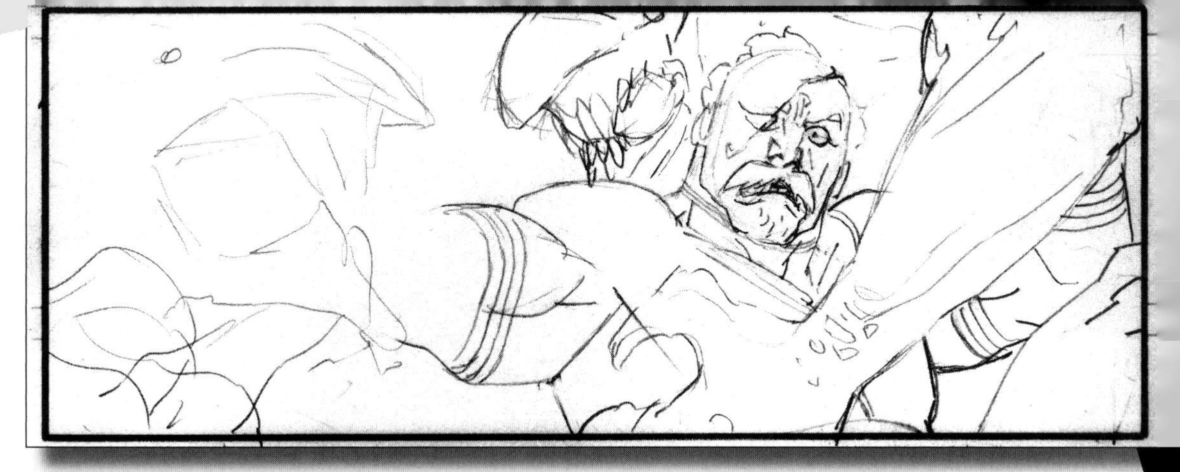

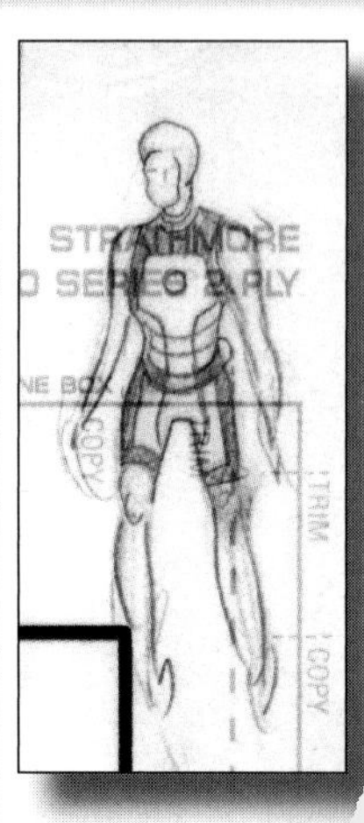

KIRKMAN: Random stuff from Cory's issues. I feel like I'm talking too damn much! Cory... explain what this stuff is.

WALKER: Well, most of it is pretty self-explanatory, but here you see the design work I did for those alien brain nerds in the gutter space of the very page they first appear on. You can also see my first pass at Thaedus from the giant head two page spread from issue 67, where I worked it to death and made it look like garbage, and then, there's little drawing I did to replace it. Also, that panel of Nolan holding the pillow over his ears is probably the best drawing I have ever seen.

OTTLEY: I Love it!

KIRKMAN: Here's the cover to 68. DINOSAURUS! Oh, Dinosaurus. You're the first comic book character my son kind of created... or well, named at the very least. We were playing with dinosaurs one day and I asked him to name his and he replied "Dinosaurus!" He was three at the time. I think I called Ryan about three seconds later to get him started on designs. Such a cool name. And I've got big plans for this guy, we'll be seeing much more of him very soon.

WALKER: Dinosaurus? Pfft. The Elephant is where it's at. Totally awesome cover, though. Ryan Ottley is the king of it.

OTTLEY: It is a fun name, even moreso after Robert told me the story. Oh and thanks Cory. *blushes*

KIRKMAN: More female villains! I've been wanting to do that for a while and that's what brought about Universa here. Excellent design by Cory Walker, which was drawn on the set of the movie PAUL.

WALKER: I remember sitting there, on the set of the movie PAUL, thinking, "I am going to design a Universa. Panty cape." So I did. As you see, though, my original color choices were not so well thought-out. Peach skin? Barf. Seriously, though, smooth making her green was smooth a smooth move, Kirkman. I think she turned out pretty good for a character that was designed on the set of the movie PAUL.

OTTLEY: Way rad, I love her design!

KIRKMAN: SEQUIDS! **Ryan's inks for the cover to issue 70.**

WALKER: SO good. I love any time Ryan draws a sequid.

OTTLEY: I love YOU guys!

KIRKMAN: Last year at Comic-Con, Erik Larsen was drawing a bunch of commissions for people, so I threw my money in the hat and asked him to draw me an Invincible. I dug it so much that I asked if he'd be okay with me having Ryan ink the thing up so that we could use it as a cover. Erik, great guy that he is, agreed and it became a variant cover for INVINCIBLE: RETURNS #1.

WALKER: SO good. I love any time Ryan teams up with Erik Larsen.

OTTLEY: I made a few changes, I deflated that hand a bit, Erik and his huge fists. It's always great working over Larsen's pencils, he has such a fun energy in his lines.

KIRKMAN: This is a pretty awesome two-page spread by Ryan Ottley... the first time Invincible appeared in his yellow and blue costume since issue 51. Man, I did not expect him to wear that blue and black costume for 20 issues... wow.

OTTLEY: FUN FACT: Jason Howard (Astounding Wolf-Man) and I hung out with Erik Larsen at this year's San Diego Comic-Con. Jason reminded Erik that I made a big fist challenge when I drew this spread. That is HALF a page of fist there folks. I then told Erik if he wants to be the "king of fists," he needed to one-up me. Erik immediately grabbed two 11x17 pages and filled the WHOLE thing with an amazing fist, and on one side you could see Savage Dragon's face. It was absolutely glorious. I hope he uses it in a future issue of Savage Dragon, because I doubt I could ever draw a bigger fist than I did here on Invincible. Until Larsen's spread hits the printed page I am still the fisting champion. Er..you know what I mean.

WALKER: Nobody does it better. Ryan can do a lot of things that other guys only dream of. Drawing wicked-awesome spreads like this is one of them. Curious about the other things? Ask your sister.

KIRKMAN: We leave you with an awesome splash page and a goofy drawing of Invincible wearing a Ryan Ottley body. Funny stuff, Ryan.

OTTLEY: Thanks! Peace out y'all.

RYAN